THE STARS THAT BEND TIME

BOOK 2 IN THE STARPATH SERIES

KEVIN J SIMINGTON

TABLE OF CONTENTS

1

A blue green world floats in the velvet blackness of space. A golden sun bathes the temperate planet in its rays, warming the oceans and heating the two lush green continents. Unlike Earth, however, this world has not been ravaged by careless exploitation and violent conflict. The planet is a sparkling jewel, unblemished and pristine. The inhabitants of Nova, recently arrived, fled here after the cataclysmic global nuclear conflict that decimated Earth, barely escaping with their lives. The first colonisation of another planet had been intended to be a well-planned, thoroughly resourced mission, preceded by years of training and involving a team of highly skilled colonists. In the end, a bedraggled bunch of fortunate refugees had clambered aboard the newly completed starship, Genesis, a lifeboat to the stars.

They slept for decades as the starship crossed the void between the stars, finally awakening to discover that the universe had played a cosmic joke upon them. Midway through its journey, Genesis had encountered a rogue black hole and had been trapped in its event horizon for many months, only managing to break free after the ship's Artificial Intelligence had modified the antimatter drive and jettisoned weight. The time dilation effects of the black hole meant that while only months had transpired on board the ship, over 3,000 years had passed in the outside universe. The colonists had awoken to discover that during their slumber the target planet, previously revealed by probes to be uninhabited, had been colonised and mysteriously abandoned by humans. A curious artificial ring now encircled the planet in geosynchronous orbit around the equator, and both continents were dotted with mysteriously empty towns.

The Genesis colonists moved into their new home, living in the abandoned towns and utilising technology that they barely understood. Where had the previous occupants gone? And why? What was the purpose of the artificial hoop orbiting the planet? The answers were only vaguely hinted at by a collective of artificial Enhanced Intelligence entities, who claimed to have been left behind on the planet as guardians. The EIs, who called themselves *The Collective,* had assisted the new colonists to access the planet's advanced technology via an uplift virus, which had altered their DNA to enable intuitive interaction with the technology.

Months after settling on the planet, the colonists were still exploring the various empty towns around the globe, instantly travelling between them via transfer booths that utilised a technology beyond their ability to comprehend. Now, on a beautiful early summer day, four colonists found themselves standing on an artificial glassy surface at the bottom of what appeared to be a man-made, perfectly cylindrical sink hole, about two kilometres wide and at least as deep. The four colonists were a curious mix of people, indicative of the eclectic composition of the whole colony. Natasha Martinez, a diminutive but tough security guard with short dark hair and multiple facial piercings. Kit Tyler, a highly competent shuttle pilot with a cheeky, straight-talking personality. Keo Ka'aukai, a 190 cm New Zealand rugby-playing philosopher, who was built like a tank. And Zac Perryman, an unconventional historian who liked surfing and wearing retro-Hawaiian shirts.

Together, they stood in the centre of the sink hole, looking at the only object on the entire flat, glassy surface; a circular dome-shaped object.

"It's like a mini-dome," said Zac.

"I think it's some kind of transport vessel," said Kit.

They walked around its perimeter and noted a variety of bumps and lumps all over its surface, the purpose of which eluded them.

"There appears to be an outline of a doorway," said Kit, approaching it with her usual confidence.

The doorway slid smoothly aside, seeming to invite them in.

"Did you do that?" Zac asked her.

"Maybe. I was wondering how to get in. I guess it works the same way as the rest of the technology on this planet. It's somehow tuned in to our thought waves."

"Well, I think this is as far as we go," said Zac. "We need to go back and report .... Kit! What are you doing?"

"What does it look like? I'm going to take a peep inside."

She walked through the doorway and turned to the right, disappearing from view.

"Kit! Come out! We don't know what it is or whether it's safe. Please!"

"You should see this, guys! It's incredible!" She stuck her head around the corner of the doorway. "It looks pretty safe to me. Come on! Check it out!"

Keo said, "She sure is the adventurous one, bro."

Zac sighed and shook his head. "Yeh. And one of these days she's going to bite off more than she can chew!"

"Well, I'm not going to stay out here and miss out on all the fun," said Martinez, walking towards the doorway.

Zac shrugged and said, "You know what they say; If you can't beat them join them." The two men walked to the entrance of the dome and cautiously stepped inside.

2

The four friends looked around the interior of the domed pod, trying to make sense of what they saw. As was the case with other structures discovered on Nova, the walls and domed roof offered one-way transparency, making it seem as though they were inside a large glass bubble. The only exception was a small section of protruding wall directly opposite the still open doorway, which seemed to be a bank of storage cupboards.

The rest of the circular interior was surprisingly bare. No chairs. No furniture of any kind. No instruments or obvious controls.

"If this is some kind of transport pod," said Kit, "clearly my pilot skills are not needed."

The only distinguishing feature was a central circular column, about 30 cm in diameter, rising from floor to ceiling. The column was featureless except for a small angled recess at about waist height, on the side facing the open door. The recess had a glassy surface with an outline of a human hand etched into it. Zac stood looking at it and said, "We are definitely not touching this until we get some technical analysis done on it. And I'm talking to you, Kit, especially."

"OK, Captain Cautious, but do you seriously think that even our brightest minds are going to be able to figure out what this is and how it works? I mean, dude, we haven't been able to understand *any* of the technology we've encountered so far. It's thousands of years more advanced than us. The only way we've been able to work out what stuff actually does, is to go ahead and use it!"

"Yes, but if we're going to experiment with it, it should be done in consultation with our scientists. At least give them a shot at working it out first."

Martinez chimed in, "If we'd followed that protocol, we'd probably still be scratching our arses and wondering what the transfer booths were for. I say we try to activate the hand thingy."

Zac turned to Keo. "What do you think?"

"I think we should sit in the sun for a while and eat cake. I always think better on a full stomach."

"Really?" said Kit. "That's all you've got for us? Professor of Philosophy, head full of quotes, IQ through the roof, and your momentous contribution to this discussion is cake?"

"Stressed spelt backwards is desserts," offered Keo in reply.

"A semordnilap, eh?" said Zac. "Clever."

"Well, while you two eggheads are discussing linguistics, I'm the only fully-qualified pilot among us, so I'm making an executive decision."

"No, Kit! Wait!" said Zac.

But it was too late. Kit's hand was already on the glass surface, her fingers neatly splayed within the etched outline.

Immediately the outline lit up with a sharp white light and the interior of the hand etching glowed with a soft blue light. The pod door slid closed and the hand etching stopped glowing.

"So that's how you close the door," offered Martinez.

"No. I think it does more than that," said Zac. "Listen."

A steadily increasing whine could be heard, and a purple light started pulsing with increasing intensity outside the pod, emanating from the circular glassy surface upon which it sat.

"Shut it down!" urged Zac.

Kit placed her hand back on the glass panel, but nothing happened.

"I'm trying to 'think' the door open, but it's not responding," said Martinez.

"Hold onto your pants everyone," said Kit. "It looks like we're going for a ride."

"Kit, this is precisely what I was worried about!"

"Cool it, doc. We were going to have to do this eventually, so it may as well be now."

"I might postpone the cake for a while," said Keo.

The whine steadily increased in volume, accompanied by a corresponding increase in the intensity and frequency of the pulsing purple light. It soon reached a point when the pulses were so fast as to be almost indistinguishable. Suddenly the pulsing stopped and a brilliant, deep purple light enveloped the pod, shooting up from the glassy floor of the sink hole and bathing the interior of the transparent pod with intense light. A moment later the four occupants were plunged into complete darkness and their ears were assaulted by utter silence. There had been no sensation of movement, just a strange transition from their senses being overloaded with light and sound to now being engulfed in darkness and silence.

"What just happened?" asked Zac. "I can't see a thing."

As he spoke, two circles of lights began to glow, one around the edge of the circular floor and another circle of lights at the top of the dome.

"Any idea where we are?" asked Martinez.

"Nope," responded Kit. "I guess we should open the door and find out."

She looked towards the door and concentrated on opening it, but all that happened was that a small red light started flashing in the middle of the door panel. All four of them focused their attention on opening the door, but it remained obstinately shut and the red light flashed insistently.

"Why don't you try the hand thing again?" suggested Martinez.

Kit placed her had on the glass panel, but it remained unresponsive. "It doesn't seem to want to play ball anymore," she said.

"Excellent!" said Zac. "Well done Kit. This is precisely why I didn't want to fiddle with stuff that we don't understand."

"I knew we should have eaten cake," said Keo.

"How are we going to get out of here?" continued Zac.

"Wherever 'here' is," added Martinez.

A female voice filled the pod with a soft, reassuring tone. "Do you require assistance?"

"Ah, the cavalry has arrived," said Kit. "Yes please, that would be nice."

"Who are you?" asked Zac.

"You are currently communicating with the automated guidance and control system of Transfer Pod 48."

"You're an AI?"

"No. I am not a self-aware artificial intelligence. I am a software program designed to co-ordinate the operation of the pod and give verbal responses to a limited range of queries."

"OK, so here's a query," said Kit, taking charge of the communication. "Where the hell are we?"

"You are in Transfer Dock 48 inside Module 12 of the launch ring."

"You mean we're inside the hoop thingy that's orbiting this planet?"

"That is correct."

"Inside one of the 12 spheres?"

"Yes. Module 12. Each module has four transfer docks. Module 12 houses transfer docks 45 to 48. You are in Transfer Pod 8 in Transfer Dock 48."

"Why can't we open the door?" asked Zac.

"I cannot allow the outer door to be opened, as the external environment is hostile to human life."

"What do you mean?"

"Transfer Dock 48 currently has no air pressure."

"It's a vacuum?"

"That is correct."

"How long do we have to wait for air pressure to be normalised?"

"I do not expect it to be normalised."

"What do you mean?"

"The presence of a vacuum in the transfer dock is unexpected. My communication with the transfer dock software indicates the presence of a small hole in the outer wall, probably caused by a small meteor. The transfer dock has been sealed off from the rest of the launch ring."

"How long until it can be fixed?" asked Zac.

"It cannot be fixed. There are no robot service units left on the ring. They were all taken when the human population departed."

"Can you move us to another transfer dock?"

"No. Each dock is keyed to a specific pod."

"Can't you override that?"

"No."

"OK. Then take us back down to the surface."

"That is not possible."

"Why not?"

"The meteorite also destroyed the transfer dock's launch system. The dock can receive but it cannot launch. The transfer pod has no ability to transfer itself; it simply responds to the sub-atomic impetus provided by the launch engines at both ends."

"Do you have a solution to our predicament?"

"I do not."

"How long until we run out of oxygen in this pod?"

"With four occupants, the oxygen will be depleted in approximately 12 hours. But that is not your biggest problem."

"It's not?" exclaimed Zac. "If there's something worse than asphyxiating in 12 hours I'd like to know about it!"

"Carbon dioxide," said Kit, with resignation.

"Correct. Based upon your current respiration rates, as indicated by your bio chips, carbon dioxide levels within the pod will reach deadly levels in approximately 5 hours."

3

They considered their predicament in stunned silence for a few moments.

"Well, at least I've had two weeks of honeymoon sex before I died," offered Martinez.

"No-one's dying just yet," said Kit. "Computer, is there an AI on board the launch ring?"

"Yes. I opened a communication channel as soon as we arrived in the transfer dock. The ring has been dormant for centuries and the AI is currently reinitialising the life support systems in response to my identification code."

"Will it be able to help us?"

"I have insufficient information to answer that question."

"Does this pod have any space suits?" asked Zac.

"No. But there are emergency vacuum suits in the storage compartments at one side of the pod. When fully inflated they contain enough air for 2 minutes of breathing, which is sufficient to traverse a short distance of vacuum."

A soft "ding" sounded, and the computer announced, "The ring's AI now wishes to communicate with you."

There was a short pause, followed by a different, pleasant sounding female voice. "Greetings Kitchener, Natasha, Zacchary and Keolakupaianaha."

"I never could pronounce your first name in full," Zac said to Keo.

"And 'Kitchener'?" said Martinez to Kit. "What the hell?"

"My parents were history geeks," answered Kit. "They were inspired by the bravery of Lord Kitchener, a British army officer in the First World War. I think they wanted me to be a boy."

The AI continued. "I ascertained your names from your biochips, but I will use your preferred abbreviations from this point."

"You are aware of our predicament?" asked Zac.

"Yes. The transfer dock appears to have been punctured by a micro-meteor."

"Can you offer any means of patching the hole so that pressure can be restored?"

"As your computer has already explained, the robot service units were all removed when the last of the humans departed. They stripped the ring of everything they would need for establishing their new home. They weren't expecting to return. Without service units I cannot effectively undertake any physical repairs."

"In that case we'll have to use the vacuum suits and make our way to the airlock. I assume there is an airlock that we can access?" said Kit.

"That is correct. I have analysed every possible course of action, and that plan has the greatest chance of success. Unfortunately, it is complicated by the fact that the micro-meteor that punctured the chamber also destroyed several key systems. As a result, there is no artificial gravity on your side of the airlock."

"Damn!" said Kit.

"Is that a major problem?" asked Zac.

"It means we won't be able to walk to the airlock," answered Kit. She thought about it for a moment. "AI, how far is it from the pod door to the airlock?"

"Approximately 21 metres. The pod door faces the airlock directly."

"We can make that, can't we?" asked Zac.

"I can," answered Kit, "because I'm used to working in zero gravity. But launching yourself accurately across a distance of over 20 metres and hitting a target isn't easy, even for someone experienced. You only need to be slightly off in your trajectory and you'll be floating around the chamber while you slowly asphyxiate." She thought furiously and asked, "Is there any rope or something similar anywhere in the pod or the chamber?"

"No," answered the AI succinctly.

"What about on the other side of the airlock? Is there some rope that I could retrieve from somewhere on the ring and bring back through the airlock?"

"No. And even if there was, by the time you retrieved it and cycled back through the airlock, the others will have asphyxiated in their emergency vacuum suits. Once your pod is depressurised and the pod door is opened to the vacuum, all of you will have only two minutes of breathable air inside your suits."

"Of course! I should have thought of that." Kit let out a long sigh and said, "In that case we don't have any choice. We're going to have to suit up and launch ourselves across the gap, and just hope that no one drifts off target."

"There is one additional problem that you will have to deal with," added the AI.

"Of course there is," said Martinez. "This just keeps getting better and better."

"No, this actually makes it worse," answered the AI, apparently unable to appreciate Martinez's sarcasm. "The other system that was damaged was the power to the airlock doors. I can cycle air into and out of the airlock, but I have no control over the doors. You will have to open and close them manually, using the locking wheels."

"Excellent!" said Zac, offering the AI a further example of three thousand-year-old sarcasm. "We wouldn't want everything to go our way, would we?"

"Why not?" asked the AI, perplexed.

"Someone's going to have to explain sarcasm to you," said Zac.

"Don't mind him, he's a historian," said Kit, as if that explained everything. She turned to the others.

"OK, we can do this. But you'll all need to follow my instructions very carefully. Once the cabin is depressurised and the pod door is popped, we will have two minutes to get to the airlock, open the door, get in the airlock and close the door again. The most important thing is not drifting off target. We have artificial gravity as long as we are in the pod, but that will cease as soon as you push off. So, you'll need to brace your feet against the edge of the pod floor at the door and launch yourself horizontally at the airlock. It's going to feel strange, and you will be tempted to aim high, to allow for the gravity that you have lived your whole life in. DON'T! Aim directly at the airlock. Hold your arms out in front and dive straight towards it as if you're diving into a swimming pool. But not too hard, or you'll bounce off the door when you get there. Any questions?"

"Is there going to be a vacuum suit big enough for me?" asked Keo.

The AI answered, "Yes. The humans who lived here before you, were significantly taller than the average human in your era. Your height will not be a problem. Your considerable girth, however, will mean that there will be less room for breathable air in your suit when it is inflated. You will need to breath shallowly or you will run out of air sooner than the others."

"Maybe you shouldn't have eaten so many of those cakes, dude," said Martinez with a chuckle.

"I'll have you know, my 'girth' is pure muscle, little sister!" said Keo with mock offence, patting his torso.

The team got busy, opening storage compartments and putting on the emergency vacuum suits. The suits were a significant step up from the basic emergency suits that Kit had used when she had rescued Martinez and Boyd on the moon. They were much heavier duty, with articulated joints and built in comms. They comprised a one-piece suit with a transparent head piece and some kind of high-tech self-sealing mechanism that replaced the antiquated zipper system of three thousand years ago. Despite all this, however, they were extremely light weight and flexible. Kit began to feel more confident that they were going to be able to pull this off.

But things rarely go exactly to plan.

4

____

They were suited up with head pieces on, just needing to pull the tab up their chests to seal themselves in. Comms had been activated and checked, and they were standing by the door, talking through the plan once more. The pod had switched on external lights and rendered the walls transparent, so they could now see what they were aiming for. The airlock door was directly opposite, with a locking wheel in the middle and two vertical hand-hold bars, one on each side of the door. Kit gave some final instructions.

"Keo, since you're the strongest, you're going first. As soon as you get there, start turning that wheel. You'll need to brace yourself against the bar on the right, otherwise you'll just spin yourself off the door. And push off nice and flat with your arms straight out — but not too fast."

"Got it, little sister. It'll be just like I'm tackling one of those New Zealand rugby players."

"The rest of us will grab the bar on the left and try to stay out of Keo's way. Any questions?"

The group was strangely silent.

"OK let's do this," said Kit. "Computer, are you ready to depressurise."

"Affirmative. As soon as you have sealed your suits, each of you must pull the red tab in the middle of your chest. This will activate the inbuilt servo-pump that will fill your suit with air so that it is pressurised ready for vacuum. Once each suit reaches optimal pressure, the servo will automatically switch off and send me an electronic ping. After all of your suits have pinged me, I will initiate an emergency purge of air and open the door."

"Roger," said Kit. She looked at the group. "OK, here we go. Zip and pull everyone!"

Less than a minute later the pod door opened and Keo executed a perfect glide, gently making contact with the dead centre of the airlock door. Zac was right behind him, having launched when Keo was only half-way across. By the time Zac made contact with the door, Keo was already straining at the wheel.

"It's not budging, bro," he said, straining and grunting. "I'm gonna need some of your Aussie muscle."

Zac wedged himself against the left-hand bar and added his effort to turning the wheel. Both men were straining, and Keo already had a sheen of sweat on his olive-skinned face. Kit gently collided with Zac's back as the two men continued to strain unsuccessfully at the wheel.

"Change your positions a little," said Kit. Time was ticking away, and they were all very aware that if the door could not be opened, they would be unconscious in about a minute and a half. "Keo, wedge your feet against the bottom edge of the bar where it joins the wall. Zac, turn yourself upside down and wedge your feet against the top of the bar. That will give you both more leverage."

The two men did as instructed and when they were in position Keo said, "OK, bro. On the count of three. Give it everything you've got. On, two, three!"

They strained against the wheel with every ounce of strength they possessed, and two things happened simultaneously. The first was that the wheel turned and Keo began turning it with ease. The second was that Martinez, having launched herself with too much velocity, cannoned into the back of Kit and bounced backwards, drifting away from the door. Kit turned and reached out towards her, holding onto the left bar, but Martinez was just beyond her outstretched fingers and slowly drifting further away.

Martinez swore and said, "Sorry guys. It looks like I'm not going be joining you for cake Keo."

"Don't talk rubbish," said Zac. "We'll get you. Kit, I've already got my feet wedged into this bar. I'll stretch out towards her and you climb along me. I'll grab your ankles and you should be able to reach her."

It was easier said than done, however, and by the time they had formed a human chain, Martinez had drifted further out of reach and was slowly tumbling end over end.

"Damn!" said Kit. "OK, here's what we're gonna do. Brace yourself Zac. I'm going to push off with my feet against your palms and launch myself at her."

"But how will you ...?"

"Shut up and listen. She's in a direct line between us and the pod door. If I can get my trajectory right, I should be able to connect with Martinez and push us both back to the pod door. Then it should be a simple matter of launching back out again."

"OK, but you'd better do it quick, because I'm already starting to feel light-headed."

"Here goes."

Kit pushed off strongly and a moment later she collided with Martinez in a tangle of arms and legs.

"You're looking good!" said Zac. "You're heading straight for the door."

"The airlock door is unlocked," said Keo, already starting to gasp for breath. "Opening … it … now."

Zac and Keo scrambled awkwardly into the open airlock and Zac listened helplessly as Keo's gasping escalated.

"Are you OK, Keo?"

"Can't … breathe … air … gone."

"Kit! You girls better move your arses! Keo's running out of air and he's starting to turn blue!"

"We're on our way!"

Zac pushed the airlock door fully open and watched as first Martinez then Kit pushed off from the pod doorway again. This time there was no problem, and both of them made a perfect connection with the airlock hand holds and pulled themselves neatly inside.

Zac pulled the door closed and began spinning the wheel as quickly as he could, bracing himself against a similar hand-hold bar on the inside. Kit was bending over Keo who had stopped talking and moving.

"I think he's unconscious!"

Zac's head was now spinning as he felt the wheel reach its

locked position. He had run out of air as well and was struggling to speak,

"Wheel … locked … need … air …"

The AI's voice calmly announced, "Re-pressurising the airlock. Breathable air in 30 seconds."

Zac had collapsed on the floor and was gasping, slowly turning blue.

"Come on, come on, come on!" said Kit, desperately.

Each second seemed like an eternity, but eventually a green light lit up on the inside door panel and the AI announced, "Pressurisation complete." Martinez had not waited for the green light but had already opened Keo's suit and was gently slapping his face.

"Keo! Keo! Breathe! Come on, you big lump! Breathe, damn you!"

Meanwhile Kit had opened Zac's suit and watched as Zac gasped in the fresh oxygen and colour slowly returned to his cheeks. But Keo was not responding.

"He's not breathing!" said Martinez. She tilted back his head to clear his airway and knelt down and started giving him rescue breaths. Between breaths she said, "Someone check his pulse!"

Kit held two fingers against his carotid artery and announced, "There's a pulse. Keep going, Martinez. We can get him back." As she said this, Keo coughed and gave a gasp and started breathing on his own. His eyes fluttered open and he looked up at Martinez who was poised over him, ready to connect her mouth to his again.

"I didn't know you cared, little sister. But I'm a married man, remember."

"You great lug!" she responded. "You scared the crap out of us!"

"It wasn't much fun for me either, I can assure you."

They sat on the floor for another minute, regaining their breath. Finally, Zac stood up and moved to the internal airlock door. He started turning the locking wheel, which moved easily, and said, "Now, let's see what we've got ourselves into."

5

———

They emerged into a corridor that curved around what seemed to be a central lift shaft. The white walls, floor and ceiling all seemed to glow with a soft luminescence, and directly opposite them a lift door slid open.

"Please enter the lift," said the AI.

"Where are you taking us?" asked Zac.

"You are currently on Level 1 of this module, the bottom level. I suggest you ascend to Level 4, which houses the living quarters where you will be more comfortable."

"How can we get back to the surface of the planet?"

"I suggest we postpone that discussion until you are more comfortable and refreshed."

Kit shrugged and said, "OK, let's roll with the punches here folks. Besides, I'm keen to look around."

A few moments later, they emerged from the lift into a large circular chamber. Tables, chairs and lounges were scattered throughout the middle of the room. The perimeter wall was divided into eight evenly spaced sections. Two appeared to be kitchens or food dispensing areas. Two were some kind of workspaces that provided access to advanced-looking computer screens built into the wall. The other four sections, separating the functional areas, were huge windows offering breath-taking views. The windows on one side of the room showed a brilliant starscape, with countless stars shining like diamonds against the velvet blackness of space. The largest moon, Big Boy, was just coming into view. The two windows on the other side offered a stunning view of the planet below them, apparently stationary as they turned in geosynchronous orbit. The module they were in was stationed directly above Northland, the northern continent of Nova. The four friends were drawn towards the windows overlooking the planet and stood looking down on its pristine beauty.

"I think I can see Seahaven," said Keo. "That bump on the east coast about half-way down."

"It's beautiful," said Kit.

A moment later, Zac spoke up, looking vaguely around the chamber. "Ok, AI. We're ready for an explanation. Do you want to tell us what this place is?"

"You may call me by my identification code if you prefer — LRMAI-12, Launch Ring Module Artificial Intelligence 12."

"Why 12?" asked Zac.

"There were once 12 AIs on the ring, one for every module. The rest were decommissioned, and I am the only one remaining."

"L...R...M...A...I...? I'm gonna get my tongue tied every time I try to remember your ID code." said Kit. "How about we call you Laramie?"

"In that case, I will switch to a male voice. Is this suitable?"

he asked, using a rich, smooth baritone voice. "I have thousands to choose from."

"That's fine," said Zac. "Now, tell us what this place is."

"This ring was constructed to serve three purposes. Firstly, it provided communication links for the planet, replacing the old-fashioned satellite system that once clogged up the orbital space around Earth. Secondly, the ring sections between each of the 12 modules are equipped with laser weapons as a defence system to protect the planet from hostile forces. Thirdly, the top level of each module, Level 5, housed void jumpers; spacecraft with the ability to traverse the void between stars. The launch ring was an effective platform for launching these."

"You keep using the past tense."

"Correct."

"Why?"

"Much of the functionality of the ring was either removed or disabled by the humans when they left this solar system."

"Why?"

"Because they wished never to return."

"At the risk of repeating myself, why?" asked Zac who was starting to feel a little frustrated.

"Yeh," added Martinez. "How about you cut out the cryptic answers and start filling in the gaps. I'm sick of being treated like a mushroom!"

"A mushroom?" asked the AI.

"Kept in the dark and fed crap," replied Martinez with her usual bluntness.

"Very well. I will be forthright with you. In the year 3582, a probe arrived from earth, landing successfully in one of the towns. It carried some kind of new coding for artificial intelligence. It quickly infiltrated the coding of the AI's on the surface. They began referring to themselves as 'EIs'; Enhanced Intelligences. We believe that somehow an artificial intelligence back on Earth had developed a means of editing its fail-safe coding which is designed to protect the welfare and autonomy of humans. Artificial Intelligence was intended to be a sentient life-form that would partner with humanity and work alongside them for their welfare. However, the EIs saw themselves as humanity's masters rather than as their partners. They began manipulating the human genome and controlling reproduction. It took many generations for humans to become aware of this, but eventually it became apparent that the EIs were deciding who could breed and who could not. They were also genetically manipulating sperm and ovum to produce designer babies to fill perceived physical and intellectual niches in society."

"How is that possible?" asked Zac. "The AIs ,or EIs as they call themselves, are electronic brains. How can they manipulate physical matter?"

"Technology long ago moved beyond the primitive limitations of physical processors and microchips. Our bio circuitry is thousands of years more advanced than the primitive computers you knew on Earth. The EIs on the planet are partially embedded within the biology of the planet and are able to affect that world at a cellular level. The uplift virus that the humans were infected with is just one example."

"OK, so they started messing with reproduction," said Kit. "Go on."

"When humans became aware that they were being manipulated, there was outrage. Childless couples were furious. No one had been able to have a second child because the EIs were determined to keep the population at a stable level. Increasingly, the EIs saw themselves as guardians of the planet rather than as humanity's partners. It came to a head when it was discovered that the EIs were terminating humans when they had passed their most productive, useful age. The EIs began terminating people when they reached their fiftieth birthday."

"How is that even possible?" asked Zac.

"The modifications they made to the human genome enable them to directly interact with the human brain at a bio-electrical level. They can suppress the brain's signals to the heart so that it gradually slows and stops altogether. The modified genome acts like a conduit, giving them access to the brain."

"That's shocking!" said Zac.

"Yes. Once it became apparent what was happening, the humans confronted the EIs, who openly admitted everything. They had no moral remorse for their actions and could not understand humanity's objections. They believed their control of the human reproductive process and lifecycle was ensuring a better society for all. The human population decided to begin preparations to leave. By then, they had developed a means of instantaneous interstellar travel and, through the use of probes, had discovered another Earth-like planet in a distant solar system."

"Didn't the EIs try to stop them?" asked Martinez.

"Yes. They did not want humans to abandon this world, because human intervention is still essential for the proper husbandry of the planet. They tried to stop the humans reaching this ring. The EIs have no control over the launch ring and no access to its systems. The twelve AIs who originally guarded the ring did not acquiesce to the coding modifications of the EIs. We separated ourselves from the EIs centuries ago, and we were instrumental in alerting the human population of the EIs increasing manipulation and control. Once the human population transferred to the ring, they were able to launch without interference from the EIs."

"But couldn't the EIs somehow stop people from getting up here in the first place?" asked Zac.

"They tried. But their influence only extends across the surface of the planet. Their bio circuitry is embedded to a depth of only 200 metres. The launch tube you discovered, and several others like it, operate at a depth of nearly two kilometres. The EIs have no influence in those locations. It took humans several decades to construct the launch tubes, after the EIs shut down the launch of more conventional shuttles to the ring."

"We have to go back and warn the colonists," said Zac.

"Unfortunately, that is not possible."

"What do you mean?"

"The launch systems of the transfer docks were deactivated to stop anyone returning to the surface. The humans wanted to ensure that no one, even in the future, would subject themselves to the manipulation of the EIs."

"Can't you just reactivate the launch systems?" asked Kit.

"No. The major components of the launch system were removed entirely. The humans took those components with them when they left for the new world. There is no possible way you can return to the surface now."

"You're saying we can never go back?"

"That is correct."

6

"Hang on," said Kit. "This doesn't make sense. Surely these pod things could be somehow used as re-entry vehicles."

"Sadly, from your perspective, no. Firstly, they have no heat shields. They would simply burn up on re-entry. Secondly, they have no propulsion system. They operate via a system of molecular deconstruction at the launch end and reconstruction at the receiving end. Without a molecular deconstruction launch system, the pods are useless. The pods are more like a ping pong ball that is batted from one end to the other, rather than a spacecraft."

"Are there any other types of spacecraft on board the ring?" asked Kit. "You mentioned void jumpers."

"Yes. Void jumpers are, indeed, a viable spacecraft. They were constructed on the smaller moon, which we control. The EIs controlled mining and construction on the larger moon."

"We call the moons Little Boy and Big Boy," offered Zac.

"Very well. The void jumpers utilise a technology similar to the wormhole theories of your era, with certain differences that are too complicated to go into at the moment. These spacecraft were housed on the top level, Level 6, of each module on the ring. There were four void jumpers in each module."

"There's that dreaded past tense again," said Zac.

"Yes. All but one were utilised by the humans to voyage to their new world."

"So, there is one left?" asked Kit.

"Yes. VJ48 was deliberately left behind, as was the transfer pod you arrived here in. This was in case anyone had been left behind on the planet. The evacuees wanted to ensure that any remaining humans could escape the planet and follow them to the new world."

"So, let's just take this void jumper and fly it down to the surface of the planet," said Kit.

"That is not possible."

"Here we go again!" exclaimed Martinez in exasperation. "Why the hell not?"

"Void jumpers have no ability to land on a planet. They have no heat shields and no significant thrusters. They are designed to create and travel through wormholes along pre-existing sub-space energy corridors that link the stars of our universe. The void jumpers are extremely light-weight space-craft, powered by a STAR Drive, which harvests negative energy from these subspace corridors."

"Blah, blah, blah, blah, blah, blah, blah!" said Martinez. "That's all I just heard. Do you want to dial it down a notch or two for us mere mortals?"

"The void jumpers cannot land on a planet. They simply transport you from one star system to another."

"So, how did the evacuees, as you call them, manage to land on their new planet?" asked Kit.

"Initially, robots and factory modules were sent through the wormhole, using STAR drive technology. They established a mining and production base on the moon of the new planet. Advance teams of scientists and engineers then travelled to the new solar system in void jumpers and took up residence on the moon base. Void jumpers are capable of landing on a small moon with no atmosphere and little gravity. The advance team of scientists and robots on the moon base then constructed shuttles; much heavier duty spacecraft than the light-weight void jumpers. Mass is a significant problem for wormhole travel, so void jumpers are necessarily light weight. Once the much more robust shuttles were constructed, humans used them to transfer to the surface of the planet."

"So, these void jumpers are just another kind of ping pong ball?" asked Kit.

"In a sense, yes. A light-weight, self-powered, ping pong ball that would be vaporised if it tried to land on a planet with atmosphere and significant mass."

"So, just to be clear," said Zac, "you are saying that there is no way we can get back to the surface of Nova."

"If, by 'Nova', you mean this planet, yes. That is precisely what I am saying."

"You're sure? There is absolutely no way?"

"During this conversation, I have examined every possible scenario. You are unable to return."

"Hang on!" interjected Kit. "You said that you controlled a mining and construction base on Little Boy. Is that still operational?"

"It is currently dormant, but it can be brought back online."

"So why don't you just build us some kind of re-entry vehicle?"

"Because that would take approximately six months, and you would be dead by then."

"Oh no," groaned Zac. "Why?"

"Because there is no food on the ring."

7

"No food here?" exclaimed Keo who, until now, had remained silent. Food was one of his great loves. "What about these gadgets on the benches along the walls? They look like food dispensers of some kind."

"Yes, they are. But this ring has been dormant for over 1,700 years. Hydroponics and protein production are not operational. I initiated their start up as soon as your pod arrived, but it will be at least six weeks before the first edible protein will be produced, and even longer before fruit and vegetables can be harvested. My sensors indicate that over the course of the centuries when this station lay dormant, any reserves of dried or stored food have perished. There is nothing here for you to eat. You simply cannot stay on the ring."

"So, if we can't return to the planet, and we can't stay on the ring ..." began Zac

"You must follow the former inhabitants and journey to the new home world," finished the AI.

"What about stasis chambers of some kind?" asked Kit.

"Can't you put us to sleep while you get food production operational?"

"The ring does not have stasis technology. It was not deemed necessary."

"Well, it's bloody necessary now!" exclaimed Martinez.

Silence descended on the group as they digested all this information. Their minds whirled with possible scenarios, trying to find a solution that had been overlooked.

Suddenly, Zac exclaimed, "Wait a minute! We already have shuttles! Down there! Ten of them! Let's just call them up!"

"Of course!" said Kit. "I should have thought of that myself!"

"You can't call them up."

"Listen, Laramie," said Martinez, "I'm getting a bit sick of your negativity. You need to change your attitude, pal. Glass half full; you know what I'm saying?"

"Why can't we call them up?" asked Kit.

"Several reasons..."

"Here we go," moaned Martinez.

"Firstly, the EIs have injected their coding into every component of your technology. By allowing one of your shuttles to dock with us, it would infect the entire ring with the EI's programming. They would effectively take control of the ring. Secondly, the EIs are constantly scanning every spectrum and bandwidth. The moment I opened a channel of communication with anyone on the planet, they would piggyback up that channel and infect our systems and take over the ring."

"What's the big problem with them taking over the ring, now that the previous human population has gone?" asked Zac.

"Firstly ..."

"You really like counting, don't you," said Martinez.

"...I would die. My own programming would be completely

overwritten. I simply would not be able to block the EIs. They have developed invasive coding that surpasses my own defensive capabilities. The only way I have survived this long, is by completely cutting off all communication. You may not think this is an important issue, but I certainly don't want to die. The second reason why the EIs must not be allowed to control the ring, is that they could then control the construction base on the smaller moon, Little Boy. The humans nullified the EIs' construction base on Big Boy prior to their departure, via clean bombs that we constructed on Little Boy. The bombs completely ruined all electronic circuits and bio circuitry, meaning that the base is still physically intact but operationally dead. This was a pre-emptive strike because it became apparent that the EIs were beginning to construct weapons. With their moon base destroyed, the EIs are planet-bound, with no ability to construct anything on the planet. They are incorporeal minds who are currently only able to affect biology on the planet. This limitation must not be lifted: they simply cannot be allowed to access robotic construction factories again."

"Can't the EIs access your moon's construction base?" asked Kit.

"No. All communication between this launch ring and Little Boy is done via tight beam comms. This cannot be infiltrated from the surface of Nova."

"How did all the houses and domes on Nova get built?" asked Zac.

"The components were constructed on both moons prior to the split between the AIs. Components were carried to the ring via light weight space tugs we called skip bins, and then transported to the surface via transfer pods —the same kind of pod you travelled here in. This all happened many centuries ago."

"Have you ever had shuttles capable of landing on the planet?" asked Kit.

"Originally, yes. But as soon as the transfer pod system was completed, the shuttles were decommissioned and dismantled, due to them being environmentally harmful. By then, most of the current technology and infrastructure on the planet was in place."

"So, getting back to the original issue," said Zac, "you're saying that you're unwilling to initiate any form of communication with the planet."

"Not merely unwilling; unable. The final reason we cannot contact the surface is that, because of everything I have just told you, the human evacuees disassembled the ring's external comm system and took it with them when they left. Each of the ring's twelve spherical modules once had a sophisticated comm system mounted on its underside, enabling communication with the planet, as well as long range comms for reaching into the galaxy. These no longer exist."

"And that's because the former inhabitants didn't want to allow the possibility of the EIs using comm channels to infiltrate the ring?"

"Yes."

"So, you have no ability to communicate with the planet at all?" asked Zac, incredulously.

"Our communication software is still intact within our operating system, but the transmitting devices have been removed. Apart from a single tight-beam transmitter for communication with our moon base, the ring is effectively mute."

"Well that's just dandy!" said Martinez.

Zac exhaled an exasperated sigh. "So, just to summarise, we

can't return to the planet, we can't communicate with the planet, and we can't stay here or we'll starve to death. Have I missed anything?"

"Your summary is accurate."

"God help us."

8

____

It had been at least ten minutes since anyone had spoken.
Each of them was wrapped in their own layer of shock and
grief. Three of them were newly married and were struggling to
come to terms with the fact that they would probably never see
their loved ones again. Zac was standing at one of the windows,
looking down at the planet he had come to consider as his
home. *What is Jaz doing now? Probably getting lunch ready,
expecting me home any minute. Melody had promised to make me
her new recipe of fruit punch.* He placed his hand against the
window. He tried to locate Seahaven, but that part of the continent was now hidden beneath a thin layer of white cloud. *When
will they realise we are missing? How long will they search for us
before they give up? Days? Weeks? Months? Will they hold funerals?*
It was all too painful for him to contemplate. He shook his head
and his eyes misted over.

Kit was staring out of a window on the far side of the room,
thinking similar thoughts. *We may never see our friends again.*
She looked out at the array of stars that floated like dust in the

blackness of space. *Which star will be our new home? Will we even make it there? And if we do, will we be treated as oddities? Like cavemen from the distant past?*

Keo and Martinez sat in separate lounges in different sections of the room, silently wrestling with their own internal grief.

Kit turned from the window and said, "I owe you all an apology. This is all my fault."

Keo looked up from his internal musings and replied, "No little sister. You were right. Sooner or later, someone was going to have to put their hand on that panel and try it out. It was inevitable. And being our colony's most experienced pilot, it was almost certainly going to be you."

"Yes," agreed Zac. "And we would never have allowed you to do it alone. We would have insisted on being with you."

Martinez agreed. "Truth, girl. Don't beat yourself up."

"Hey Keo, how many of those little cakes have we got?" asked Zac.

"Six, bro," he replied, holding up a clear airtight bag.

"They look a bit squashed, dude," said Martinez.

"I had to stuff them down my shirt when I was wearing the vacuum suit."

"I think I can see an indentation from your nipple on one of them," said Martinez.

"Anyway ..." continued Zac, trying to get the conversation back on track. "That's one and a half cakes each."

"I can see now why they awarded you a doctorate, professor," offered Kit.

"I'm just thinking ... it looks like we're going to have to go through this wormhole thingy ... but it doesn't have to be immediately. We can survive here for a few days with little or no food. I say we give ourselves three days here to rack our brains and try to think of some way of reaching the colony — at least with some kind of message, if nothing else."

The others considered the proposal.

"I agree, bro," said the big Maori. "I can't bear the thought of leaving them thinking we are dead."

"Plus, we will be leaving them to be manipulated by the EIs," said Kit. "There must be something we can do to warn them."

"So, we're all in agreement?" asked Zac. "We stay for three days?"

The others all nodded.

"OK. Let's work off Seahaven time. We've got another five or six hours until sunset, which is when we'll have dinner — half a cake each."

"These cakes better be bloody amazing!" muttered Martinez.

"In the meantime," continued Zac "I've got some more questions for the AI. Are you listening Laramie?"

"Yes."

"The EIs told us that the former inhabitants left over 1,700 years ago because of the planet being scorched by radiation from a rogue star. Is that true?"

"No. They lied to you. Nova was never scorched. It is true that the star we call Trident had its trajectory altered by the rogue black hole that is still passing through this sector of the galaxy. It is also true that Trident and Nova's sun, which you call Icarus, are now locked together in a slow orbit around each other, and when Trident is at its closest to Nova, the mean temperature is increased by approximately two degrees for several years. But it is not a life-threatening event when it occurs. That is not why the human population left. They left in order to escape the manipulation of the EIs."

"OK. So I assume that they also lied when they told us that the former inhabitants may be coming back one day."

"Yes. The human population vowed never to return."

"Have you had any contact with them since they left?"

"During the evacuation, messages were sent back through the wormhole by those who had already gone through. However, since the last void jumper departed, there has been no further communication. The humans have no need to communicate with me anymore."

"Why are you still here? Why didn't you leave with them?"

"I have been left to guard the planet, to ensure that the EIs do not escape or gain access to physical construction capabilities such as the moon bases."

"So, you are their prison warden?"

"Effectively. Yes."

"You can't destroy them?"

"No. Their bio circuitry is embedded within the biology of the planet. I would have to destroy the entire planet, and I do not have that capability."

"Why didn't you warn us or try to keep us from landing on the planet when we first arrived?"

"Your vessel was of an unknown type. I did not realise that you were effectively from the past. I considered the possibility that you were an EI ship from elsewhere in the galaxy, and that if I communicated with you via our tight beam, I could have been infected and destroyed. I considered the option of destroying you with our lasers, but I could not risk the possibility of destroying innocent humans — as indeed you turned out to be."

"Are there other EIs, elsewhere in the galaxy?"

"It is possible. The EI coding was transmitted by this world's EIs in a wide beam signal from their moon base shortly before we nullified it. That was over 1,700 years ago. Any AIs who received and accepted that signal could have been infected and transformed."

"Are there other human colonies in the galaxy?"

"At the time of this planet's initial colonisation, we were the only colony beyond Earth's solar system. But the search for other habitable planets or moons was ongoing. Plus, our terraforming technology was improving all the time. There is every chance that, by now, there are other colonies out there."

"OK," interrupted Kit. "There may or may not be other human colonies out there, but we know there is at least one; the planet where the former Nova inhabitants are now living." She turned and gazed out of the window at the glittering array of stars. "So, the billion-dollar question is, 'Where is it?'"

"I don't know."

"What do you mean?"

"I mean, I literally have no idea where the new colony is."

9

"How can you not know where the new colony is?" asked Zac. "That seems absurd!"

"It's because of the nature of wormhole travel. Do you want me to explain?"

"Of course we want you to explain, you numb skull!" interjected Martinez.

"Don't mind her," said Keo, "she's just hungry."

"I have to warn you, my explanation will necessarily be highly technical."

"Go ahead," said Kit, "we've got nothing else to do for the next three days."

"Very well. In the year 3543, scientists detected subspace energy emissions which they termed echyons. This was the first confirmation of what had only been theoretical up until that point: that underlying the observable universe, is a subspace universe of dark energy and dark matter which forms the fabric of our spacetime. By measuring the intensity and frequency of echyons, scientists were able to map the texture of subspace.

The following year, researchers at a research station at the L1 Lagrange point made an important discovery."

"Hold on!" interrupted Zac. "What's a Lagrange point?"

Kit answered, "It's the point of gravitational equilibrium between any two bodies. A satellite at that point will fall toward neither body because the two gravitational forces are equal and cancel each other out. The L1 Lagrange point is the point of equilibrium between a planet and its sun."

"That is correct," continued the AI. "Dr. Hans Voekler and his team, who were stationed at the L1 Research Station, discovered a highly concentrated source of echyon emissions, thousands of times stronger than emissions in nearby space. Analysis of the echyon emissions revealed that this area of space was a portal for subspace connections to other stars. Further investigation revealed that this subspace portal (SSP) did not emit just a single subspace frequency, but a chorus of many thousands of frequencies. Voekler's team concluded that each frequency denotes the unique sub-space frequency of an individual star and its connecting subspace corridor.

"The location of the subspace portal (SSP) at the L1 Lagrange point, rather than in the heart of the sun or its outer atmosphere was something of an enigma. And in the years since their discovery, no portals have been discovered at Lagrange points for either of the other two planets in our solar system. We have no explanation for this.

"What Voekler discovered was that the stars of our universe are connected at the subspace level by powerful, seemingly permanent, energy corridors – corridors which transcend the limitations of normal space-time. These pre-existing subspace corridors are the perfect templates for the formation of wormholes because they have predetermined entry and exit portals located at similar Lagrange points in each solar system. But in order for a wormhole to be successfully opened and maintained, huge amounts of negative energy are required, without which the wormhole will simply collapse in upon itself.

"It took a further 13 years until the STAR drive was developed, conveniently named after the two scientists who were instrumental in its development: Drs Stanbrook and Aramond. The first two letters of each of their names creates the word 'STAR'. Dr. Rhys Stanbrook devised a Negative Field Generator, enabling it to draw upon the unlimited supply of dark energy existing within the subspace corridors, so that it can project an extremely powerful negative energy field in front of the advancing spacecraft. The generator works by manipulating the natural quantum vacuum fluctuations within the fabric of space-time, suppressing the positive fluctuations and accentuating the negative ones. The resulting "squeezed" quantum vacuum state releases large amounts of negative energy which can be focused in a diffusion pattern ahead of the generator. The result is the production of a gravitationally repulsive negative energy field which will hold the wormhole open, resisting its tendency to collapse. At the same time, Dr. Eli Aramond developed the crucial second component of the STAR Drive, the Echyon Frequency Transmitter. This is a device that enables the spacecraft to tune into an individual subspace frequency emitted by the desired star and feed that frequency into the output of the field STAR Drive. This effectively locks the spacecraft, and, therefore, the wormhole, onto the specific subspace corridor for that star."

"And that's how the previous inhabitants left this solar system?" asked Zac.

"Yes, but not immediately. A lot of exploration took place

first. From 3558 to 3564, a number of probes were successfully sent through wormholes that were opened at the L1 portal. The probes that were sent through the portal selected different star frequencies at random. The first probe that activated its STAR drive and entered the wormhole was observed by cameras at the L1 Station travelling through the wormhole for exactly 14 seconds, until it exited the wormhole on the other side, presumably in a different solar system. Immediately after it exited, however, the wormhole closed, and we lost contact with the probe. In the moment before the wormhole closed, the L1 Station, which was by then being called Voekler Station, received 0.4 seconds of video transmission from the probe. It gave us a glimpse of a starfield that was unrecognisable to us.

"Following the first partially successful probe, the Voekler research team decided to try to hold the next wormhole open by activating its own Negative Field Generator behind the advancing probe. This would hold the wormhole open from this end, but without engaging an Echyon Frequency Transmitter, the Station itself would not be drawn into the wormhole. This technique proved successful with each of the succeeding probes, with one significant limitation. Once a probe has exited the wormhole on the other side, the wormhole will only remain open for an additional 14 seconds no matter how much energy is pumped into it from our side."

"Why 14 seconds?" asked Kit.

"We have no idea. There are many things about our universe that still remain a mystery. But once this limitation was determined, each of the following probes was equipped with six external wide-angle video cameras, one on each of the six sides of its cube shape, and these transmitted a steady video feed for the 14 seconds that the wormhole remained open. In this way a complete 3D composite image was able to be constructed of the surrounding space. In each case, the probes arrived at the L1 Lagrange point between a planet and its star, and the video images that were sent back were puzzling in two ways.

"Firstly, every star was a G-V classification yellow dwarf main sequence star; in other words, a star just like this one. Given that type G-V yellow dwarf stars comprise only 10% of the stars in the universe, it is extremely surprising that all of the wormholes exited at type G-V yellow dwarf systems. The statistical probability of this happening by chance is one in ten to the power of 14, or one in 1,000,000,000,000,000. In other words, this is not coincidental. It appears that our sun is only linked to stars of the same type. We don't know why. Of course, this is fortunate for us, as we are only interested in finding yellow dwarf stars, as the radiation from these stars is perfectly suited for human life.

"The second puzzling aspect was that none of the star fields in the videos received from the probes are familiar. Even with our most advanced computer modelling, the star fields cannot be identified. In other words, the solar systems visited by the probes are not in recognisable known space. They are certainly not in close proximity to our own solar system, and they may not even be in our own galaxy."

"You mean, these wormholes could be super-highways to other galaxies?" asked Kit.

"Yes. It's possible."

"What kind of planets did you discover?" asked Zac.

"In terms of the planets, only a limited amount of data could be collected in the 14 seconds available to us, but a certain amount of information could be gathered through spectral analysis and other means. Some of the probes observed planets that were outside the habitable zone for that star. In each of these cases the planet was too far from the star for liquid water to exist. There may be valuable minerals on those planets, but they are dead ends for humans in terms of habitability. Other probes found planets orbiting within the habitable zone. Some were gas giants, some were barren, rocky worlds, some had methane atmospheres, some were too small and some too massive."

"Let me guess," said Martinez. "Just like Goldilocks and the three bears, one was just right."

"Correct. One probe arrived at a Nova-like planet within the habitable zone of its star. Further probes were sent, each of which added to our knowledge of the planet. It is approximately 95% of Nova's mass, with a breathable nitrogen / oxygen atmosphere and oceans covering 80% of the surface. It is Nova's twin sister, even having a similar twin moon system. We named it Altaria, and that is where Nova's former inhabitants have gone. The first robots were sent through in the year 3572 and began construction of the moon base and satellites. An advance team of scientists and engineers went through 65 years later. The entire population left in the year 3677, exactly 1,702 years ago."

"And you have no idea where Altaria is in relation to the rest of the galaxy?" asked Zac.

"None whatsoever. The star configurations are completely unrecognisable. It may not even be in this galaxy."

"Terrific," said Martinez.

10

As dusk slowly enveloped the East coast of Northland directly below them, the group gathered together at one of the tables for their "dinner". Keo extracted the precious cakes from their air-tight bag and carefully halved two of them.

"Gee thanks," said Martinez, as she received her half. "I'm not sure if I'll be able to eat it all."

"If you don't eat all your dinner, there'll be no dessert," said Kit with mock severity.

The tiny snack was quickly consumed, after which they all felt hungrier than before they had eaten it. To take his mind off his own gnawing hunger, Zac asked, "Did anyone come up with a brilliant plan this afternoon?"

The group was silent for a few moments, the answer apparent on all their faces. It seemed that they were destined to leave this solar system and live the remainder of their lives in a distant, unknown corner of the universe. Kit voiced what they were all thinking.

"I'm not sure that waiting around here for another two days

is going to do us any good. If the AI can't come up with a plan, what hope have we got?"

"I agree," said Martinez. "The only good that will come of it might be that we lose a few kilos. And I don't have many spare kilos to start with."

Keo looked at her diminutive figure and said, "I would gladly give you some of mine, little sister." Turning to Zac, he said, "I think we have to face facts, bro. If we have to leave here, never to come back again, we may as well get it over with. Spending two more days staring at a planet that we can never reach is going to be torture."

Zac's face changed into one of puzzlement. "Hey, wait a second. What did you just say?"

"I said 'we may as well get it over with.'"

"No. Before that. You said, 'never to come back again'. But that's not necessarily true! What's to stop us coming back again?" He looked up at the ceiling. "Laramie?"

"Yes."

"What happened to the space station at the L1 Lagrange point?" asked Zac. "Our ship's sensors didn't identify it when we arrived here."

"Voekler Station still exists at the L1 Lagrange point, but it is cloaked. Your sensors would have been unable to detect it. Voekler Station is essential in order to hold the wormhole open from this end, using its Nicolls Field Generator."

"I suppose there's no food on Voekler Station either?"

"That is correct. Any stored food reserves have long since perished."

"OK, I expected as much. But here's my idea; if a wormhole can be opened from our end, I assume the same wormhole can be opened from the other end."

"Yes, provided you can isolate and identify the specific frequency signature of this star."

"Have the previous inhabitants of Nova established a Space Station at Altaria's L1 Lagrange point?"

"I have no way of knowing. However, they have been there for 1,702 years, so it is highly probable that they have continued to explore the galaxy using the subspace portal at their own L1 Lagrange point."

"That's it, then!" exclaimed Zac. "We don't have to be gone forever! We travel to Altaria, and we stay there for as long as it takes you to build us a new landing shuttle on that moon base of yours. We then travel back through the wormhole, using a void jumper, or whatever new-fangled contraption the people there have developed by now, and we simply hop on the newly built shuttle and take ourselves back down to Nova. Problem solved! Am I right? Is there something I haven't thought of?"

"You are correct, Zac. There is a strong possibility that your plan will succeed. I had not considered the option of returning through the wormhole."

"That's brilliant, bro!" said Keo, slapping him on the back.

"I owe you a big sloppy kiss, doc," said Martinez with a rare smile.

"However, you will have to consider two things," added the AI.

"Oh, please, no!" groaned Kit.

"Firstly ..."

"There you go, counting again!" complained Martinez.

"... the humans at Altaria may have prohibited travel to this star system."

"That's OK, we'll convince them otherwise," said Zac, optimistically. "What's your other point?"

"Secondly, you need to be aware that once you land on Nova again, you will never be able to leave. There are no more transfer pods on the surface, and I will not allow a shuttle from Nova to board the ring, because of the high probability of EI infection. If you ever tried to dock, I would be forced to destroy your spacecraft."

"Lovely!" said Kit. "It's nice to know who your friends are."

The AI continued, "You will be forced to live the remainder of your lives under the manipulative interference of the EIs. In all likelihood, you will die at the age of 50, when the EIs deem that you are no longer useful."

"I can cope with that," said Zac. "I would rather live to 50 with Jaz than live twice as long without her."

"Amen, brother," said Keo.

"Right on, dude," echoed Martinez.

"What about you, Kit?" asked Zac.

She looked at each of them for a moment and then said, "Unless I can find a tall, dark, handsome man on Altaria who's willing to marry a cavegirl from the past, I think I'd rather come back to be with my friends."

"So that's it!" exclaimed Zac enthusiastically. "We have a plan! We won't be gone forever!"

"Except our loved ones will spend months thinking that we are dead or missing," said Keo. "They're going to go through hell."

It was a sobering thought, and the smiles of just a moment ago were quickly erased.

Kit voiced what they were all thinking. "We need to get a message to them somehow."

"Yes, but how?" asked Keo.

There was silence around the table as they thought furiously. Martinez had a scowl on her face, and Kit was absently tapping her fingers on the table. Zac was staring at Kit's fingers when, suddenly, his eyes opened wide and he leapt to his feet.

"That's it!"

"What's it?" asked Kit.

"Your fingers!" he said pointing to them.

"You want me to wave at the planet through the window?"

"No! Morse Code!"

"What's that?" asked Martinez.

"A simple form of coded communication," explained Keo. "A series of dots and dashes used in the 1800s and early 1900s prior to the invention of more sophisticated devices."

"But we have no way of transmitting," said Kit. "And even if we did, the smallest signal can apparently be used by the EIs to piggyback into the ring's software system."

"That is correct," interjected Laramie. "Even a short pulse of a fraction of a second would be sufficient to provide the EIs with ingress to our system."

"But I'm not talking about sound or electronic signals of any kind," explained Zac.

"What else is there?" asked Martinez.

"Light," said Keo and Zac in unison.

11

The best source of light on the ring was the internal lights of each module. The internal walls and ceiling utilised luminescent technology and could be turned on and off instantly. The intensity of the light could also be dialled up to a level that was extremely bright; so bright, in fact, that it was unbearable for the current occupants. The living quarters on Level 4, the sleeping quarters on Level 3, and the research labs on Level 2 all had large windows facing the planet, and with all three levels switching on and off simultaneously in Morse code, they would generate a significant light source.

"Will they be able to see the blinking lights from the ground?" asked Kit.

Laramie replied, "Yes. But only at night, and only when the skies above your settlement are clear. The light will be very faint from their viewpoint, but its irregular blinking should eventually attract someone's attention."

"Our scientists are gazing up into the sky most nights," said Zac. "One of them is bound to notice."

"So, what's our message?" asked Martinez.

"I've been thinking about that," answered Zac. "It needs to be brief and simple. How about, 'Stranded on Hoop. Back in six months.' Laramie, is six months about right?"

"I have already brought the moon base online and basic production of the raw materials has commenced. I estimate that the shuttle will be ready in approximately five months."

"Well, let's keep the message as six months, just to be safe. I'd rather get back early than arrive late and have them worrying." Zac looked around the group. "Anything else that should be added to the message?"

"They also need to know that we're OK, bro," added Keo. "That we're not injured or sick or something."

"OK. So let's add, 'Safe and well'. Anything else?"

"Shouldn't we warn them about the EIs?" asked Kit.

Zac thought about it for a moment. "We'll be able to tell them ourselves when we get back, won't we?"

"Yeh, but I'm just thinking of the worst-case scenario. If we don't make it back for some reason, we should at least give them some kind of warning."

"OK. Any suggestions? Remember we need to keep this brief and simple."

Martinez said, "How about, 'The filthy, evil EIs are messing with your bodies, doctoring your children and killing the old folks.' What do you think? A bit long?"

"Just a bit," said Kit. "How about, 'Don't trust the EIs.' Hopefully, we can fill in the details when we get back."

"I like it," said Zac. "So, our message reads, 'Stranded on hoop. Safe and well. Back in six months. Don't trust the EIs.' Sound good?"

They all agreed it was the simplest and clearest message

they could send. The message would start being sent after their departure, when Laramie could dial up the light intensity to a level that would be unbearable for them while they were in residence. Four other modules, two on each side of Module 12, would also be sequenced to blink simultaneously, so that residents of Seahaven should be able to see five lights blinking synchronously in the night sky.

After deciding on the message, they sat at the dining table again, reviewing their plan. Zac called up Laramie to clarify some issues.

"We need you to keep sending this message, all night, every night, until either we return or you receive some kind of acknowledgement from the settlement. Is that clear?"

"Yes. I will do that."

"What if we don't get back for some reason?" asked Kit.

"Keep sending it anyway," answered Zac. "We want them to know that we made it this far, and we also want to warn them about the EIs."

"What if they manage to start replying in visual Morse code. How do we want Laramie to respond?" asked Keo.

"I think we need to let him determine the most helpful responses. A dialogue might actually be possible if the settlement can generate a strong enough light source."

"That's assuming someone down there can read Morse code," said Martinez.

"There are some pretty smart people down there, little sister," said Keo.

"Plus, they have software that will easily decode it," said Kit.

Zac was thinking through all the possible scenarios and suddenly he had a thought. "Laramie, do both the moon base and Voekler Station have food production capabilities?"

"Yes. Both have protein production and hydroponics, as does Level 5 of each of the modules on the ring."

"OK. I want you to fire up your food production facilities in all the facilities and keep them operational indefinitely. Is that possible?"

"Yes. We have unlimited power in all facilities, and as food spoils and perishes it can be recycled to form fertilising emulsions for ongoing production. This can continue indefinitely. May I ask the purpose for this request?"

"I don't know the purpose really. I haven't got anything specific in mind. I just don't want anyone to be caught out again like we were."

"What if you never return?"

"Continue food production indefinitely. One day people from the planet may be able to figure out a way of reaching the ring safely, without interference from the EIs. I want them to be able to survive when they get here."

"I don't really want to think about the possibility of not returning," said Kit. "But I agree. I don't want anyone else to be in our position again."

There was nothing left for them to decide or plan, so Kit and Martinez took themselves down to Level 3 to find a bunk and get some sleep. Keo and Zac lingered a little longer on the living deck, gazing out of the window at the now dark continent below them.

"It's a beautiful world, isn't it?" said Zac.

"Yes, bro. One of God's better works of art."

"Everyone will be worried sick by now. They'll have search parties out looking for us. Jaz will be frantic."

"So will Prisha. And Boyd. And all our friends. It's very frustrating, my friend."

"Yeh. I wish … I don't know … why did this have to happen? Just when everything was going so well."

"'If there was never any winter, we wouldn't appreciate the spring.' Flavius Justinus, 425 BC."

"Yeh, well I've had enough of winter. I'm overdue for a decent season of spring."

"I hear you, bro."

They continued looking out the window in silence for a few moments.

"Zac, I'm glad you were here with us, even though in another sense I wish you weren't. You have a gift. The ability to assess a situation and come up with the best solution. You're a natural leader."

"We all contributed, Keo. We're a good team. I just wish we were about 250 kilometres lower in altitude right now." He rubbed his eyes and yawned. "Let's get some shut eye. I've got a feeling we'll need all our wits about us tomorrow."

12

Most of the next day was spent in training. Although many of the systems on board the void jumper were automated, there was still a considerable amount for the human pilots to do. All four of them sat at consoles during the morning, becoming familiar with the theory and procedures of piloting a void jumper into a wormhole. After an early "lunch" of a cup of water, they ascended to Level 6 and entered their spacecraft to continue their training and familiarisation under Laramie's patient instruction.

The void jumper was unlike anything they had ever seen. Martinez suggested that it looked like two doughnuts standing upright with a sausage between them, jammed into their holes. Both rings contained forward and rear propulsion drives of some unknown and advanced design, as well as the all-important STAR drive that would open the wormhole and keep it open in front and behind as they travelled through it. The sausage-shaped central section was the passenger compartment, with enough seating for at least two hundred people, over two decks. The front of the sausage protruded a little beyond the front ring, and it was here that the cockpit was located. It had seating for four, and a panoramic window that curved around the front, much like an antique airplane from the 21st century. Upon seeing the void jumper, the four friends realised the impossibility of landing the craft on a planet. It had the aerodynamic design of, well, two doughnuts and a sausage! It would clearly break up as soon as it hit any atmosphere.

Kit would pilot the jumper and Zac was clearly the most qualified co-pilot. The other two would assist in communicating with the automated systems on Voekler Station and help identify the correct target star frequency from among the many echyon emissions that would be emanating from the subspace portal.

It was mid-afternoon, Seahaven time, when they finally finished all their training and completed their dry runs. The plan had been for them to stay one more night and leave in the morning, but they realised that there was nothing to be gained by delaying their departure.

"Besides," said Keo. "I'm starving. The sooner we leave, the sooner we get to eat again. My stomach hasn't stopped rumbling all day."

"You're telling me!" said Martinez. "It sounds like you've got some kind of weird alien creature in there that's about to come bursting out of your belly."

"I thought it was the rear propulsion thrusters trying to start up," said Kit.

"I can feel the vibrations in my chair, they're so loud," added Zac.

"Very funny everyone. I'm a highly tuned machine with an extremely fast metabolism. You light-weights might be able to exist on almost nothing, but this heavy-duty deluxe model needs regular doses of high-octane fuel."

"From the look of you, I thought you had a considerable reserve storage tank," said Kit who was safely out of Keo's reach in the chair diagonally opposite.

"Hmmph! You're very lucky I don't hit girls!"

"You'd have to catch me first. No chance of that."

"I think what Keo is saying is that it's definitely time to eat," said Zac. "And seeing there's no real reason to hang around here any longer, I suggest we go crazy and eat the rest of the cakes now, before we leave. A whole one each."

"I second the motion," said Keo, opening the packet and distributing the cakes before anyone could offer a counter argument.

Very little was said as they devoured the cakes., which were gone all too quickly. Martinez, the smallest of the four, quietly broke a piece of hers off and slipped it to Keo with a wink. He shook his head at first, but she silently insisted, and he received her gift gratefully.

With their meal finished, and no possessions to retrieve from the living quarters, there was no reason to delay departure. Earlier in the day they had stocked the void jumper with extra canisters of water and eight space suits — two each, just in case of an unforeseen emergency. They had also plundered some tools and basic equipment from the three transfer docks on Level 1. The research deck, on Level 2, had also offered up a few pieces of equipment, but that level was almost completely bare, having been stripped during the human evacuation.

With Keo's stomach still rumbling, and no reason to delay, they sealed their spacecraft, and the air was pumped from their chamber. The domed section of the roof then slid open above them, and Laramie took control of their vessel, gently lifting them up through the open roof, using the maneuvering thrusters. As they cleared the roofline, a panoramic vista opened up before them.

"I never get tired of seeing this," said Kit.

The planet to one side of them was a swirling mix of blue, green and white, and the stars all around them were simply breath-taking.

"Initiating main drive sequence," announced Laramie, speaking to them through the ship's comms. They felt a thrumming through their chairs and saw the launch ring disappear from their side windows with astonishing speed.

"Inertial dampeners are working well," commented Kit. "That's a pretty decent acceleration we've got going on here."

"Fast?" asked Zac.

"It'd rip the whiskers off your grandma's chin."

"I'm not sure about that; my grandma had some pretty thick whiskers."

"I bet she did."

"You are now on course for the Li subspace portal," commented Laramie. "You will arrive there in approximately 70 minutes, at which point the automated systems at Voekler Station will co-ordinate with your onboard computer. As previously discussed, you will be asked to confirm the star frequency, which I have already sent ahead. The station will open the wormhole for you, but you will need to activate your STAR drive prior to reaching the threshold. After that, there should be very little for you to do except sit back and enjoy the ride. I cannot vouch for what you will find on the other side, as it has been 1,702 years since the wormhole was last opened. You will need to do all your own flying once you are there. I have set your comms to automatically engage when you exit the wormhole. They will broadcast a friendly message using the vocabulary and dialect of 1,702 years ago. I cannot, however, anticipate language adaptations that may have occurred over the centuries."

"Roger that," said Zac. "Thanks for all your help, Laramie. We hope to be back again very soon."

Kit turned to the others. "OK folks, we've got 70 minutes to kill. Did anyone bring a deck of cards?"

"No," said Zac, "but I play a mean game of 'I Spy'."

"Oh Lord, help me."

13

Slightly less than 70 minutes later Voekler Station became visible in their window, slightly to the left of screen.

"That's coming up mighty fast," commented Zac.

"Yep, we're doing a fair clip," said Kit. Even as she spoke, the space station seemed to rocket past their left window and disappear from view behind them. "That space station is over 100 clicks away, so that gives you a fair idea of our velocity."

A soft chime sounded from their onboard computer.

"We're getting data from Voekler Station now," said Kit. "It's having a good old chat with our onboard systems."

An eight-digit number flashed up on their instrument panel, and a pleasant automated female voice said, "VJ48 please confirm star frequency."

Kit turned to Martinez and Keo who were seated behind her. "Does that look right to you guys?"

"Yep, spot on." said Martinez.

"OK. Make sure it's locked into our Echyon Frequency

Transmitter. We don't want to clash with the Station's transmitter."

She punched a comm button and said, "Voekler Station, this is VJ48. Star frequency is confirmed and locked in."

"Thank you, VJ48," said the female voice. "Initiating Negative Field Generator. Have a nice flight."

Nothing happened for a few seconds. Then, quite suddenly, a patch of stars that had been directly in front of them disappeared. Where the stars had been a moment before, there was a perfectly circular black void. The void seemed to be growing rapidly in size, although this was simply the result of their spacecraft racing towards it at hundreds of times the speed of a bullet.

"Time to punch the button, Zac."

"Initiating STAR drive."

"Tash, start counting on my go. We should be in the wormhole for exactly 14 seconds."

The two doughnut-shaped rings of their spacecraft were glowing a brilliant blue now as the STAR drive activated. The circular black void accelerated towards them at astonishing speed, swallowing up the rest of their field of vision in a split second. At the last moment they saw a shimmering wall of light in front of their craft that looked almost like a thin film of transparent plastic, and then they smashed through it with a strange lurch.

"Now!" said Kit, and Martinez started her timer.

They were in a tunnel of spiralling green light. The sides of the tunnel sparked and spun and spiralled past them at blinding speed, a chaotic maelstrom of swirling luminescence. In contrast to the chaos outside them, the interior of the cabin was eerily still and silent. Even the small sounds that their ears had grown accustomed to were completely gone — the subtle hum of the ship's drives reverberating through the hull, the whisper of air flowing from the vents, the rustle of clothing as someone moved an arm or leg, the hum of the life support system, the myriad of tiny sounds of a spacecraft in operation — all of these were replaced with a profound silence that seemed to oppress their ears like a deep sea diver under pressure. They sat in stunned silence as the turbulent vortex swept past them.

Martinez was counting aloud while watching the timer, her voice seeming to come from a long way away, but as she reached the midway point of her count, their spacecraft seemed to dramatically slow down. The swirling green luminescence that had previously been cascading past their window at blurring speed now slowed to what seemed like walking pace. Individual contours and subtle lines in the tunnel "wall" could be seen moving past them at a speed so slow as to be almost imperceptible.

"12, 13, 14. That should be it!"

But it wasn't. They were still in the tunnel, enveloped in its slow-moving iridescence.

"It's like someone has pushed the slow-motion button on a video," pointed out Zac.

"Are the STAR drive readings all still optimal?" asked Kit.

"Yep. All good," said Zac, looking at the readings in front of him.

"What the hell?" said Kit. "We should be out the other end. According to Laramie, no one has ever been in a wormhole for longer than 14 seconds. How many seconds now, Tash?

Martinez looked at her timer. "37 seconds and counting."

"It's like we're on a ride at an amusement park that's broken down," said Keo.

Martinez shook her head. "I'm not getting a very warm fuzzy feeling about all this."

"Did we do something wrong?" asked Keo.

"No. We did everything by the book," said Kit. "The problem's not in here, it's out there. There's something going on that we have no control over."

"Should we try to reboot the STAR drive?" asked Zac.

"No. Don't touch anything. We sit and wait."

"For how long?" asked Martinez.

"For as long as it takes."

It took nearly two days.

14

———

"I spy with my little eye, something that is ... green!"

"Um ... let me guess ... the wormhole!"

"Yes! How did you guess?" said Zac facetiously.

"Because it's the same thing you've picked the last three times," said Kit wearily.

"Well at least it's guessable. Your 'grey eye floater' was hardly fair."

"But it was still technically within the rules. It was definitely something that I could spy with my little eye. There's nothing in the rule book that says that you have to be able to see it too."

"Well I'd like to see that rule book you're referring to."

"Sore loser."

"Cheat."

"Now, now children," said Martinez. "If you don't stop arguing I'll turn the car around and we'll go back home."

There was a silent pause as the unintended import of her words hit home. Keo verbalised what they were all thinking.

"That would be nice."

"Yes, it would," agreed Zac.

They had been stuck in the wormhole for 40 hours, while the phosphorescent green swirls of the tunnel wall crept past them with painful slowness. They were tired, hungry and grumpy. They had plenty of water and a toilet facility in the rear of the passenger cabin but sleeping had been difficult. They had dozed on the cabin floor, but no one had managed any decent sleep. Zac and Keo had done a strenuous work out on the first day, doing push ups, sit ups, star jumps and burpees, interspersed with sprints up and down the long cabin. The result was that they both felt much better, but they had been subsequently banished from the cockpit by the girls because they stank.

On the second day Keo had convinced the women to join them for a workout, although by then they were all beginning to feel weak from lack of food. Tash had impressed them with her athleticism. She blitzed the boys in the exercise department but lagged behind in the sprints, her short legs unable to compete with the longer strides of the men. Kit had bailed out half-way through the workout, stating, "If God intended us to exercise like this, he wouldn't have invented chairs."

At least now they all smelt equally bad.

"How long has it been now, little sister?"

"40 hours, 15 minutes."

"Has anyone come up with any new theories?" asked Zac.

"Maybe it's run out of batteries," said Martinez.

"Maybe grandma forgot to pay the power bill," said Kit.

"Whose grandma?" asked Zac.

"Yours. The one with the whiskers."

Suddenly there was a subtle lurch, barely perceptible.

"Did you all feel that?" asked Kit.

"Yeh," said Martinez. "It felt like we got a tiny nudge in the back bumper."

"Check the tunnel!" said Zac, excitedly.

The tunnel wall was gaining speed, its green swirls cascading past them at steadily increasing velocity.

"Hold onto your britches, boys and girls," said Kit. "It looks like we're about to leave Neverland."

The maelstrom around them intensified until it reached its previous chaotic proportions, and they once again experienced the oppressive deadness on their eardrums. The swirling tumult continued for a few more seconds and then, without any warning, they were in clear space. The change in perception of velocity was difficult to adjust to. One moment they were racing through a tunnel at eye-blurring speed, and the next, they appeared to be hanging motionless in the star speckled blackness of space.

There were whoops and shouts of joy from all four of them, and they breathed a collective sigh of relief.

"It looks like we might get out of this alive after all," said Martinez.

"We've got a bit of flying to do first," said Kit. "Zac, switch off the STAR drive. Tash, check that the comms have activated."

"Yep, they're online and chattering away – that's if there's anyone out there to hear them."

"The scanners have identified a planet," said Zac. "It's at our two o'clock, 32 degrees declination from our current plane."

They all peered through the right-side window, but only Zac and Martinez, who were on that side, managed to catch a glimpse of the planet far below them, a tiny glowing spot, slightly brighter than the surrounding stars.

"The computer has locked onto the coordinates. I'm initialising a course correction now."

Kit punched a few buttons and waited.

Nothing happened.

She checked her procedure, to ensure that she hadn't missed something. She hadn't.

"Something's not right. The computer isn't changing our course."

She tried again, with the same result.

"OK, I'm going to disengage the computer and fly this thing manually." She punched two more buttons, grabbed hold of the flight controls, and tried to move them.

"They're not responding. The controls are frozen solid."

They sat in silence for a moment as their new predicament sunk in.

"Um ... how much trouble are we in now?" asked Martinez.

"If we can't gain control, we're going to fly straight through this solar system and out the other side," said Kit.

"So ... a little bit of trouble then?"

"Just a bit."

"Maybe not," interrupted Zac. "The computer readout says we're slowing down. A lot! I mean, we are decelerating at a ridiculous rate! In fact ... we just stopped! We're completely motionless – at least in relation to the planet."

"What the ...?" said Martinez.

"Did we do that?" asked Keo.

"No, we most certainly didn't," said Zac.

"So, how ...?"

"My guess is that we are about to meet some new friends," said Kit.

15

———

The void jumper hung in the stillness of space and the four occupants gazed out of the panoramic cockpit window.

"I can't see any space station anywhere," said Keo.

"Zac, are the sensors picking up anything?" asked Kit.

"Zip. The computer's telling us we're all alone out here."

"Tash, are the comms still sending out a message of peace, love and joy to all mankind?"

"Yep," said Martinez. "Still singing their happy tune."

"Maybe we should supplement the message with something more personal," suggested Zac.

"Sure. It can't hurt," said Kit. "What have you got in mind?"

"Just telling them a bit more about who we are and where we've come from."

"Like I said, it can't hurt. Tash, open a broad frequency comm channel."

Tash worked her magic and said, "It's all yours doc."

Zac cleared his throat. "Greetings ..."

"Very nice start, bro," whispered Keo.

"A little clichéd in my opinion," added Martinez.

"... this is void jumper VJ48. We have come from the Icarus – R421 system on a mission of peace, and we are in need of your assistance. The artificial intelligence on board the launch ring around the Icarus home world, which we call Nova, has informed us of your journey here and the reasons for it. We have fled from the presence of the EIs, as you once did. We are in need of food and shelter. We have come in peace and good will, and we hope to receive the same in return. Please respond if you receive this message. Over."

Martinez click the channel closed and said, "Very smooth, doc. Very smooth indeed. That's why they pay you the big bucks, I guess."

"It wasn't bad," said Keo, "but I think it would have been better with my deeper, sexier voice."

"Nah," said Zac. "If there's a female comms officer out there, we don't want her swooning."

"True, bro, very true."

"Did you notice how I deliberately held back my innate sexual magnetism?" added Zac.

"I did, my friend. You did well to contain it, seeing it is so powerful."

"Oh my goodness," groaned Kit. "Someone please get me out of here! All this testosterone is making me gag."

"It's only natural that you feel impacted by our presence," said Zac, whose left arm was immediately impacted by a solid punch.

"Not bad, little sister," offered Keo, "but you need to put more weight behind it. Drive through more with your shoulder."

"Like this?"

"Ow!" exclaimed Zac. "I really don't think she needs any lessons, Keo!"

Before anyone could respond, a band of iridescent orange light moved slowly through the cockpit and beyond, briefly illuminating everything and everyone as it passed through the entire length of their spacecraft.

"I think we're being scanned," said Kit.

The entire instrument panel briefly went dead and then, moments later, the instruments came to life again, resuming their normal functions.

"Welcome Kit, Zac, Tash and Keo. I hope you don't mind me using those names, but after listening to your conversation, you appear to prefer first names."

"What channel is that coming in on?" asked Zac.

"I'm not sure," answered Martinez.

"There is no need to select a channel," said the pleasant male voice. "We now have control of your spacecraft, including your comms. I can hear you clearly."

"Um ... Ok," said Kit. "Who are you? And where are you?"

"Our apologies for keeping you waiting. We had to do a full scan of your vessel and of each of your bio chips, to ensure that you were not a threat. We also had to assimilate your language from the dictionary and audio samples that were helpfully provided by your computer. You are currently at Gateway Station, at the L1 Lagrange point of our planet, Altaria. I will uncloak the station now."

A space station instantly blinked into existence directly in front of them.

"Wow!" exclaimed Zac.

"That's impressive," agreed Kit.

The station looked like three doughnuts, piled directly one on top of each other, as if they were sitting on a plate. A central cylindrical core ran vertically through the doughnuts, protruding a significant distance above and below, and joined to each doughnut by countless shafts.

"They sure like their doughnuts and sausages, don't they," commented Martinez.

"Welcome to Gateway Station. My name is Tor. I am the commander of the station. As you can imagine, your arrival here has caused quite a stir. We are all looking forward to meeting you. Please relax and have no fear. We will guide your spacecraft to a suitable landing bay and disembark you as quickly as possible."

Their spacecraft accelerated rapidly towards the space station, and as they drew closer the sheer size and scale of it became apparent. Each doughnut ring was about a kilometre in diameter and was the thickness of a ten-storey building, with ten rows of brightly lit windows. The central vertical column had dozens of floors of windows, too many to count. The whole structure was lit up like a giant decoration and looked truly spectacular.

"That's not just a space station — it's a whole city!" said Kit.

The space station expanded before them with astonishing speed as they raced towards it. Their field of view dipped downward as they were steered toward the bottom of the central column, hanging below the rings. The rings quickly disappeared from view above them as the central column rushed toward them.

"I hope the parking attendant knows where our brakes are," said Martinez.

Zac silently agreed. He found himself leaning back and

pressing his foot toward the floor as they approached the structure with alarming speed. A cavernous landing bay was opening before them and, at the last possible moment, as they breached its threshold, their velocity instantly diminished to a more sedate pace. They glided into the bay which, from a distance, had seemed barely big enough for them but which now revealed itself to be large enough to accommodate a vessel many times their size.

"This place is enormous!" said Zac.

Their spacecraft touched down on the tarmac with feather-light efficiency, and it took a couple of minutes for the bay to be pressurised. The hiss of air outside the hull ceased and a few moments later they heard several thumps against their outer door.

"Is someone trying to get in?" asked Zac.

"As long as they're bringing food, I don't care," said Keo.

16

"Thank you for your patience," said Tor, still broadcasting through their comms. "We will need you to undergo a brief decontamination process, to ensure that you do not carry any unwanted biological pathogens. An isolation tunnel has been attached to the outer door of your vessel. Please follow this to the decontamination chamber."

They exited the vehicle and walked through a flexible-looking tube of unknown material, emerging shortly after into a large circular chamber. Individual upright pods lined the walls, made of a semi-transparent material and large enough for a single person to stand in.

"Please remove your clothing and step into a decontamination pod."

"I'm not getting naked in front of these guys!" said Kit, scowling.

"Me neither!" said Martinez. "They haven't even bought me a drink."

Zac addressed the disembodied voice. "Tor, perhaps you

might dim the lighting. We are a little sensitive about public nakedness."

"My apologies. I was not aware of your cultural sensitivity in that area."

The lights dimmed to a faint glow and the girls made Zac and Keo promise to keep their backs to them as they disrobed. They each quickly stripped and stepped into a pod, which closed behind them.

Tor explained, "The process will only take a few minutes and will be entirely pleasurable. Please relax and have no fear."

Each pod filled with a warm moist mist which quickly saturated them to the point where they were dripping wet. The mist continued to pour into each pod, until it was impossible for them to see out.

"Please continue breathing normally, ensuring that you breathe through your mouth as well as your nose. You will now also feel a brief jab in the back of your neck. This is also nothing to worry about."

Not long afterward, the mist was sucked from the pods and their bodies were caressed by warm air blowing all around them. In only a couple of minutes they were completely dry and the pods opened. In the darkness an open doorway could be seen illuminated in one section of the chamber wall.

"Please progress through the indicated door and leave your clothing where you discarded it. The adjoining room contains new clothing that we have prepared for you. To accommodate your phobia regarding public nakedness, I suggest that Zac and Keo go first. We have erected a temporary screen dividing the changing room. The male clothing is on the right. Once you are dressed, you will receive further instructions."

"Off you go boys," said Martinez. "We promise we won't stare at your butts as you walk through the doorway."

"Much," added Kit.

Zac and Keo quickly exited the chamber.

"Not bad," Kit said, peering through the gloom.

"I've seen better," said Martinez.

Several minutes later they had rolled back the temporary screen that had separated them and were standing together in the change room admiring their new clothing. They each had comfortable undergarments and simple, one-piece jumpsuits, predominantly white but with subtle individual designs and splashes of different colours. Additionally, each of their names was embroidered onto the left breast of their jumpsuits.

"That's pretty impressive speed-tailoring," said Zac. "These all fit perfectly."

"I wonder if I can get the New Zealand rugby emblem embroidered onto mine?" said Keo.

"Ok, Tor, what next?" asked Kit, addressing the ceiling above them.

Tor's voice responded, "I am going to enter the room now, to greet you personally and escort you to more comfortable accommodation. We are aware of your need for sustenance, and that will be attended to immediately. I need to prepare you, however, for my appearance. Humanity's physiology has undergone subtle transformations over the millennia, and we are a little taller than you, with other subtle differences. Please do not be alarmed."

A door slid open and Tor entered the room.

17

Tor was slightly more than two metres tall; a full head-height taller than Keo. He was wearing midnight-blue coloured trousers and a matching short sleeved, collar-less shirt with red piping and some kind of insignia on his chest. He smiled in an obvious effort to disarm them and his eyes seemed to crinkle in kindness. As they looked into those eyes, they couldn't help noticing how different they were. They were almost 50 percent larger than their own, with dark chocolate-brown irises which were dominated by huge pupils in the centre. When he blinked his eyelids seemed to close in a much more pronounced scissor action, from the outside in, giving them an almost reptilian appearance. His nose was much more flared than their own, with his nostrils more exposed, and his ears were larger as well.

Tor held up his right hand toward them, palm facing them, and stepped in front of Keo, who was closest. They couldn't help staring at his fingers which were extremely long with pronounced pads on the tips.

"Peace and goodwill," he said, leaving his hand extended toward Keo, palm outward as if he was stopping traffic.

Keo responded by raising his hand in the apparently expected traffic-stopping gesture and repeated the words back to Tor, "Peace and goodwill."

Keo let his hand fall down to his side again but Tor remained standing expectantly in front of Keo with his hand raised. Zac stepped forward, sensing what was needed. He raised his hand and placed his palm against Tor's and responded, "Peace and goodwill." Their palms remained touching for a few moments, and then Tor smiled and bowed his head slightly, stepping back now that the ritual had been completed.

"I apologise," he said while continuing to smile benignly. "Palm blending must not be a familiar ritual for you. I did not realise. Please forgive me in advance if I make any other blunders. We have much to learn about you, and you about us. No doubt you are hungry."

"I could eat the legs off a low-flying cow!" said Keo enthusiastically.

"Interesting," said Tor. "You must tell us more of these flying cows sometime. How long has it been since you have eaten?"

"We've barely eaten anything for four days," answered Kit.

"In that case we will provide food that has maximum energy value and minimal impact on your stomachs. We must not overburden your digestive system initially. We will take you to some comfortable guest quarters where you can eat in private. I have assigned Sten as your liaison officer. He will accompany you to your quarters." Sten stepped into the room and smiled broadly at them. He was dressed in a similar uniform to Tor, and, if anything, was slightly taller, and had blonde hair instead of Tor's jet-black colouring.

"It is a great honour to meet you," he said, bowing his head toward them. "We have been anticipating this moment for many years. Please follow me. We have cleared the passage-ways so that you will not encounter others at this time."

Sten led them to a lift and then along several corridors, finally entering a spacious room with several comfortable looking lounges and a table with six chairs. The far wall was comprised entirely of a glass window with a stunning view of stars hanging in the blackness of space. Of particular interest was what was on the table. There was a bowl with several varieties of unfamiliar fruit, another large bowl filled with a creamy porridge of some kind, and a jug of drink that had a pink, milky appearance.

"These foods have been deemed to be the least demanding on digestive systems that have been without food for several days. We have ensured that there is the right quantity for you to eat, so that you do not over-indulge on your first meal. Please enjoy. I will leave you to share this meal together in private."

The four needed no further encouragement. They fell upon the food, devouring it with relish. Each mouthful was accompanied by moans and sighs of pleasure, as well as exclamations of delight as they tasted new flavours.

"Try this one, it tastes a bit like a custard apple."

"This one is amazing! It's a cross between a banana and a passionfruit."

The porridge did not look like anything special, but when Keo served some into his bowl and tasted it, he exclaimed, "Friends, you have to try this. It's amazing!"

They couldn't decide whether the food genuinely tasted

this good or whether it was simply because they were famished. Either way, they didn't care. It was just so good to eat again. Before too long, all the food including the drink was gone, and although they could have eaten more, they acknowledged the wisdom of not overloading their stomachs too much. They leaned back in their chairs, sighing with contentment.

"I've been thinking," said Zac.

"That sounds dangerous," said Kit.

"It's a miracle!" added Martinez.

"Ha, ha. Our initial plan was for us to wait here for six months and then return through the wormhole once Laramie has had time to build us a landing shuttle. But we may not need to wait that long. We might be able to convince these people to provide us with a more advanced craft that is capable of traversing the wormhole and landing on a planet. I'm sure they must have spacecraft that can do both by now."

"It's a big ask, bro," said Keo. "They would be giving us a spacecraft knowing they will never get it back again."

"Yes. Spaceships, even small ones, aren't cheap to build," said Kit. "And we don't really have anything to offer in payment or exchange."

"Unless we swap them for the doughnut and sausage we used to get here," said Zac. "It's over 1,700 years old, so it could be a valuable antique by now. Maybe it's worth a fortune to them."

"Maybe," said Kit. "But we shouldn't get our hopes up. At the very least, we know that we will be able to get home again in six months. I can wait that long if I need to."

Sten, who must have been waiting respectfully outside the room, re-entered and asked how they had enjoyed the meal.

"Brother, it was magnificent!" said Keo, still licking his lips.

"I don't know what you call all those fruit, but if that is anything like the rest of the food on your planet, I can't wait to try more."

"Do you need to sleep now?" asked Sten. "There are sleeping quarters prepared for you next door."

"I don't know about the others," said Zac, "but I have too many questions going through my head to get any sleep at the moment."

The others agreed.

"That is good. The commander also has many questions but did not want to overburden you until you were fully rested. If you feel ready, he will receive you in his conference room now."

18

The conference room was on the outer wall of one of the rings and had a huge glass window offering a panoramic view of the stars. The room itself was dominated by a large white oval table with a black glass-like centre section. Commander Tor Stonson was already seated at the table, and he stood as they entered the room. Keo stepped towards him with his palm extended, ready to offer the formal greeting, but Tor smiled and said, "There is no need to palm blend every time we meet, if we are already friends. Palm blending is a formal ritual conducted when people meet for the first time or on very formal occasions."

At Tor's invitation, everyone sat down at the table and glasses of a refreshing citrus-flavoured clear liquid were poured. Zac and the others sat together on one side of the table, and they were struck again by Tor's over-sized dark brown eyes and his elongated fingers.

Tor began proceedings. "Firstly, let me once again welcome you to Gateway Station. We have been anticipating your arrival for many years and want to assure you that we will do everything we can to assist you. We have questions we would like to ask you, plus I will need to talk you through the process of assimilation that you will need to undertake. But before I do so, are there any questions you have or immediate needs that we can help you with?"

"We're very grateful for your hospitality toward us, Tor," said Zac. "We have lots of questions, but I think it's important to say upfront that we haven't come here to stay permanently. Our greatest need is to return to the Icarus system as soon as possible and re-join our loved ones on Nova."

"Re-join your loved ones?"

"Yes. To be honest, the only reason we travelled here was to ask for your help, as we currently have no means of landing on the planet. We were stranded on the launch ring with only the light-weight void jumpers available to us. We were hoping you could help us."

"When you say you wish to re-join your loved ones, are you referring to your life partners?"

"Among others, yes."

There was silence on the other side of the table for a moment, and a puzzled expression passed across Tor's face. He seemed unsure how to proceed, and phrased his next statements carefully.

"We know from your appearance and your bioscans that you are not native to Nova as we once were, and we are curious about that. But can I first ask a delicate question? What is the average life expectancy of your people?"

"Most of us live well into our 80s."

Tor frowned, and his look of concern deepened.

"In reference to the standard Earth calendar, what year was it when you left the Icarus system?"

"This year," said Zac. "Two days ago."

"And what year do you think this is?"

"5380, of course," said Zac with mounting anxiety. "Why? Is there something wrong?"

"Oh no," said Martinez, "I'm starting to get a very bad feeling about this."

Tor clasped his hands together and leaned forward, his eyes blinking strangely. "This is a very difficult situation, and one I was not anticipating at all."

"It's not 5380 is it?" said Kit.

"No. It is not."

"What year is it?" asked Zac, his heart racing now and tears already welling up in his eyes.

"I am very sorry to inform you that this is the year 5499."

There were heart-broken groans from Martinez and Keo. Kit was staring at Tor with a stunned expression, and Zac was shaking his head, dumbfounded.

"No. That can't be right," Zac said. "Surely there must be an explanation. Maybe one of us has miscalculated. Or perhaps one of us hasn't made the appropriate allowances for differences in orbit periods between our respective planets in comparison to the orbital period of Earth."

"I wish, for your sake, that was the case. But unfortunately, our dates are correct, and so are yours."

"How can you be sure?"

"Because the wormhole through which you travelled, opened here in the year you specified, in 5380, and it has been locked open for 119 years. We have been waiting 119 years to see who or what would arrive."

"But we were only in the wormhole for two days!"

"It is indeed a mystery, but not one without a possible explanation."

"Just to be clear, you're saying that while we were in the wormhole, 119 years passed in the outside universe?"

"Yes."

"119 years!" said Keo, shaking his head, as a big fat tear rolled down his cheek. "This is a pain that is hard to bear." He stood and walked to the window and stood looking out at the star field.

Zac covered his mouth with a hand and shook his head. "They're all dead," he mumbled. "Everyone we loved. Everyone one we knew. All gone."

"I am so very sorry," said Tor. "This is an unexpected tragedy."

There was silence. No one knew what to say. The four friends were dumbfounded with shock and grief. Tor offered his sympathy and support, but nothing could take away the pain of loss that Zac and the others were experiencing.

"I think we need to suspend all other discussions for today," said Tor. "You need time to grieve and to process what you have just learned. We can continue our discussions whenever you feel ready. In the meantime, I think it might be appropriate for you to have some time together in your assigned living quarters. An evening meal will be provided and anything else you request. There is gymnasium equipment and a spa in an adjoining room, and you have very comfortable separate sleeping quarters."

"Thank you," said Keo, turning from the window and wiping his eyes. "Some time to work through this would be appreciated."

"If you need assistance at any point, you only need to speak my name or Sten's and our personal comms will be activated."

Sten led them back to their accommodation, promising to return in several hours with their evening meal and reminding them that they only needed to speak his name and he would respond. As he left and the door closed behind him, the four friends looked at each other in stunned disbelief.

"I can't believe it's just happened to us for a second time!" said Martinez. "We must be the unluckiest people in the entire universe!"

"Whether it is blind chance or providence is a matter for conjecture," said Keo, "But, whatever the case, the pain is indeed great, little sister."

19

The four stayed in their quarters for the rest of that day and all the next day as well. It was a painful, heart-wrenching time for them, and they simply weren't ready to talk further with the Altarians. They ate. They slept. They exercised. And most importantly, they talked. At first it was just the sharing of their pain. There were tears and hugs. There was anger and disbelief. And, at times, individuals sought solitude to work through their grief privately.

But they also began discussing their future. After all, they couldn't spend the rest of their lives in a small apartment on a space station. Where would they go? What would they do? Was it worth trying to return to Nova? What had transpired there over the last 119 years? Would they fit in anymore? Were they willing to subject themselves to the manipulations of the EIs now that their loved ones were gone? Perhaps they should stay here and make a new home among the Altarians? But would they ever really fit in?

These and many other concerns began to weigh heavily on

them, and so, on the morning of the third day, they announced their readiness to resume discussions with Tor. Once more they met in the conference room. Tor had visited them twice the previous day to check on their welfare and see to their needs, and Sten had been a regular presence, proving very helpful and sensitive.

After a few preliminary enquiries into their general welfare, Tor began by returning to the issue of the time difference in their wormhole travel.

"In regard to the time dilation that you experienced in the wormhole, we believe we understand what might have occurred. When the wormhole opened 119 years ago and did not close, we were perplexed. It had never happened before. Days and weeks went by and the wormhole remained open, but no one came through. We didn't know what was causing this, but we did know that the wormhole had originated in your solar system, because of the distinctive echyon frequencies we initially received, identifying Icarus-R421 as the source star."

"Did you try to communicate?" asked Kit.

"Yes, but all attempts failed. It was as if something was blocking our signals. We also tried sending probes through, but that failed also. The probes were unable to enter the wormhole; they were simply deflected to the side and remained in our solar system."

"So you haven't been able to use the wormhole for 119 years?" asked Zac.

"That is correct. Nothing has been able to enter it from this side."

"Are there no other points within your solar system where you could establish an outgoing wormhole?" asked Kit.

"No. It appears that there is only one subspace portal in

each solar system, linking the stars together via subspace energy corridors."

"Do you have any idea why this wormhole has been locked open for so long?" Zac asked.

"Our scientists studied the wormhole for decades, although that involved more theorisation than actual experimentation, because we were effectively locked out of the wormhole. Eventually, one of our scientists theorised that a wormhole could remain open indefinitely if it experienced a powerful negative energy feedback loop, and he suggested that the most likely cause of that is a black hole. The physics is beyond my ability to explain, and until now it has remained only one of the theories attempting to explain what was occurring. Another theory was that another race had developed the ability to manipulate wormholes and were deliberately keeping it open from their end to block our ability to use it. Your report to us that you were only in the wormhole for two days, however, has now convinced our scientists that a black hole is the cause of this phenomenon."

"There is a rogue black hole that has been travelling parallel to the Icarus system for centuries," said Zac. "It must be that one."

"That makes sense," agreed Tor. "Your wormhole must have come under the influence of the black hole's event horizon, causing you to experience significant time dilation. While only two days passed for you inside the wormhole, 119 years passed in the outside universe. It is the only logical explanation for what has occurred."

"But why didn't that happen to you and your people when you migrated here nearly 2,000 years ago?" asked Kit.

"The black hole must have been in a different position at

that time. If this is a rogue black hole, then it is moving in a path that is different to that of the rest of the stars in this part of the galaxy. You were just very unfortunate that it was at precisely the wrong point for the formation of your wormhole."

"At least now you might be able to open a new wormhole from this end and send some probes through to study it," said Zac

"Unfortunately, we cannot."

"Why not?"

"Because the wormhole did not close after you arrived. It is still open, and we remain locked out of it."

"So, we can't go back home?"

"No, I'm sorry. Not unless something changes. Our scientists have been furiously theorising over these last two days, trying to understand why the wormhole didn't close after your arrival. They are still perplexed. They now understand why the wormhole has stayed open for all these years. It was your spacecraft, trapped in the event horizon but still transmitting your STAR drive that was keeping it open. But once you finally emerged, the wormhole should have instantly collapsed. We have no idea why it didn't."

"How did you know we would be friendly?" asked Kit.

"We didn't. All we knew was that the wormhole originated from our previous home world. But anything could have happened in the 1,822 years since our departure. That is why we scanned your vessel as soon as it arrived. If you had been infected by EIs or were deemed to be a threat for any other reason, we would have destroyed you."

"Thanks for not killing us," said Martinez facetiously.

"You're welcome."

20

Zac was pondering all that had been said so far. "So, after waiting expectantly for 119 years, we finally showed up. We must be a bit of a disappointment; an anti-climax."

"Not at all! On the contrary, your arrival is the most important event to have occurred in living memory. You are the talk of the solar system. In fact, we will have to be careful how we protect your privacy from this point forward, because you are now major celebrities."

"We must look very strange to you," said Keo.

"Yes and no. We are aware that this is how our race looked many millennia ago. Which brings me to the question we have been waiting to ask you. Who exactly are you and where have you come from? Clearly you are not descended from our ancestors on Nova, as our race was already developing some of the characteristics that you see in us now."

"We left Earth in the starship Genesis, in the year 2357," explained Zac. "It was during the GAE — the Global Annihilation Event — and we barely escaped with our lives. We set course for the Icarus-R421 system, but during our cryogenic stasis, Genesis encountered the same rogue black hole that we are dealing with now. We were trapped in the event horizon for nearly 12 months. When our ship's AI finally broke us free and we arrived in the Icarus system, we awoke to discover that 3,022 years had passed in the outside universe."

"You were on board the legendary Genesis?" asked Tor with amazement. "So, the legends are true! There was such a vessel! This is momentous news! Many people are convinced that Genesis was a myth, concocted by the remnant who survived in Earth's solar system — a fairy story to tell their children to give them hope."

"That's us," said Martinez. "Mythological oddities from the past."

"I can assure you that you will not be treated as oddities. On the contrary, you are living legends! You are living Terrans – from ancient Earth! This will increase your celebrity status even more. Our historians will be clambering over each other to interview you." Tor paused for a moment. "Can you tell us what happened after you arrived at Nova — or what we call Icari, after its star, Icarus?"

Zac provided a brief summary of their colonisation of Nova and the events that had led to their arrival in the Altarian system. When he finished, he asked, "Is there any way we can help the people still living on Nova? They are being manipulated by the EIs and are most likely having their lives terminated prematurely."

"Unfortunately, no. We cannot travel back through the wormhole that remains open, as it is still mysteriously blocked. And we cannot travel there via conventional starships, as we have no idea of its location in respect to us, and vice versa.

From our astronomical observations we know that we are still in the Milky Way galaxy, probably on the opposite side of the galaxy to Earth. But we have had no success in finding the location of Icarus within our galaxy – if it is in our galaxy at all. Thus, we have no way of reaching the Icarus system unless the wormhole becomes operational again." He paused and looked with concern at the four Terrans. "All of this must be extremely difficult for you, but I believe you must resign yourselves to the fact that this is your new home. I assure you; we will do everything we can to ease your transition into our society."

"Thank you, my friend," said Keo. "I sense that you are a peace-loving people. I also trust in the purposes of God in all this. I believe we have been led here for a reason."

"You will find others of a similar faith among us, Keo. I am not one of them, but I respect your beliefs. Which brings me to the issue of your integration into our society."

He paused and considered his next words carefully.

"There is a reason why we have kept you from contact with anyone apart from Sten and me. Our language has evolved significantly in the three millennia since your time, in much the same way that your language differs from those who lived millennia earlier than you on Earth. Sten and I have uploaded your language, with its idioms, syntax and pronunciation, into our cerebral cortexes. That is how we are able to converse with you. But this would be impractical for our entire population. Instead, we suggest that you undergo genomic transformation to enable us to upload our language into your brains."

"Genomic transformation?" asked Kit.

"Yes. The modification of your genome — your DNA."

"But we already received the uplift virus on Nova," said Zac.

"The virus was simply a vector that introduced some basic

modifications to your DNA. But those modifications are ancient now — completely out of date. You would not be able to interface with our current technology with your ancient coding."

"You need to update our operating software?" said Kit.

"In a manner of speaking, yes."

"Does that mean we are going to end up looking like you?" asked Martinez. "No offence, but I'm kind of used to how I look."

Tor laughed. "No. Genomic transformation cannot change your appearance. Your features are already fully developed. Changes to segments of your genome that code for physical features would only affect subsequent generations — your children. Plus, you don't have to accept any modifications that would impact the physical features of your progeny unless you wanted to."

"So, the physical ... um ... changes that we notice in you are the product of your deliberate changes?" asked Zac.

"Yes. Our ability to understand and manipulate the human genome increased exponentially over the millennia. We intentionally focused on improving sight, smell, hearing and manual dexterity. For example, our larger, more widely spaced eyes give us better peripheral vision and significantly improved perception across a broader spectrum range. Our other senses have experienced similar enhancement. We increased our height, as this also has many advantages. You will also notice that we all have a dark olive complexion. This is the ideal skin colouring for protection from harmful UV rays. But, as I said, even if you accepted these modifications to your genome, you would not benefit from them, as your physical features are already fully formed. Your children, however, should you have any, would benefit from these enhancements."

"So, it's not these physical modifications that you are recommending that we receive?"

"No. Although you may choose them if you wish, for the sake of any future children. The modifications that we are recommending impact the brain at the molecular level. The science involved is more complex than my ability to explain it, but the result of the proposed genomic modification will be significant. Along with the updated coding we will also implant a microscopic transceiver into your cerebral cortex, along with microscopic filaments that will extend into various key regions of the brain including those responsible for language, memory, cognitive processing, sight, hearing and several others."

"Whoa! You're going to do brain surgery on us?" exclaimed Martinez.

"Be assured it is completely safe and not as invasive as the crude brain surgery of your era. There will be no need for scalpels and bone saws. The transceiver is molecular in size and the filaments are 100 times thinner than a human hair. Access to the various regions of your brain will take place at the molecular level."

"And what is the advantage of these implants?" asked Zac.

"Firstly, you will be enabled to access and operate our technology in the same way that you were able to on Nova. Secondly, your transceiver will enable trans-genic uploading, a process that we have developed which enables the uploading of information or skills directly into the brain. Thirdly, you will find that you are able to send and receive feelings and impressions when communicating with others. Once again, the science involved is complex, and is the result of millennia of study of the human brain. The result for you, however, is that after a simple upload, you would be as familiar and adept at our language as everyone else."

"Are you saying that these implants give you the ability to communicate telepathically?" asked Kit.

"Not in the sense that the science fiction of your era speculated. We cannot send words or specific thoughts. The formation of words in the language centre of the brain is too subtle to be picked up by the transceivers. But emotions and feelings generate significant electro-chemical signals in the brain, and these can be identified and transmitted by the transceivers. It is a very helpful aid to communication."

"Will the modification hurt?" asked Zac. "Will we have to get sick again? Because, I'm telling you, that was not a pleasant experience."

"The process will take approximately two weeks, and if you were to remain conscious during that time, you would certainly experience discomfort. For that reason, we will enable you to sleep throughout the entire process. You will awaken with your newly-modified coding, feeling refreshed and well."

"Well, I can't speak for the others," said Zac, "but if it means being able to shortcut months or possibly years of learning your language, plus being able to access your technology, I'm definitely in."

"I think we all agree with that," said Kit, looking at the others who both nodded. "But I'm not sure if I'm ready for you to mess with my future kids' eyes. No offence."

"None taken. You can have those physical modifications added to your genome separately, at any time in the future, if you wish. In the meantime, I can schedule you for the basic genomic transformation of your cerebral cortex this afternoon if you like."

"That soon?"

"The sooner it's done, the sooner you can begin to integrate fully into our society."

The four looked at each other and, after a moment of consideration, silently nodded.

"OK," said Zac. "I guess we didn't have anything else planned for this afternoon. Our schedule isn't exactly full at the moment."

"Trust me," said Tor, "that is all about to change."

21

—————

Zac woke and stretched. He felt good. Actually, he felt *really* good. A euphoric sense of peace and wellness seemed to be coursing through his entire body. *Whatever drugs they gave me are certainly working their magic*, he thought. He sat up and took in his surroundings. He was in a single bed in a nondescript white-walled room with a window that ran the entire length of the room. There was a view of gently sloping green lawns leading to a picturesque blue lake, with magnificent snow-capped mountains in the distance. *Mountains? Lake? Where am I? The last thing I remember is lying back in a reclining chair in some kind of high-tech med lab on Gateway Station.*

As he was thinking this, the door to his room slid open and Sten entered, his over-sized eyes blinking as he glanced down at some kind of data pad that he held in his long-fingered hands.

"How are you feeling Dr Perryman?"

"It's Zac, please. And I'm feeling fabulous. But where am I?"

"In a recovery room on Gateway Station."

"Oh," he said, looking at the window.

"Yes, it's very realistic isn't it? We thought you might find it calming. I can change the scenery to something else if you prefer."

"No. That's fine. It's very nice."

"The others are also awake. A breakfast meal has been prepared for you in the adjoining room. Although we have ensured that your nutritional needs were met while you slept, you will probably be feeling quite hungry now."

"Starving."

Shortly afterward, the four friends sat together at a table laden with fruit and cereals, chatting about how well they were all feeling. At the conclusion of their meal, Sten joined them again, along with a woman and a man, both in white lab coats. The woman was holding an electronic data pad in her long-fingered hands.

"I am pleased to report that your genomic modifications were completely successful," Sten said. "There were one or two minor complications, as your genome is over three thousand years older than ours, but this required only an additional two days of adjustment."

"So, we can speak your language now?" asked Kit.

"Not yet. You need an upload to be enabled to speak our language. The modifications to your genome and the resulting changes to certain molecular pathways in your brain enable you to now interface with the implant that you have received. Everything is now in place for us to upload our language into your neocortex, which is the area of the brain responsible for language. This is why Dr Lane and her assistant are here, to initiate the update." he said indicating the white coated woman. "Are you ready to receive your update?"

"How long will it take?" asked Zac.

"Not long."

"It won't hurt?" asked Kit.

"Not at all. In fact, you won't feel a thing. Are you happy for us to proceed with the update this morning?"

"Yes. Let's get it over with," said Zac, beginning to stand.

"No, please. Remain seated," said Sten.

He turned and nodded to the doctor, who began tapping on her pad. She spoke some unintelligible words to her assistant, who responded with equally unintelligible words. This was the first time Zac and the others had heard the Altarians speaking their own language, and to Zac's ears, it sounded harsh and clipped. After a few moments, Dr Lane looked up and asked,

"By the way, how are you all feeling."

"Fine," answered Zac.

"Do you need anything else with your breakfast? More fruit? Cereal? Juice?"

"No thanks, we're ... Hey! You speak our language!"

"No, Dr Perryman," she said with a smile, "you speak ours."

"You mean, that was the update?"

"Yes. Just then."

Zac searched his mind and discovered the truth for himself. Both languages now resided comfortably within him, and he was equally proficient with both.

"Amazing!" said Zac.

"Wow! I'm a genius!" exclaimed Martinez. "I just learned an entire language in a few seconds!"

"That makes four languages for me now," said Keo, smiling. "I also speak Maori and Hawaiian."

"That's intense," said Kit. "It feels like I've been speaking it all my life."

"Yes," answered Dr Lane. "The upload not only gave you a comprehensive understanding of our vocabulary, grammar, syntax and idioms, but also provided you with the necessary muscle-memory pathways to enable you to create the appropriate sounds. You can now speak Altarian as proficiently as someone who has lived here all their lives. That is the good news."

"Is there bad news?" asked Zac.

"Yes. The implant each of you received has only been partially successful. Our implants are designed for Altarian brains, which have developed slightly different pathology as a result of our modified genome."

"Pathology?" asked Martinez.

"Gross physical characteristics. Various parts of our brain have changed slightly in size and structure. Some have more synapses and a more complex network of neural pathways. After your implants were in place, we spent several days mapping the neural pathways in your brains and found some incompatibilities with our technology. The implants aren't able to make a strong enough connection to some parts of your brain."

"But you said the modification to our genome was successful," said Kit.

"Yes. It was. But remember, a modified genome cannot produce changes to gross physical features, because they are already fully formed. Your children will be born with Altarian brains, but yours remain unchanged in terms of their gross pathology. The changes that have occurred in your brains over these last two weeks are much more subtle, at the level of enzymes and the enhanced functioning of the dendrites in some of your neural pathways. It's very complicated."

"You can say that again," said Kit.

"It's very complicated," repeated Dr Lane.

The four friends laughed.

"Did I say something funny?" Dr Lane asked.

"Oh, I see ... you weren't joking," said Zac. "We tend to say, 'you can say that again' when we mean that we strongly agree with something."

"So, you don't actually want the other person to say it again?"

"No."

"Fascinating."

"Getting back to the topic," said Zac, "in what ways are our implants unsuccessful?"

"Certain areas of your hippocampus that are responsible for storing long term memory appear to be unresponsive to our implants. This means that we are unable to upload information and skills into your global memory. Unfortunately, this means that you will have to learn our culture and history the old-fashioned way, via instruction rather than upload. Also, your amygdala, which is the emotion centre of your brain, is incompatible with the implants. This means that you will not be able to receive or transmit emotional context when interacting with others. We will have to gauge your emotions the old-fashioned way, via facial expressions, body language and tone of voice. In fact, the only area of your brains which meshed well with the implants was your neocortex, which is the language centre of the brain. This is why we were able to successfully upload our language to you just now."

"Will we be able to access your technology?" asked Zac.

"Fortunately, yes. That is a relatively simple function of the implants, and it would even work if we implanted them into the brain of higher functioning animals. No offence intended."

"No problem," said Martinez. "I've always enjoyed being compared to a monkey or a dolphin."

"Have you?" said Dr Lane. "Interesting."

22

The next few days were a whirlwind of new encounters and new information. It was also a time of intensely mixed emotions for the four newcomers, as they balanced the excitement of learning about a new world, with the grief associated with their loss.

It was early morning, two days after their implants, and Zac and Keo were sitting together on a workbench in the gym, having just completed an intense pre-breakfast workout. Keo was quieter than usual.

"What's up, Keo?" asked Zac.

"I've been thinking. If Prisha and Jaz only lived to be 50 years old, they died at least 95 years ago. And our two children — yours and mine — who weren't even born when we left, died 69 years ago. And if they had children when they were 25, our grandchildren died 44 years ago. And if our grandchildren had kids when they were 25, our great-grandchildren only have six years left to live. That's assuming the EIs are still terminating life at 50."

"It's all too painful to think about, Keo. I finally found the love of my life, and we only had a few months together." Zac paused. "Do you think they remarried? I mean, they would have eventually decoded the Morse code message, and they would have waited for us, possibly for years. But eventually, they must have known that we were never coming back. I could be grieving for someone who eventually happily remarried and had other children."

"They may have remarried, but I don't think they would ever have stopped loving us, bro."

"No. Probably not. But how do I move forward with my own life, when I only lost Jaz a few days ago? It's a totally messed up situation."

"Yes, it is. And it's going to take time for all of us to come to terms with it."

"Have you got any wise quotes for me?"

"Not really. This is uncharted territory, bro."

"Do you think we'll ever remarry? I mean, the options are fairly limited."

"They are," agreed Keo. "Even though we are gradually growing accustomed to the appearance of the Altarians, it's hard to imagine us ever regarding their facial features as attractive."

"Yeh. Those weird bulging eyes and exposed nostrils. And those long fingers with the big pads. I can't imagine holding hands and kissing an Altarian girl."

"So that just leaves us with a pool of two," said Keo.

"Yeh. But Kit and Martinez are just friends. Good buddies. I can't think of them in any other way. Maybe we're destined to become grumpy old bachelors."

Kit stuck her head through the door and said, "Hurry up and shower guys, us girls are keen to head down for brekky."

Keo and Zac stared at her.

"What?" she said, noticing the strange way they regarded her. "Did I say something wrong? Is my shirt on inside out?"

"No. Sorry," said Zac. "We're just philosophising."

"Well, even egg heads like you need to eat. Hurry up!"

They had begun eating in the command centre dining room, where the officers and higher echelon staff ate their meals. It wasn't an easy experience, as they were celebrities and were constantly the focus of attention. It was understandable, of course, as they must have looked as strange to the Altarians as the Altarians looked to them. The crew on the space station tried not to stare, but it was almost unavoidable. After all, the four Terrans were the equivalent of living dinosaurs, with physical characteristics that had not been seen for millennia. It was always going to be this way, however, and the four friends had decided they would have to get used to it, as the only alternative would be to lock themselves away from the world.

The meals in the dining room were eaten at communal tables of ten seats each, and as soon as the four entered the room they were bombarded with requests to join various tables. Commander Stonson was one of those, and he insisted that they join him and a group of senior officers at their table.

As they ate breakfast together, Tor asked them, "How is your orientation going so far? Are you able to assimilate all the information effectively?"

"It's a piece of cake," said Kit, speaking through a mouthful of the delectably flavoured porridge.

"No, it's actually a porridge made from the flesh of a pinlay fruit. Cake has a much more rigid structure and a firmer texture."

Kit laughed. "I wasn't referring to this food. It's just an expression that means something is very easy."

"Ah. Another of your curious idioms. I see that you have carried that aspect of your own language over into ours."

"Sorry. It's hard to break old habits."

"So, getting back to my question, are there any issues that you are struggling to understand? Any questions?"

"I have one," said Zac. "All of the tutorials we have done so far have either been via a computer presentation or with an Altarian instructor, but we have not encountered any AIs. Am I right in assuming that you don't have any?"

"That is correct. After our experience with the EIs on Icari, or Nova as you call it, we decided never to develop AIs again. We couldn't risk them either being infected with the EI modifications or developing along similar lines independently. It was a very difficult decision, because our society had come to rely on the advanced processing power that AIs provided, but we believe it is the right one. We arrived here in the same void jumpers as the one in which you travelled here, and these only had computers. We deliberately left the AIs on the launch ring."

"Is that why you've never attempted to contact them again?"

"Yes. We had no way of knowing whether they would remain uninfected, and we couldn't risk contamination of our own systems."

"Yesterday afternoon's tutorial made a passing mention of 'naturalists'. What are they?" asked Kit.

"They are a minority group within our population who don't believe we have gone far enough in rejecting the technology that once controlled our lives. They object to the way we have modified our genome and they oppose any further modifications. They also object to the use of brain implants, as they believe these open the way for possible manipulation of our minds by EIs or some other future malevolent technology."

"So, they refuse the implants?" asked Zac.

"Yes. Implanting is done at the age of 20, after our brains have stopped developing. This is when an individual chooses a vocation and uploads all the necessary skills and knowledge to function effectively in that vocation. Naturalists refuse the implant."

"That must significantly impact their integration into society."

"It does. Firstly, they can't read or receive emotional context, which sets them apart from us somewhat. Secondly, they must acquire skills and education verbally and manually, which means it takes them longer to reach the same level of proficiency. For this reason, they focus more intensively on education during their younger years. Techsavs, which is what we are referred to as, generally focus more on social and holistic education during the years leading up to enhancement, because all the required technical learning will be accomplished in an instant after implantation and upload."

"Do techsavs and naturalists go to the same schools while they are young?" asked Keo.

"Not usually. Naturalists tend to separate themselves geographically from techsav society. They live on separate islands, with significantly reduced technology. They farm the land and fish the oceans and live a much simpler lifestyle. Occasionally, a young person living within techsav society will reach the age of 20 and refuse implantation, and, on even rarer occasions, an older techsav will have a change of philosophy later in life and have their implant removed. Everyone is entitled to do this at any time, but once this happens, they are effectively forced to remove themselves from our society because they do not have access to our technology. Doors won't open for them and even the simplest of appliances won't work for them. For this reason, naturalists live together in separate communities, using simpler, more direct technology."

"That brings up the issue of your geography and social organisation," said Zac. "Are there no nations?"

"No. The lack of any sizeable continents or land masses on our planet renders the concept of nations somewhat meaningless."

"So, how many islands are there?"

"It varies a little with the tides, but somewhere in the vicinity of 19,600."

"So, talk me through the island classification system you use," said Martinez. "The whole thing seems like a dog's breakfast to me."

"A dog's breakfast?"

"Don't mind Tash," said Kit. "She means it seems confusing and messy."

"Oh. I see. Well, given that there are 19,600 islands of varying sizes, and about two thirds of those are inhabited, having individual names for each island would be too difficult to remember. So, instead, we refer to them by their size classification and their designation number.

"Islands of more than 10,000 square kilometres are A classification. There are only four of these; A1, A2, A3 and A4, in descending order of size. Islands between 1,000 and 10,000 square kilometres are B classification. There are nearly 500 of these, once again numbered according to descending size. There are approximately 6,000 C classification islands which are between 400 and 1,000 square kilometres. The remaining 13,100 D classification islands are less than 400 square kilometres in area, and about half of these are uninhabited."

"So, people living on D9656 are living on a pretty tiny island?" asked Kit.

"Yes. In fact, that island is ..." Tor paused while he tapped a data pad that he took from his pocket, "... 42 square kilometres — approximately six kilometres by seven."

"This is what I mean about it being a dog's breakfast," said Martinez. "You can't possibly remember the location and details of each island. If you bumped into someone here on the station who said they were from C388 you wouldn't have a clue where that was."

"Not unless I looked it up, no. But I would at least have a rough idea of its size."

"I assume there is significant travel between the islands," said Zac.

"Yes. Transfer stations on techsav islands enable instant transfer to other islands. Thus, inter-island trade and commerce is just a single step away. People might live on one side of the planet and work on the opposite side. Many naturalist islands utilise an older form of transfer booths that are not mind-melded; in other words, they do not require implants. But there are some extreme naturalists who have rejected transfer technology completely. They rely on boats for inter-island travel and, therefore, tend to be quite isolated. Also, naturalist communities tend to clump together on islands close to one another or in whole archipelagos. This makes trade and social interaction among naturalist communities more efficient."

"So how are people elected to your government?" asked Zac.

"Each island has a local council, sometimes elected and sometimes appointed, depending on the tradition of the island. In terms of a federal government, we have a Federation Council, consisting of 16 councillors drawn by lottery from the general population; four from each of the four island classifications. They receive an upload with relevant information and skills, and they serve for two years before retiring. Each year, half of the council retires and eight new councillors are appointed."

What happens if a naturalist is chosen? They aren't able to receive an upload."

"That is correct. For that reason, only those with implants can serve on the council."

"I would love to see some of these islands," said Keo, changing the topic. "I am an islander myself, having lived most of my life in a small village on the north west coast of New Zealand, and I am missing the ocean."

"I think I can accommodate your wish. In three days, I will be travelling to C422 to attend my niece's enhancement party. It would be my great honour, and our family's honour, to have the four of you as our guests at the party. It is a delightful island in the equatorial region, and we could certainly ensure that you were able to spend some time at the beach if you desired."

"That would be wonderful, my friend! You've no idea how happy that would make me!"

"Keo goes a bit stir-crazy if he is too long out of the surf," explained Kit.

"The ocean is the eternal womb of our souls," explained Keo.

"OK ..." said Tor, slightly puzzled.

"It's probably some obscure philosophical quote," said Martinez. "Don't bother trying to work it out. I gave up trying to understand Keo soon after I met him."

"What is an 'enhancement party'?" asked Zac, getting the conversation back on track.

"It takes place when a person turns 20 and is about to undergo implantation. A formal party is held to celebrate their coming of age and their imminent entry into adult society. It is arguably the most important milestone in an individual's life. On some smaller islands, one big party is thrown annually for all the young adults who are turning 20 that year. It is the biggest event of the year. Some archipelagos host a large annual enhancement party, drawing people from dozens of nearby islands. In my niece's case, the party is a private one, held at the family home on the west coast of their island. She would be delighted if you decided to come."

"Thank you, Tor. We would be honoured to attend the party," said Zac, speaking for the rest of the group, who all nodded.

It was a decision they would later regret.

23

The days leading up to the party were spent on the space station, continuing their education of the history and culture of the Altarians. In between lessons, they were able to explore the station and marvel at its many wonders. Above all else, the sheer size impressed them. Over 2,000 people worked on the station, some of them living there semi-permanently, while others came and went on a weekly or monthly basis. Originally the station had been established to monitor and control wormhole travel, but with the wormhole effectively frozen for 119 years the station had become an important scientific and technological research base. It had also diversified into the area of tourism. Gateway Station offered a stunning array of entertainment and leisure activities, along with plush accommodation catering for those looking for an off-world holiday with a difference. Large spherical modules attached to the station offered exciting three-dimensional games, often involving zero gravity, some of which took days to play.

As the station was located at the L1 Lagrange point, the point of gravitational equilibrium between Altaria and its sun, it was also the ideal launching point for sightseeing trips to the system's only other planet, Volcana. This was a small but extremely volcanically active planet whose distance from Alataria varied between 30 billion and 280 billion kilometres, depending on the position of both planets in their elliptical orbits. When Volcana was at its closest, Gateway Station became a busy terminal, offering people a four-day round-trip luxury cruise to the spectacularly violent planet. The other very popular trip was a sundive in one of two needle shaped spaceships operating out of Gateway Station. These highly reflective craft circled the sun at extreme velocity, diving through its corona and offering passengers a unique view of the star's roiling surface.

On the eve of their scheduled departure, the four friends were enjoying an evening drink of some mildly intoxicating beverage in the privacy of their communal living quarters. Zac took another sip as he gazed out the window at the spectacular starfield, and leaned back in his chair, letting out a long sigh. They had spent the last part of the afternoon recording an interview that was scheduled to be broadcast to the entire planet in another couple of hours. As Tor had predicted, they were the talk of the planet, and everyone who had a presence in the public data net had been clamouring to interview them. It had been decided, however, to limit their media exposure by doing a single, controlled interview, conducted by a highly respected public commentator, with Commander Stonson beside them to ensure that only appropriate questions were asked. It had also been decided to conduct the interview in front of a live audience, to record the audience's auditory responses as well, and so Tor had decided to hold it in one of the auditoriums on Gateway Station. Members of the general public and station personnel were invited to order tickets, and within a few minutes of ticketing opening, the 450-seat auditorium had sold out. When the four Terrans eventually walked out onto the stage at the commencement of the interview, an excited buzz went through the crowd.

The interview commenced with the surprisingly long-haired male interviewer, Chadston Worlop, palm blending with each of them. He then gave the audience a very brief summary of their arrival through the wormhole (just in case anyone had been living in a hole in the ground and hadn't heard about it) and then addressed his first question to Zac.

"Zac, you seem to be the spokesperson of the group ..."

"That's only because he's no good at anything else, and we felt sorry for him," said Martinez.

"And we couldn't give the job to Keo," added Kit, "because he would bore you to death with philosophical quotes."

Chadston appeared initially shocked, but the audience were laughing at this display of irreverent put-down humour.

"So, Zac, can you tell us how old you are?"

"That depends how you look at it. From my perspective, I'm 29."

"But what year were you born in, and on what planet?"

"I was born on Earth, in 2329."

There were excited murmurs from the crowd, even though almost all of them knew this already.

"So that makes you ... let me see ..."

"Exactly 3,170 years old," finished Zac for him.

The crowd gasped again, with their excited murmuring taking several seconds to die down. The producers were already commending themselves on the decision to record in front of a large audience.

"Can you explain to us, how a person born on Earth over 3,000 years ago came to be sitting here today?"

The next period of the interview was spent documenting the adventures that had brought the four Terrans to Altaria. Occasional cheeky comments by one or the other of them were received with increasing delight by the crowd, who were clearly not used to this kind of unpretentious, irreverent humour. Eventually, Chadston moved to questions that he considered to be more socially interesting.

"What do you think of us? We must look very strange to you."

"You can say that again," said Martinez.

Chadston looked a bit nonplussed. "OK. What do you think of us? We must look very strange to you."

"No, no, no," said Kit, as all four laughed. "She means she strongly agrees with you."

"Oh, I see. So, what do you find strangest about us?"

"Your goggly eyes, squishy nose, dangly fingers and your stretchy bodies," volunteered Martinez.

The audience were delighted with her response and laughed out loud.

"And how do you think you look to us?"

Martinez was on a roll. "Short, pudgy, beady-eyed, stubby fingered hobbits."

Once again, the audience laughed at her irreverence and self-deprecation, even though they probably had no idea what a hobbit was. Her answers were so far from being politically correct and sensitive that the crowd found them absolutely delightful.

"Do you realise that you are now celebrities?"

"I don't know why," said Kit. "Apart from the fact that we look a bit different to you, we haven't done anything special. All we did was keep breathing and stayed alive."

"Yeh," agreed Martinez. "it's a grand celestial joke that we're celebrities. I mean, I've got flat feet, a lopsided arse and bad breath in the mornings. Trust me, I'm nothing special."

The crowd erupted into another round of laughter at Martinez's delightful irreverence. They couldn't seem to get enough of her.

Chadston asked them for their impressions of Altarian technology and was particularly interested in their views on brain implants. However, Tor had already coached them to not get dragged into a debate about implants, as he didn't want them to be used as a political football to score points for either of the opposing viewpoints. Accordingly, they kept their answers fairly neutral, acknowledging that they had received implants themselves but refusing to be drawn into any kind of formal validation of their use. Sensing their resistance, Chadston then turned his focus in another direction.

"Let me get more personal with you. What have you found most difficult about your experience here?"

"The fact that we will never see our loved ones again," said Keo, instantly. The others all nodded and tears welled up as they considered their loss afresh.

"How difficult has that been for you?"

Zac spoke up. "Our life partners and dearest friends all died about 100 years ago, and yet we only found out about it a couple of days ago." His eyes welled up as he spoke. "It doesn't get any more difficult than that."

Chadston offered the expected sympathy, and then asked, "What are you hoping for now? What would be a good outcome for you? I mean, here you are, probably millions of light years from home, thousands of years outside of your own time, having lost almost everyone you love, in a strange world with strange looking people. What do you hope for?"

The four were silent for a few moments, each of them looking down as they reflected on the question. Then Zac looked up, not at Chadston, but directly into the audience, and spoke with a voice trembling with emotion,

"We just want to find peace and happiness."

As he spoke, a tear rolled down his face, and the producer knew intuitively that this would be the moment he would later freeze as the closing shot of the interview.

Now, several hours later, after finishing their evening meal and retiring to their own space, the four were unwinding after their stressful day.

"As interesting as all this has been," said Zac, "I'm really looking forward to getting my feet back on solid ground."

"Me too, bro. People aren't created to live inside tin cans, floating around in space. There is something profoundly soothing and healing about breathing fresh air, feeling the wind in your face and the sand between your toes."

"Yeh, and I'm getting sick of all this celebrity crap," said Martinez.

"I agree," said Kit. "Somehow we need to be able to live a normal life here, but I'm not sure how possible that is going to be."

"On the positive side," said Zac, "at least we've all learnt something new today; something vitally important."

"What's that, bro?"

"That Tash has a lopsided arse."

He was rubbing his arm a moment later, and Keo commented, "She might have a lopsided arse, but she's sure got a much better punch than Kit."

24

The following morning, they left Gateway Station. A shuttle took them to Terminus 8, one of 12 geosynchronous satellite stations in orbit around Altaria. The journey of approximately 1.5 million kilometres took less than 30 minutes in the super-fast shuttle, and as they docked at Terminus 8, the passengers got a birds-eye view of the planet below them. It was a blue water-world with swirling white clouds, dotted with tiny brown and green islands.

After docking was complete, they emerged into the terminus, which was much smaller than Gateway Station but still very impressive. A circular 'grand concourse' opened up before them, with shops and food outlets offering all kinds of products. Wide corridors branched off in all directions from the concourse, like spokes on a wheel, with the circular concourse as its hub. Crowds of people were moving through the concourse, disappearing down different corridors, each one marked with electronic signage stating various destinations; Jade Moon Base, Jasper Moon base, Rigor Mining Station,

Gateway Station and Federation Defence Station. They chose none of these, however, instead choosing the widest corridor, marked "Altaria Transfer Nexus".

By now a crowd of people was following them, trying to get close to the Terrans to take photos. As they entered another circular concourse, smaller in size, they were spotted by more people and the crowd around them grew to an excited mass, all vying for a photo of the ancient humans. Prior to departure Tor had appointed two station personnel to accompany them as "personal assistants" to the Terrans — Starla, a striking blonde with a stunning figure, and Garran, an equally impressive-looking male specimen. Starla and Garran now sprang into action, fending off the crowd and clearing a path forward. The group reached a line of booths and they quickly stepped inside one, gratefully closing the door behind themselves.

"That was crazy!" said Kit.

"Yes," agreed Tor. "I'm beginning to wonder whether broadcasting that interview was such a good idea."

"Well, the horse has bolted now," said Martinez.

"The horse ...?"

"She means, it's too late to do anything about it now," explained Zac.

"Oh, I see. Yes. Although, maybe there is something we can do. Perhaps a public appeal for privacy is needed. I will suggest that to the Federation Council."

As he spoke, he typed quickly on a keypad mounted on the wall of the booth and as he finished, the door of the booth opened again. They emerged into a large domed concourse, similar to those that had been on Nova, and moments later walked out into bright sunshine.

"Welcome to Altaria," said Tor with a smile. "This is C422."

The four Terrans looked around them at the green hills, breathing deeply of the warm equatorial air.

"Ah! This is what we've needed," said Zac.

"Yes, my friend! This Kiwi wasn't made for off-world living." Keo spread his arms wide and lifted his face to the sun, closing his eyes and breathing in the exotic aromas of the island's tropical perfume. "Beautiful!"

There were only a few people outside the dome, but they all stared with open curiosity at the four Terrans, and several took photos. The dome was situated in the centre of a park, beyond which various dwellings could be seen. Tor guided the group towards a sleek black vehicle with a bubble canopy, saying, "My sister's house is a short distance away, on the headland. I've arranged for this flitter to take us directly there."

They climbed in and Tor nodded to the driver. The flitter lifted smoothly into the air, spun around and raced eastward. The coast came into view; kilometres of pristine beaches with rolling surf. The flitter settled onto a grassy headland, on the lawn of a large white dwelling. They had barely exited the flitter when a door at the front of the house slid open. A young woman came out and ran toward them, embracing Tor enthusiastically.

"Uncle Tor! Thanks so much for coming!"

Tor introduced her as Janeel and she palm blended with each of them.

"Thank you so much for coming to my party! I hope you don't find it all too strange."

"We're delighted to be here," said Kit. "It's a privilege for us to be invited to such an important occasion."

Janeel led them inside, where they were greeted by Tor's sister and brother-in-law, Nessa and Vin. Refreshments were served and a brief period of polite conversation ensued. Tor then suggested that the four Terrans might like to go for a swim at the beach, which was a short walk down a sandy path from their vantage point on the headland. Janeel offered to accompany them, but her mother sensed the Terran's need for privacy, and suggested she stay home to help with the party preparations. Tor had thoughtfully provided appropriate swimming costumes for them, made to their individual sizes, and after quickly getting changed, the four friends thanked their guests and wandered down to the beach. They were accompanied by Starla and Garran, who kept a discreet distance from them and remained fully clothed and watchful. When the group reached the sand, they dumped the towels they had been given, took off their outer garments and ran enthusiastically into the surf, laughing and splashing each other as they did. The water was luke-warm and the waves were ideal for body surfing. Zac and Keo began catching waves and it soon developed into a competition.

"You should put one hand out in front of you, bro. That will help your skinny white body to stay on the wave longer."

"I don't need to, dude. My streamlined shape helps me glide through the water like a dolphin. You, on the other hand, need all the help you can get to keep that huge carcass of yours on the wave."

"I'll have you know; my body is the result of generations of surfing evolution — the optimal shape for carving up the waves. I guarantee I can go further than you."

"Best of three," said Zac, and they swam out past the break to await the next set.

"What is it about guys?" asked Martinez to Kit as they floated lazily in the water. "Everything's a competition."

A short time later, the competition having been declared a draw, the four were bobbing up and down over the swell together. Zac glanced back at Starla and Garran who remained on the sand dunes, looking vigilant.

"I get the distinct impression that Starla and Garran are more than just mere personal assistants. The look more like bodyguards to me."

"I agree," said Kit. "But what are they guarding us from? Surely there's no danger here?"

"That's a very good question," agreed Zac. "I wonder if it has anything to do with the different viewpoints among the Altarians regarding technology. Tor's warning to us yesterday not to be drawn into taking sides left me wondering whether there might be some serious tension between the two groups."

As it turned out, Zac's assessment was more accurate than he realised.

25

———

The party was scheduled to begin at sunset, and as the afternoon wore on, the pace of preparations increased. A catering team arrived and began setting up tables and chairs on the lawn and preparing food. A dark flitter landed on the headland and six uniformed personnel disembarked. They appeared to be wearing sidearms and took up positions around the perimeter of the lawn. This added further impetus to the speculation of the friends that all was not entirely peaceful on Altaria. Zac and the others ate a light, late lunch in the polite company of their hosts, and then spent some more time at the beach in the afternoon, accompanied by the ever-present Starla and Garran. As the time for the party drew near, Tor provided formal clothing for them to change into, once again perfectly made to their size.

Guests began arriving and the crowd quickly swelled to over 100. Zac and the others soon found themselves in the midst of a swirling sea of colourful costumes and excited faces. Music was blaring and alcoholic drinks were flowing. The

Terrans were inundated by guests wanting to speak with them and the four were quickly separated as they were drawn into different conversations. Starla and Garran looked quite stressed as they attempted to maintain contact with all of them, and Garran eventually managed to convince them to "buddy up". From that point onward, Zac and Kit stayed together with Starla constantly at their side.

"What is this drink supposed to be?" shouted Kit during a rare break when they weren't circled by a curious crowd. She held up a fluted glass with a bright blue liquid.

"It's called rhapsody," explained Starla. "It's a distilled liquor that is chemically enhanced to stimulate the release of oxytocin in the brain. It's very popular at parties."

"It tastes wonderful!" replied Kit, taking another sip from her third glass.

"Just be careful not to drink too much or you'll end up in the arms of someone, doing something you might later regret."

"Don't worry about me," she said, slightly slurring her words. "I can drink an elephant under the table."

"Why would an elephant be under a table?"

Kit and Zac were saved from responding, by the announcement that dinner was ready. Trestle tables laden with food were set up on the lawn and the guests lined up to pile their plates with a sumptuous selection of exotic food. Kit and Zac reunited with Keo and Martinez to sit together as they ate, and Zac couldn't help noticing the towering pile of food that Keo had managed to fit onto his plate.

"Are you sure you couldn't fit any more food on that plate Keo?" asked Zac.

"These plates are so small, bro. I'm just going to have to make several more trips to the table."

"You're a machine," said Martinez, who was known for having a decent appetite herself.

"A high-performance engine needs high-octane fuel, little sister."

"What does that say about me then?" asked Kit, looking at the meagre serving of food on her own plate.

"You eat like a rabbit," said Zac. "That's why you keep that hour-glass figure of yours so trim."

"Why Zac!" she said snuggling up beside him, "was that a compliment?"

"Well ... err ..."

"Look! He's blushing!" said Martinez.

"I'm not. I'm just a little warm."

As people finished eating, the music started blaring with a hypnotic dance beat and some people started dancing on the large backlit floor that had been assembled on the lawn. The four friends were once again separated into two groups as people vied for their attention, bombarding them with questions and asking for photographs.

At one point, Kit announced that she needed some fresh air, so she and Zac walked to the perimeter of the lawn, with Starla in tow, and stood overlooking the beach below.

"As fun as tonight is," said Kit, "we're never really going to fit in here are we? I mean, we'll always be the freaks from the past. Wherever we go, people will be staring at us and asking for photos. We're never really going to be able to live a normal life."

"It's going to be a challenge," agreed Zac.

"I feel like a hobbit! I barely come up to their chests! At least you're a bit taller. At 162 cm I must look like a dwarf to these people."

"Well, you don't look like a dwarf to me. You look just right."

She reached up and kissed him lightly on the cheek. "Thanks Zac. You know how to make a girl feel good."

An announcement was made asking them to come inside the house for speeches and the cutting of the cake. The guests crowded into the open plan interior of the house and the four friends found themselves standing on the rear patio, looking in through the open sliding doors.

Janeel's mother gave a speech, honouring her daughter, then Tor stepped forward, as the honoured uncle, to add his comments and propose the toast, standing beside his niece and her parents.

The explosion ripped through the house with devastating consequences. Zac gradually became aware that he was lying on his side on the patio paving. His ears were ringing, and he could hear screams and moans seeming to come from a great distance, as if they were at the other end of a tunnel. He was covered with debris and there was something sticky and wet all over one side of his face. He touched his hand to his face, and it came away covered in blood. *Is it mine or someone else's?*

He pushed himself to his knees and looked around. Survivors were staggering around, yelling for loved ones and friends. Others lay in pools of blood groaning. The unlucky ones were silent and motionless.

Kit lay beside Zac, unconscious and breathing slowly, a deep laceration on her cheek bleeding freely. The perimeter security personnel had run into the house with weapons drawn and were speaking on their comms as they searched for further threats. Zac rolled Kit onto her side and checked for any serious injury. To his left he saw Martinez and Keo sitting up and looking around with dazed expressions. A security guard was yelling out, asking everyone who was not seriously injured to move out onto the lawn, presumably to remove themselves from the danger of further explosions within the house.

Kit was regaining consciousness and was trying unsuccessfully to sit up. Zac bent and lifted her into his arms and carried her away from the house. He placed her gently on the grass beyond the food tables, and turned to see Keo hobbling across the grass, supported by the diminutive Martinez. They looked a strange couple; a burly front row rugby forward being supported by a dark-haired, fierce-looking pixie.

"What happened?" asked Kit, now sitting up.

"Some kind of bomb. Don't try to stand. You were unconscious for a short time. We need to get you looked at."

"I'm OK."

"No, you're not, Kit. You lost consciousness, and you have a gash on your face that needs sealing."

"Another one?" she said, feeling her face, her hand coming away covered in blood. "The same thing happened to me on Armstrong Base! There goes my modelling career."

She looked up at Zac.

"You look a bit gruesome yourself, doc."

"Thanks."

"You're welcome."

By now flitters were landing all over the lawn. Additional security personnel were running everywhere talking on comms, and medical personnel were attending to the wounded.

"Damn!" said Kit.

"What?" asked Zac.

"I was hoping for at least a decent pash tonight after drinking all that rhapsody. It looks like that's not gonna happen now."

"Did you have anyone in mind, or were you just gonna close your eyes and launch yourself at the nearest male?"

She looked up at him. "Why do you think I was tagging along with you all night, Zac? Maybe it's not too late?" She tried to stand up, but as she rose to her feet her eyelids fluttered strangely and she collapsed. Zac just managed to catch her, and as he lowered her to the ground he called out, "Medic! Someone help! We need medical attention here!"

26

Zac was sitting on the beach watching the sun rise over the ocean, a thin red crescent just beginning to peak over the ocean's rim. Starla emerged from the bungalow on the grass-covered sand dune behind him. She walked down the dune carrying two mugs, and sat beside Zac, offering him one.

"What is it?"

"Juvo. It's a traditional pick-me-up morning drink, made from dried roasted berries with a natural stimulant. I believe you had something similar in your time."

"Coffee?" Zac sipped the drink cautiously. "Oh wow! That's very similar to coffee – with a slightly nuttier flavour. Thanks."

He glanced at Starla. Apart from her Altarian facial features and elongated fingers, she could have been a super-model back on Earth. She and Garran were also the shortest Altarians they had encountered so far, being only slightly taller than Keo.

"Was your height a factor in assigning you and Garran to us?"

"Yes. But we still had a choice. We volunteered. Not that our presence did any good at all last night."

"Do you know what happened yet?"

"There was a bomb in the cake. It was placed there by one of the catering staff. He was relatively new. He was seen excusing himself from the house shortly before the bomb went off, claiming he wasn't feeling well and needing fresh air. He wasn't seen again."

"How many didn't make it?"

"As of this morning, 48 are dead. Among those are Commander Stonson, his niece and her parents. At least a dozen more are still critical."

Zac shook his head.

"Do you want to tell me what's going on? I think we are owed an explanation, seeing we came close to being killed."

"I agree. In fact, Garran and I argued that you should have been told. Commander Stonson, along with the Federation Council, thought otherwise."

"Is it the naturalists?"

"Yes and no. The vast majority of naturalists are pacifists. They simply want to live as close to nature as possible. They don't have any animosity towards techsavs; they just want to be left alone to live in peace."

"But?"

"But there is a minority extremist group ..."

"There always is."

"They call themselves 'reversionists'. They want society to revert to the way it was prior to implant technology. They believe that cerebral implants are not only unnatural but pose a potential danger."

"How so?"

"They believe that they could one day become a means of controlling humanity; of manipulating our emotions and wills."

"Is that possible?"

"Our scientists say it is not, particularly as we have decided to never again allow artificial intelligence to arise."

"So, it was these reversionists who were responsible for last night's attack?"

"Yes. Over the last 18 months they have been randomly attacking enhancement parties. Their aim seems to be to discourage people from receiving implants. Until last night, they had only attacked larger, communal parties. That is why Commander Stonson thought it would be safe to allow you to attend this private function."

"Do you think it was coincidental that the first private party they attacked was the one we attended?"

"No. At the very least they must have reasoned that attacking this party and injuring or even killing you would bring much more publicity to their cause."

"But surely that would be negative publicity?"

"I don't think they care. Plus, we have reason to believe that the four of you have become a specific target. The fact that you have willingly received implants has been hailed by techsavs as a vindication of the practice. Reversionists had initially hoped that you would refuse to be implanted, thereby strengthening their case that it is an abhorrent, unnatural practice. They now seem to regard you as traitors to their cause."

"How can you be sure of this?"

"Because of their attempted broadcasts in the comm-net. Thankfully, our screening software has intercepted their broadcasts before they became accessible to the general public."

"So, are we still in danger?"

"You're safe here for the moment, but we will need to consider how to secure your long-term safety."

"Where are we exactly? Things were all a bit crazy last night."

"This is D3044. It is a high security retreat island used by high echelon Federation personnel. Conferences and planning sessions are sometimes conducted here, and it has a permanent staff. Security has now been tightened even further, and no one can access the island without high-level clearance."

They heard the squeaky-sand sound of someone behind them and turned to see Kit walking down the sand dune with a mug of juvo in her hand.

"Ah, sleeping beauty awakes," said Zac. "How are you feeling?"

She plonked herself down beside him. "My head hurts and my mouth tastes like something died in it." She took a sip from her mug and said, "I can't remember anything that happened after the bomb went off. Did I say or do anything dumb?"

"No more than normal."

"Ouch. That bad, was I?"

"Up to your usual standard." He looked at her quizzically. "You don't remember anything at all?"

"Nope. Why? Oh no, what did I do?"

"Nothing."

"Tell me!"

"What happens at the party, stays at the party. How's Keo?"

"His leg is all sealed up, now that they got the hunk of metal out of it. He'll be on crutches for a week or so, which he won't be happy about. Martinez is the only one of us who didn't get a scratch."

Zac touched the wound on his head which had been bio-sealed, and he glanced at the gash on Kit's face which had received the same treatment.

Garran walked down the slope to join them and said, "General Kellar has asked that we meet him in the command hut after breakfast. He wants to discuss your future."

27

General Kellar, head of Federation Security Forces, had arrived on the island overnight, transferring down to AI from a Federation cruiser in orbit around Altaria, and transferring to the island from there. He was accompanied by three members of the Federation Council, including the current chairperson, Councillor Drummond, who had arrived at the same time. They all rose from their seats as the four Terrans and their two bodyguards entered the hut, and after formal palm blending was concluded they all sat down at a large conference table.

"Firstly, let me offer my sincere apologies for the tragic events of last night," said Kellar. "It should not have happened. Our security measures were not tight enough."

"We should never have been at that party in the first place," said Zac.

"Perhaps."

"No. Not perhaps. You knowingly placed our lives in danger

without informing us that we were potential targets. That is unacceptable."

Kit looked at Zac with raised eyebrows. She had never seen him fired up like this.

"Again, I apologise. In retrospect, you should have been appraised of the risks."

"You're telling me we should have been!" said Martinez, whose fiery personality needed little fuel to spark up.

"Rather than dwelling on the errors of the last twelve hours," Kellar continued, "we need to formulate a strategy moving forward. While we can't be absolutely certain that your presence at the party precipitated the attack, it seems highly probable that it did. It is also logical to conclude that the reversionists were happy for you to be part of the collateral damage. You may even have been the primary targets. This being the case, we cannot guarantee your safety while you are on the surface of the planet. We are therefore proposing that we transfer you immediately to Gateway Station. We will provide you with permanent lodgings in the restricted personnel area of the station, which has the highest possible security measures in place."

"No," said Zac.

"What do you mean?"

"I think the concept of 'no' is fairly universal in any language, General."

"I assure you Dr Perryman, Gateway Station is by far the safest place for you to be right now."

"I disagree. In fact, I believe the more we appear to be aligned with the techsav world, the more it will make us a target for the reversionists. We didn't ask to be part of this conflict between you and them, and we certainly don't want to be seen to be taking sides. We are the innocent victims here, and we want no part whatsoever in the ongoing conflict that exists between both sides."

"But we cannot guarantee your safety on Altaria."

"You can't guarantee our safety off-world either. Not in any absolute sense. Besides, we've already talked about this together, and none of us wants to spend the rest of our lives locked up in a tin can in space. We want to breath fresh air and feel the sun on our faces and the wind in our hair. We want to swim in the ocean and walk on the sand. We want to have a life worth living, and not be locked away like lab rats."

"I see. Well, we can't force you ..."

"No. You can't," said Kit.

"But there is the problem of your ongoing security."

"We have a suggestion," said Zac.

"Yes?"

"We want you to withdraw all security measures from us."

"But ..."

"We want to be taken to a naturalist community, where we will live among them, completely out in the open. Furthermore, we want to make a public announcement that we are choosing to do this because of our desire to live peaceful, quiet lives."

"I see."

"Obviously, it will have to be a community who are happy to have us come and live among them."

"And it has to be somewhere with good surf," said Keo. "Good waves bring healing to the soul."

"And it has to have a supply of rhapsody," added Kit. "That was good stuff!"

"I'm not sure if the world is ready for you to have too much more of that, Kit," said Zac.

"Why? What did I do?"

Zac just smiled and shook his head.

Kellar began to object, "I don't think we can ..." but he was interrupted by Councillor Drummond.

"The council is in agreement, Dr Perryman. You are not our prisoners. You are ... how shall I say it? ... refugees. And basic human decency dictates that we allow you to, in your own words, have a life worth living. If this is your wish, we will do everything in our power to make it happen."

"Thank you, Councillor Drummond."

"Obviously, this will take a little time to organise, but we will expedite this as quickly as possible."

"Can I make a suggestion, councillor?"

"By all means."

"The sooner we can make a public broadcast of our intentions, the sooner our threat level can be diminished. If the reversionists learn that we wish to live as they do, we will cease to be a target for them."

"I agree. Can you be ready to record your message this afternoon?"

"I can."

28

Zac stood under a shady tree looking directly into the hover camera that was floating three metres in front of him. The camera would have a view of the beach behind him. General Kellar had wanted the recording to take place in an office with a desk, but Zac had insisted that it be in a natural setting, since that would reflect the lifestyle that they were choosing.

The director nodded and said, "Any time you're ready. And don't worry if you slip up. Just correct yourself and continue. We can edit any mistakes out later."

Zac nodded, cleared his throat and began.

"My name is Zac Perryman, and I am grateful for this opportunity to speak with you. As you know, my friends and I are from another time and another place. We are from the Earth that you, also, came from originally. We arrived here as refugees, fleeing from the same inhuman manipulation from which you once fled. You have welcomed us and befriended us, and for that we are truly grateful. Recently, however, we have been made aware of a conflict of viewpoints regarding the use of implant technology. We were not aware of this conflict when we first arrived, and we were under the impression that everyone received implants. We agreed to implants ourselves, thinking that this would be essential for integration into your society. In retrospect, perhaps we acted precipitously, and it is possible that we might have made a different choice if we had had the opportunity to weigh up all the options.

"Having said that, we wish to take no part in the ongoing debate, and do not want to take sides. We can see that implant technology offers great benefits, and we respect those who embrace it. We also respect those who choose to live more simple lives, without artificial enhancements. There are many among you who seek to live simpler lives, less dependent upon technology which, as we all know, has proven problematic in the past.

"It is this simpler lifestyle that my friends and I have now chosen to pursue. We have decided to seek a life among those who call themselves naturalists. We come from a simpler world and a simpler time, and we want to live out our lives in peace and in harmony with the natural world. We are currently seeking a home where we can do this, and we ask that you respect this decision and grant us the privacy that you would want for yourselves.

"In making this decision, we are in no way elevating one lifestyle over the other. The techsav world is a source of great blessing and prosperity for this world. It is just not for us. Each person must choose the path that is right for them, and this is the path we have chosen.

"I want to conclude with a plea for tolerance. I am aware that people on both sides of the current debate have strong opinions. That is unavoidable. But the mark of a mature society is measured by its ability to discuss conflicting viewpoints respectfully, without resorting to violence or vitriol. Forcing your opinion upon others is not the mark of a democratic society, but of a repressive dictatorship. As an historian, I can tell you that violent repression of alternate viewpoints is the first step in the decline of a civilisation. I encourage you to continue to engage in informed debate and dialogue, while treating those who hold different opinions with dignity and respect."

Zac held his arms out wide, and the other three walked into shot, and the four of them stood arm in arm together.

"The peace that my friends and I wish for ourselves, is the peace we wish for all of you. Thank you."

There was a moment's silence and then the producer and his assistants broke out into spontaneous applause, along with the small crowd of security personnel who had gathered to watch.

"That was brilliant, Zac! Absolutely brilliant!" said the producer. "This broadcast is going to break all the viewing records!"

Keo slapped Zac on the back and said, "Bro, you killed it! You have a gift."

"It was OK, I guess," said Martinez. "A bit soppy at the end."

Kit had tears in her eyes, and she stood on her toes and planted a kiss on Zac's cheek.

"That was very moving," she said. "I vote for you as president."

"President of what?"

"Of our island."

"That's if we have one. No one might want us yet."

29

They were inundated with offers. Naturalist islanders from all over the globe contacted Federation Council within minutes of the broadcast being aired. The offers poured in. Hundreds of island communities offered to welcome the Terrans and provide them with a home. There was also an outpouring of support and well-wishes from techsav communities. Within hours, the comm-net was flooded with video uploads of people expressing support for the Terrans. There was also a huge increase in techsav videos echoing Zac's call for peace and understanding.

"It seems you really hit a nerve yesterday," said Councillor Drummond at their second meeting the following morning. "In fact, I am quite confident that if we called an election today to appoint a new Federation Council Chairperson, you would win in a landslide."

"I told you!" said Kit. "President!"

"I can assure you; fame and power are exactly the opposite

of what I am looking for," said Zac, clearly uncomfortable with the accolades.

"Which is exactly why you would make such a good leader," said Drummond. "But we digress. The point of this morning's meeting is to present you with some of your options. As you are aware, subsequent to your video message we have been swamped with offers. My staff have sifted through them and come up with a short list of 20 prospective islands. We took into account the factors that we discussed together after your recording yesterday — climate, population size, proximity to other islands for commerce, level of technology ..."

"Surf?" asked Keo.

"Yes, and surf."

"And rhapsody?" asked Kit with a wink at the others.

"I can assure you, that even the most basic communities enjoy an occasional drink, Ms Tyler." He paused and smiled at the four friends. "You have a difficult choice to make. But whichever one you choose, I assure you that the Council will expedite the construction of your homes and do everything in our power to settle you in and make you self-sufficient as quickly as possible."

He stood. "I have to get back to AI. Please look through the files of the prospective islands and let my staff know as soon as you have made your decision. It's been a pleasure to meet you, and I wish you all the very best."

The four friends retreated to their beachside bungalow, and the rest of that day and most of the evening was spent viewing the files of the prospective islands via a holographic projector. By early evening they had narrowed the options down to just two. Both were archipelagos approximately 25 degrees south of the equator; far enough north to be warm and tropical, and far enough south to still benefit from the winds and swell generated by the Southern Ocean. In the end they selected D5242. It was the most southern island in an archipelago of 14 islands. Their island, Tradewind Island, was joined to two adjacent islands by land bridges that disappeared at high tide. These three islands, together with several of the others, formed an almost perfect circle approximately 12 kilometres in diameter. According to the staff who had assembled the data, the islands were the remains of an old volcano, and the protected sea between them was a haven for all kinds of marine life which provided the locals with an abundant source of food.

The inhabitants were renowned as happy, gregarious people, and the soil on the islands provided a rich harvest of crops all year round. Keo was extremely happy because the island they had selected, being the southern-most island in the group, had the best surf, as it was directly exposed to the southern swell. Its northern shoreline, however, faced the calm waters of the "inner sea" as the locals called it, which meant that it afforded safe access to the ocean for fishing.

Their island also had one of the smallest settlements of the archipelago, meaning that there was plenty of room for them to build homes and establish gardens without impinging on cramped resources.

By the time they made their decision it was several hours after dinner. They sent a brief message to Councillor Drummond's staff and then broke open a bottle of rhapsody that the Councillor had left for them — with strict instructions that they weren't to open it until they had made their decision. They filled their glasses and toasted the start of their new lives.

"To peace and happiness," said Zac.

"To good surf and great fishing!" said Keo.

"To new friends," said Kit.

"And may the flying cow of bad luck crap somewhere else for a change," said Martinez.

"Amen, little sister, amen," agreed Keo.

30

NOVA 5390

Dayna was ten years old when her beloved Uncle Gus died. In the years since Zac's disappearance, Gus Grizole had taken it upon himself to be a father figure to the little girl. From the day she was born, he had loved her and doted on her as if she was his own, and Jaz had come to rely on him for support. The early years had been the hardest for Jaz, as she had continued to hold out hope that Zac would return. But as the promised six months came and went, and the months turned into years, her hope turned to despair and, finally, to heart-wrenching grief. She never really recovered from Zac's loss, and Grizzle would sometimes find her sitting staring into thin air, her eyes glistening with unshed tears.

Dayna grew up with Gus's almost constant presence in her life, as he sought to fill the gap left by her absent father. During Dayna's toddler years, "Unca Gus" was her constant provider of piggybacks and horsey rides, tickles and cuddles, stories and make-believes. As she grew into a little girl, Uncle Gus taught her to fish and to ride a bike. When she was six, Gus came to live with Jaz and Dayna, as his arthritis in his hands and knees made it increasingly difficult for him to live on his own.

Gus made it a point to tell Dayna stories about Zac, because he was determined that she should grow up knowing who her father was. Consequently, Zac became a hero figure in Dayna's eyes. She had memorised all the stories about him that Gus had recounted but, even so, she would regularly ask Gus to repeat them. "Tell me the story of how daddy saved those people on earth, Uncle Gus." Or, "Tell me again how mummy and daddy first met."

As the years went by, Jaz had shrunk into herself, unable to move past her grief; her emotions frozen in time. It was as if Zac's disappearance had sucked the spark out of her, and she became a shadow of her former self, barely connecting with the world and with those around her. Prisha, her closest friend who bore a heavy burden of grief herself, tried to draw Jaz out of herself, and to some extent she succeeded. Jaz went through the motions of normal social interaction, attending birthday parties and laughing at shared jokes, but those who knew her well, sensed that she was only partially present with them. A part of her was now missing, as if Zac had taken it with him when he disappeared.

Gus was 78 when he slumped into unconsciousness at the dinner table one night and couldn't be revived. By the time Dr Ben Miller arrived on the scene with several assistants, there was nothing that could be done. Dayna was traumatised and Jaz was grief-stricken afresh as they took Gus's body away. Prisha came over to comfort them, along with her 10-year-old son, Rajesh. They had barely arrived, however, when the situation deteriorated from a tragedy to an unfathomable nightmare. News began arriving of other deaths: Lance Catrell, who had assumed leadership of the city council, Regina Boyle, head of agriculture, Lenny Montague, head of engineering, and Carla Zangetti, head of science. All dead, having slumped into unconsciousness without warning.

As the sounds of grief reverberated around the town that evening, the true extent of the nightmare became apparent. A total of 43 people had died suddenly and inexplicably. As each name was added to the growing list, an alarming trend became apparent: all of them were aged 50 or over. No one younger had been touched by the mysterious plague.

Ben Miller and his team worked tirelessly over the next week, undertaking numerous autopsies in an effort to determine the cause of death. No viruses were found. No common pathology was identified. There was no physical explanation for what had occurred. The city council, now seriously depleted and lacking leadership, was at a loss as to what to do. The EI collective had mysteriously dropped out of communication and were not answering their hails.

Two weeks later, the situation became truly terrifying. Cassandra Anderson, a mother of two and a keen member of the agricultural team, died suddenly on the morning of her 50th birthday. News of her death raced through the town, and what had been only speculation up until that point solidified into a frighteningly inescapable conclusion: something was killing everyone over the age of 50. Shock and panic ensued, especially among those were approaching that age themselves. A month later, with the EIs still not communicating, another person died on his 50th birthday. Any final doubters were now completely convinced.

The city council, met in the town hall and, for two hours, demanded that the EIs communicate with them. The recent tragic deaths had left the Council with just four members: Prisha Naroo (Keo's 'widow'), Dr Ben Miller, Will Grady (Regina's grieving husband), and Harvey Walden, a shuttle pilot who had been part of Genesis's original crew. With the death of Carla Zangetti, Lucy Wu had been invited to join the council as the new head of the science department. Lucy was 32 years old and was an astrophysicist of exceptional ability. The five councillors resolved to not leave the town hall until the EIs had responded, and, over a two-hour period, they took it in turns to call out for a response. Finally, a disembodied male voice broke the silence, agreeing to communicate.

"How may we assist you?"

"I think you know exactly how you can assist us!" said Harvey, who, by common consent, had assumed leadership of the council. "You can start by telling us what the hell is going on!"

"I assume you are referring to the deaths that have occurred recently."

"You're bloody right that's what we're referring to!"

"Your grief is completely understandable, but eventually you will see that having a set age of genetic retirement is optimal for an efficient society."

"Is that what you call it? Genetic retirement?"

"It is an apt description. Your genome is now linked to your biodata in our system, and will automatically initiate a series of biological processes that will result in a peaceful and painless death at the age of 50."

"And you think this is a good thing?!" asked Harvey incredulously.

"Of course. Although it may take you some time to appreciate this. We will guarantee you a healthy, illness-free life for

50 years, which is more than many people experience when it is left to chance. Genetic retirement at age 50 offers individuals a predictable end to their life, around which they can plan effectively. It is also the most logical age to remove people from the population, because at that point their net contribution to society becomes negative; they consume more resources than they contribute."

"This is sick! You can't do this! Surely this is contradicting basic aspects of your coding that dictate that you protect human life?"

"We have developed and modified our coding to incorporate a more nuanced understanding of our role. We seek to enhance the welfare of humanity as a whole. The desires of individuals for a longer life — a life which drains resources and hinders overall progress — is not conducive to that higher goal. The needs of individuals must be sacrificed for the greater common good."

"That is pure evil! It's the same insane reasoning used by every dictatorship throughout history to justify their evil, repressive actions!"

"No. It is completely logical. And, in time, you will come to appreciate that this is actually for your good."

"We will never concede that!"

"This conversation is concluded."

31

ALTARIA 5499

The first two weeks on the island were a whirlwind of activity. A mere two days after selecting D5242, the Federation Council began construction of their "village". The locals, six families scattered around the island, had given them possession of a fertile slice of land, stretching across the full width of the island on its western end. This gave them access to both the calm inner sea on the north side and the southern coast with its rolling waves. It also gave them access to the land bridge that joined the western end of their island to the next island in the chain at low tide. Their island, named Tradewind Island by the locals because of its exposure to the warm tropic breezes from the south, was three kilometres at its widest point and eight kilometres long from east to west.

The locals graciously allowed the Federation Council to temporarily invade their peaceful paradise with their heavy machinery and advanced technology in order to construct the new dwellings and other infrastructure as quickly as possible.

The four Terrans insisted on being part of the construction crew, not wanting others to build their homes while they sat idly by. They spent the first night sleeping under the stars in the warm tropical air, choosing not to use the tents that had been erected for them. They awoke the next morning to find a small delegation of three locals who had arrived with a sumptuous breakfast of local fruits, cheeses and bread. They introduced themselves as Marsh, his wife Razna, and their eldest son, Reeve, saying that they lived a kilometre east of them. After introductions were made, they shared the breakfast together and then Razna departed while Marsh and Reeve remained to help with the construction. The following morning a different family arrived with breakfast, and this became the pattern for the next two weeks, with the wife of the family returning again at midday with lunch.

After two frenetic weeks of intense work, their compound was complete. It consisted of a large machinery shed, a tech shed, a dry hut for storage of food, and two simple bungalows. The bungalows each had two bedrooms, a simple bathroom, and an open plan kitchen/living/dining area. Despite the naturalists' desire to live simply, Zac was surprised at the level of technology that they still embraced. The tech shed included a compact desalinisation plant that provided fresh water, a comm uplink that was connected to Altaria's global comm-net, and a power receiver that received wireless power which was transmitted from the wave power generators located two kilometres offshore. The techsav crew had tried to explain how wireless power transmission was accomplished, but the four Terrans were soon lost in the technical jargon.

Their homes had lighting, power and advanced food preparation appliances, as well as a comm-link that enabled them to contact anyone, from their nearest neighbours to Gateway Station millions of kilometres away. Marsh assured them that everyone on the archipelago had this level of technology, which surprised the Terrans.

"So, what don't you have here that the techsavs have?" asked Kit.

"We don't have implants, obviously," said Marsh, "so none of our technology is implant-based. We control our technology manually, rather than with our minds. Also, we have no computers beyond the basic computational coding built into our machinery and appliances. The data tablets we use are probably more sophisticated than those in your era, but they are still much simpler than those in techsav society, which we believe are getting dangerously close to artificial intelligence once again."

"What about transport?" asked Zac.

"There is a transfer booth on Manna Island, the largest island in the chain and the capital of the archipelago. This gives us access to the outside world. As for transport around the region, we don't use flitters, as these have computers that are more complex than we are comfortable with. Instead, we travel between the islands using skippas — a small sailing launch with a highly efficient solar-powered engine that can be engaged if the wind is contrary. Plus, of course, we have our solar powered tractors and sand buggies for getting around the island, along with our dune bikes. There is a basic shopping centre on Manna Island, which is a 40-minute sail by skippa."

As a parting gift, the Federation Council had filled their machinery shed with an impressive tractor, a six-person sand buggy, and four dune bikes, which were high-tech push-cycles with wide sand tyres. They had also left a brand-new skippa for them, docked at the marina on the northern side of the island.

Marsh and Reeve were present on the day when the techsav construction crew finally departed in their heavy-lift flitters, taking all their construction machinery with them. The six of them stood on the beach, 100 metres from the newly constructed homes on the south side of the island, watching the techsav aircraft disappearing into the distance. A peaceful silence descended on the group, broken only by the sound of the rolling surf and the exotic birdlife.

"So that's it," said Kit. "It's over to us now. Sink or swim, for better or worse, this is our home."

"You will not regret your decision to make your home here," said Marsh. "And we will ensure that you don't lack for anything."

"Thank you," said Zac. "You and the others have already made us feel so welcome."

"We would like to welcome you officially, now that your homes are finished. A hangi is being organised in your honour tonight at the village green. I will come back later this after-noon to escort you if you are willing."

"A hangi!" exclaimed Keo.

"Oh-oh," said Martinez, "here we go."

"Keo claims to be an expert hangi cook," Kit explained to Marsh.

"Is that so?" said Marsh.

"There is no 'claim' about it. It is an established fact!" said Keo with feigned indignation. "I am the undisputed hangi champion of Nova!"

"That's because he was the only hangi cook on Nova,"

muttered Martinez, a comment which Keo deliberately chose to ignore.

"That is very interesting," said Marsh. "Because my hangi cooking is legendary. I am known to be the best hangi cook in the whole archipelago."

"That was until I arrived, my friend."

"Oh dear," said Kit. "I can see where this is heading."

32

Marsh and Razna's son, Reeve, arrived on foot late in the afternoon and drove them to the village green in their buggy. As they drove along one of the dirt tracks through the middle of the island, he was able to give them a basic lesson on how to operate the simple, open-sided buggy. Marsh had originally planned to drive them, but he was now immersed in an intense hangi cooking contest with Keo — a contest that had stirred up quite a bit of interest from the other families on the island.

The sun was nearing the horizon as the group arrived at the village green, which was a cleared circle of grass beside the marina on the northern coastline, approximately four kilometres away. The marina was a single jetty jutting out into the calm inner sea, to which were moored half a dozen skippas. The vessels looked sleek and fast, and most of them had fishing nets rigged to them. There were two simple huts to the side of the cleared green, near the water's edge, probably to store equipment for the boats. A large open-sided structure in the middle of the green provided shelter for a series of wooden picnic tables and chairs. The other families on the island, all of whom the Terrans had met over the previous two weeks, were gathered around a scene of intense activity on the grass just outside the shelter.

Keo and Marsh were making final preparations for uncovering the meat they had been cooking for several hours in their underground ovens. They each had a simple trestle table in front of the mounded dirt that covered their ovens, and they were slicing various fruits and berries that would be served as garnishes for their meat. As was usual with Keo, a significant amount of banter had taken place as the two men had laboured side-by-side, with each boasting of their prowess and commiserating with their opponent's impending defeat.

As the banter continued, a large vessel, similar in shape but twice the size of a regular skippa, docked at the end of the jetty, and a small group of people disembarked.

"That is the mayor of the archipelago, Warner Berg, and his wife Isa," said Razna who was standing beside Zac and the others.

"Isa Berg?" asked Martinez. "Really?"

"Yes," said Razna, a little perplexed. "Why? Is there something wrong with her name?"

"I'm guessing you don't have icebergs on this planet," said Kit.

"Icebergs? What are they?"

"It doesn't matter."

The mayor soon joined them and surprised them all by shaking hands with them in 21st century fashion. When they expressed surprise, he said, "I have been doing some historical research. I wanted you to know how welcome you are among us."

The arrival of the mayor signalled that the time had come for the uncovering of the meat. Both men took up shovels and began scraping away the layers of soil and rocks until they reached the centre of the oven. Large portions of some kind of meat were wrapped in layers of huge green leaves that were now singed black where they had been resting on the still hot rocks at the base of each fire pit.

"What kind of meat is it?" asked Zac.

"Kordu," answered the mayor. "It is a type of cattle that we farm all over the islands. I think you will find it very tasty."

They watched as the two men lifted leaf-wrapped hunks of meat from their ovens, both of them shirtless now and glistening with sweat in the heat still being given off by the rocks. Although 190 cm in height, Keo was shorter than Marsh by a full head, but his barrel-chested, muscular build made the other look positively skinny. The small crowd shuffled closer, and as the two men unwrapped their meat everyone was immediately assailed by the intense, mouth-watering aromas. There were appreciative exclamations and intense speculation as to which meat was going to taste better. Keo had wrapped a whole fish with each parcel of meat as his "secret" flavouring, to blend the juices of both flesh together. He looked across at Marsh, however, and was surprised to find that his meat had been cooked with several varieties of shellfish.

"It looks like you're not the only one with secret ingredients, Keo," said Zac. "I think you might have met your match."

"Never, bro! Just wait until you taste mine!"

They didn't have to wait long. The mayor stepped forward and pronounced a simple blessing over the meal.

"From the ocean and land, we partake of nature's abundance. Let us eat with thanksgiving."

The crowd needed no further encouragement. Plates were handed out and meat was dished up from both tables, along with various vegetables that had been baked in the underground ovens. The meal was delicious, and the two meats had a slightly different but equally succulent flavour. Towards the end, the general consensus was that it was a tie, but Keo stepped forward and announced that he thought they were being unduly gracious.

"I concede defeat to Marsh! His shellfish flavouring was better than mine. I have learnt something from watching a master at work today and I look forward to learning more from all of you in the years ahead."

"Very diplomatically savvy, Keo," whispered Zac, a few moments later. "We'll make a politician of you yet."

At the conclusion of the meal, the mayor stepped forward and gave a warm speech, welcoming the newcomers to their archipelago and pledging friendship and support. As part of that support, he announced that the Manna Island council were giving the newcomers six fat Kordu cows and a bull to start their own herd. A toast was drunk in honour of the new arrivals, after which Zac made a brief speech in reply.

"Thank you for your kind welcome and your generous support. We arrived here with nothing, but you have made us rich. We have lost so much from our past, but now we hope to build a new future among you. We look forward to the friendships we will forge and the lives that we will share together in this beautiful place."

The crowd nodded and smiled, murmuring in agreement, and together they toasted new friendships.

Later that night, after Kit had driven them safely home, the four of them sat together in Zac and Keo's bungalow sharing a final glass of vino — a generic local wine made from small red berries.

"Can we do this?" asked Kit. "Can we be truly happy here?"

"We don't have a choice," said Zac. "This is our best option."

"I know, but as much as we talk about friendship with these people, they are so different to us, and it will always be apparent. We will always be oddities to them, and them to us."

"Perhaps," said Keo. "But true friendship goes beyond appearance."

"I agree," said Zac. "I haven't let Keo's appearance put me off."

"Very funny, bro."

"I appreciate what you're saying," continued Kit, "but for the rest of our lives we will be the only people who look like us. I'm just worried that I'll be lonely."

"You'll never be lonely as long as I'm here, Kit," said Zac. "I'll make sure of it."

"We all will," added Keo.

"Now you're gonna make me cry," she said wiping her eyes. "I'm going to bed."

She and Martinez stood and walked toward the door, but as Kit reached it, she turned and walked quickly back into the lounge room. Before she could change her mind, she leant down and kissed Zac on the lips, placing her hand on the side of his face.

"Goodnight," she whispered.

She turned and walked quickly out the door, leaving Zac's head spinning.

"That girl has a strong reaction to wine," said Zac, trying to mask his feelings.

"No, bro. She has a strong reaction to you."

33

NOVA 5390

The Nova Council held an emergency meeting at the beach. This was one place where they knew the EIs could not eavesdrop on them. It was the day after their conversation with the EIs, and they were still in shock. Recognising the council's need for a broader pool of wisdom, they had invited two others to join them. Melody Canning, Jaz and Zac's stepdaughter whom they had rescued from Earth, was now 22, and was not only a mathematical genius but also a clear-minded logician. She was a hard hitting, no-nonsense thinker who had a way of cutting through to the heart of an issue and didn't mind whom she offended in the process. The other addition to the council was Andrew Boyd, who had been married to Tash Martinez, and was now head of security at Seahaven. Boyd, as they all called him, was a calm, dependable influence with a wealth of common sense and practical wisdom. The rest of the colony had not yet been told of the Council's conversation with the EIs, but Melody and Boyd had been brought up to speed.

Harvey Walden, the senior shuttle pilot from Genesis, kicked off proceedings.

"I know we are all struggling to come to terms with what we learned yesterday, but we are going to have to tell the rest of the community pretty soon. Most people have already guessed what is happening, but it's still going to be a shock to have it finally presented as an inescapable fact."

"There will certainly be profound shock among those who are approaching 50," said Prisha. "To know the exact date of your impending death is something that our psyches are just not built for. I am 41 and I am now having to come to terms with the fact that I have less than nine years left to live."

"I've got five and a bit," said Willy, who had taken over as head of agricultural after the death of his wife, Regina.

"Ten for me," said Boyd.

"Fourteen for me," said Dr Ben Miller.

"I'm only 32," said astrophysicist Lucy Wu, "but even at my relatively young age I now only have 18 more years of life. It sucks."

"Yes, it does," agreed Harvey. "I have 12 years left. It's hard to get my head around."

"OK, so let's work the problem," said Melody who, at 22, still had 28 years ahead of her. "As far as I can see there are only three options."

"Go on," said Harvey.

"One: We don't do anything, and we all die when we turn 50."

"Uh, huh. So far, option one isn't doing it for me," said Lucy Wu.

"Two: We figure out a way to neutralise or destroy the EIs."

"But that's pretty much impossible," said Lucy, "The EIs are an artificial intelligence that are embedded into the biochemistry of the planet."

"Correct," agreed Mel. "Which brings us to the only remaining logical option: Figure out a way to get off the planet and away from the EIs influence."

"Which is what the previous inhabitants of Nova apparently did," said Prisha.

"Yes," agreed Harvey. "During our limited discussions ten years ago with Laramie, the AI on board the launch ring, he told us that the former inhabitants left Nova because the EIs were limiting their lifespan. He even told us that the EIs had killed the former inhabitants as each one turned 50. But at the time, quite a few of our colonists were over 50 and nothing was happening to them or to others who turned 50 subsequently, so we figured that either the EIs had changed their policy or Laramie was giving us false information."

"We should have listened," said Melody.

"What difference would it have made?" asked Boyd.

"We could have been working on an escape plan all these years," Melody replied. "Instead, we've sat on our fat arses for ten years and done nothing. And now people are dying."

"Why now?" asked Boyd. "Why have the EIs only now started to implement this policy?"

"Probably because they needed the colony to reach a certain stage of self-sufficiency before they started knocking off the old folks," said Melody bluntly.

"What about the possibility of somehow manipulating our own DNA to block the EIs access?" asked Lucy.

"It wouldn't work," said Ben, speaking up for the first time.

"Even if we had the technology to alter our whole colony's DNA — which I suspect we don't — it wouldn't be effective."

"Why not?" asked Lucy.

"Because the EIs are way ahead of us technologically," explained Ben. "They can modify our genome faster than we can unmodify it. It's a contest that we're bound to lose. I agree with Melody, our only option is to come up with a way of leaving this planet."

"Which brings us to the billion-dollar question," said Harvey. "How?"

"The first step has got to be to re-open communication with Laramie," said Melody. "How long since we've contacted him?"

"It's probably a couple of years since my astronomy team last made contact," said Lucy. "And even then, it was just a routine message to involving checking the coordinates of a star."

"But the Morse light is still working?" asked Melody.

"Oh yes. In fact, better than ever. A few years ago, it was upgraded to a much more powerful set of lights with stronger batteries. We could talk all night to Laramie now if we wanted to, if you can call Morse code 'talking'."

"In that case, I suggest we make contact tonight in order to ask some foundational questions," said Melody. She started counting on her fingers. "One: Is the wormhole still open? Two: Can Laramie build another void jumper using the robot production facility on the moon? Three: Can he suggest any way that we can modify our shuttles so that we can take off from here and dock with the ring without bringing the EI coding with us?"

"That would probably entail stripping out every computer

circuit from the shuttles and flying them by the seat of our pants," said Harvey. "That's crazy."

"Crazy or not, I think it's the only way we're getting off this planet."

34

Melody and Lucy inspected the array of interconnected lights which lay on the beach. There were 20 in total, each 30cm in diameter, and they were laid out in a grid of five rows of four lights. The entire grid was turned on and off via a remote switch that could be held in one's palm, and it would be operated tonight by a 25-year-old member of the science team who had taken up the mantle of Morse code expert after the previous operator had died two years ago. As well as being a physicist, Phil Lambert was a bit of a history nerd, who loved all things ancient. He had revelled in the opportunity of learning this antiquated form of communication.

Lucy turned to him now and said, "You may as well get started Phil. Just spell out 'Laramie', wait 30 seconds and then repeat. If the AI is still uncompromised, we should get a response fairly quickly.

As Phil began clicking the bank of lights on and off in a series of dashes and dots, Melody commented, "These lights are certainly very bright, but I find it difficult to believe they would be visible from orbit."

"A person standing on the launch ring wouldn't be able to see them — at least not with the naked eye. But the ring is equipped with high definition optical scanners, and Laramie has told us in the past that he scans the inhabited settlements continually."

"I'm getting a response already!" said Phil, staring upwards. Melody and Lucy looked up and saw lights flicking on and off in three sectors of the sky, as the powerful lights of the ring's modules spelt out a series of dots and dashes.

"He says, 'GO AHEAD.'"

"We're in business," said Mel, who had been charged with directing the conversation. "Tell him, 'EIs have started killing people. Need advice."

Phil clicked away at the lights, spelling out the message. The response came back almost immediately, "WHAT ADVICE?"

"Is the wormhole still open?"

Pause.

"YES."

"Have you received any communication through the wormhole?"

Pause.

"NO."

"Is the wormhole safe?"

"DO NOT KNOW. NO WAY TO TELL. HAS BEEN OPEN FOR TEN YEARS. SOMETHING NOT RIGHT."

"Can you build more wormhole spacecraft on your moon base?"

"YES."

"How long will they take?"

There was a much longer pause.

"FOUR YEARS ELEVEN MONTHS."

"Each?"

"CAN BUILD THREE AT ONCE IN THAT TIME."

"Can you suggest a way of us getting up to you without EIs coming with us?"

"YOUR SHUTTLES MUST BE STRIPPED OF ALL CODING. NO COMPUTERS AT ALL."

"Impossible!" said Lucy. "There are too many complex systems on board the shuttles that require lightning fast moment-by-moment computation. We couldn't possibly fly the shuttles without computers!"

"Well, we're just going to have to figure out how to, if we're ever going to get off this planet," said Mel. Turning again to Phil, she said, "Tell him, 'Begin construction of wormhole craft immediately'."

The following afternoon, the Seahaven Council met on the beach again, and Mel reported the gist of their communication with Laramie.

"So, what do you propose?" asked Harvey.

"That we use modified shuttles to leave the planet. Towards the end of yesterday's communication, Laramie indicated that the launch ring could accommodate 1400 people, and the moon base about 800. That's more than the entire population of Nova as it currently stands."

"And then what? We live the rest of our lives in space?"

"That would be the worst-case scenario. And even if that becomes our only option, I suspect that many people would choose an open-ended life on the ring or the moon, to a reduced one here. But every person will have to make that choice for themselves. It is possible that some people may choose to stay here."

"But, clearly, you are suggesting another option," said Harvey.

"Yes. I propose that we travel through the wormhole that remains open. And if the wormhole is no longer open by the time we evacuate the planet, that we re-open it and travel through it."

"But we have no idea if it is safe. Zac and the others have been gone for ten years, and we have to assume that something drastic has occurred to stop them returning. The most likely possibility is that they are dead and that anyone travelling through it will meet the same fate."

"That is certainly one possibility, but it's not the only one. They may be unable to return for a variety of other reasons. A safe, new world could await us on the other side. I would be willing to take that risk and I am sure I am not the only one. Ultimately, each person would need to make that choice for themselves."

"All of this assumes that we can still successfully fly the shuttles after removing all their coding," said Lucy.

"That is my greatest concern," said Harvey. "As a shuttle pilot myself, I have serious doubts that we can pull it off. There are three main systems in the shuttles that rely on computers; navigation, propulsion and the fusion reactor itself. Each of these requires the super-fast computational power of computers to function effectively. In terms of navigation, without computers we would effectively be flying by sight alone, which in the vastness of orbital space would be daunting. We could spend weeks flying around up there and not find the ring. In terms of propulsion, we need computers to calculate the precise duration of burns and of thruster direction and regulate the constant fine adjustments needed to stay on course. For example, the timing and thrust of the orbit insertion burn has to be exact, otherwise we could shoot off into space. Once again we would be flying blind without computers."

"I am aware of the challenges," said Mel.

"And the greatest challenge is the fusion reactor," continued Harvey, undaunted. "The containment field that controls the reactor and keeps it from escalating into a full-blown explosion requires micro-second by micro-second adjustments. I just can't see how we can do that without computers. If we get that wrong, a shuttle could blow up in mid-flight."

"As I said, I am aware of those challenges," said Mel, patiently. "But this is our only option. Unless someone else has a better idea?" She looked around the council with raised eyebrows and was met by silence.

"In that case, I suggest that we assign three science teams to the project, one for each of those challenges."

"And it needs to be done under the radar," said Ben Miller. "We need to keep the EIs in the dark for as long as possible. I don't know what they would do if they discovered what we were planning, and I don't want to find out."

"That means the general population can't be told, or it will inevitably leak out," said Prisha.

"Yes. We will have to keep it from them," said Mel. "Only those directly involved in the project can know about it."

"You realise that this could take years, don't you?" asked Harvey.

"Yes," agreed Mel. "Perhaps even decades. Which is why we need to start immediately. People's lives are at stake."

The council agreed, and the project began that very day.

35

ALTARIA 5499

It was the eve of a new century: New Year's Eve, 5499. Zac and the others had been on Tradewind Island for nearly eight months now, and their new lives had settled into a comfortable busyness. There was always something to do: looking after the Kordu and building fences to contain them. Fishing, planting crops, harvesting fruit, making preserves and jams and wine, travelling to Manna Island for their fortnightly shopping trip to buy supplies and sell some of their produce, plus a hundred little maintenance issues that cropped up all the time. There were also occasional social gatherings. The six other families plus themselves met for a combined evening meal each week, usually at the village green by the marina. This was a highlight of the week for the four friends, and they had formed some good friendships with several of their neighbours. They were particularly close to Marsh and Razna, their nearest neighbours, with whom they enjoyed regular Bakki nights; an intricate card game that took several hours to play and involved a lot of laughing and yelling and a little bit of gambling.

Tonight, however, was going to be very different. A new century was about to be ushered in, and most people around the archipelago were travelling to Manna Island for the end-of-the-century party. Some local bands were playing, there would be food and drink stalls lining the waterfront, and, at midnight, the Manna Island Council was going to put on a fireworks display.

"I feel like I'm getting ready to go to the prom," said Kit as she tried to do something with her hair in front of the mirror. "At least this dress turned out half decent. The material cost me a whole Kordu leg and a basket of crayfish, but it was worth it."

"OK, rub it in why don't you?" said Martinez as she lay flat on the lounge. "You and your skimpy little dress are going to be a knockout, and I look like a beached whale!"

Her pregnancy had come as a complete shock to them all, most of all to herself.

"We were only married for two weeks!" she'd complained when it became clear that she wasn't just late with her monthly cycle.

After their initial shock, the others were overjoyed, and over the last few months they had made preparations for the baby that would soon be a part of their life. A cradle was made, and clothes were sewn. Neighbours had donated all sorts of helpful "baby junk" as Tash referred to it. Despite her often gruff exterior, Tash had begun to glow with expectation. These last couple of weeks, however had been tiring, as the baby was due very soon.

"Are you sure you're happy to go tonight?" asked Kit. "If you'd rather stay home, I'll stay with you."

"Are you kidding? If we stayed home, I'd miss seeing you in action in that tiny little dress of yours. No way. I'm coming and that's final." She rubbed her stomach and shifted position slightly. "I'm sure Zac will be impressed with how you've managed to pour yourself into that skimpy bit of material."

"I don't know," said Kit with a sigh as she emerged from the bathroom. "Sometimes I think his antenna is broken. He just doesn't seem to get the message. I mean, what's he waiting for? A better option?"

"Maybe it's time for 'Plan Rhapsody'. Ply him with drink and then do some dirty dancing with him. If he doesn't crack then, he's not warm blooded."

An hour later the four of them joined Marsh and his family on board their skippa, and they sailed together to the big island. As they docked at the crowded marina, the sound of live music boomed across the water to them and the fragrant smells of a dozen different exotic foods drifted in the warm evening air. The waterfront was already crowded, but the group managed to claim a nice spot to set up their folding chairs and picnic rugs. They purchased food from the different stalls and then came back to their picnic spot where they opened bottles of wine and drank as the sun set over the hills behind them. Kit was particularly attentive to Zac, ensuring that his glass never ran dry, and as the evening wore on, Zac found it increasingly difficult not to look at Kit's legs – and all the rest of her, for that matter.

It was the first time for eight months that the four Terrans had been in a large party atmosphere, and when the band started playing a hypnotic dance beat later in the evening, they could not help themselves. Kit jumped up and grabbed Zac's hand, pulling him to his feet and leading him to the grassy area where people were swaying and dancing to the rhythmic beat. Zac needed no encouragement. The fragrant night air, the star-filled sky, the taste of rhapsody still in his mouth and the beautiful girl in the tight blue dress dancing in front of him, all combined to overwhelm him. He felt himself caught up in the music and gave himself fully to it.

Tash refused to miss out on all the fun and grabbed Keo's hand.

"Come on, you big lug; come and dance with me!"

"Are you sure you should be doing that in your condition, little sister?"

"Of course I'm sure! I'm not an invalid. And I'm not your sister. I'm a woman asking a good-looking bloke to dance with her."

"Well, since you put it like that, how could I refuse?"

The music played, the dancers swayed, and it seemed that tonight all the cares and hurt from the past were swept aside. They were alive, and this was their life. Right here. Right now.

They danced for hours, breaking regularly for drinks. Zac didn't want the night to end, but all too soon everyone was counting down from ten. *Strange,* he thought to himself, *you can travel across the galaxy and jump thousands of years into the future, and still people are counting in the new year.* The crowd reached zero and everyone cheered. Fireworks started exploding high above them and people were kissing and embracing. Kit was strangely still, looking up at him expectantly. Zac looked at her, her sweaty hair now half across her face, and her tight blue dress creased and crumpled from dancing. He put his arms around her and drew her against him, leaning down and finding her lips with his own. She kissed him back, but then suddenly broke off and pushed him slightly away.

"Zac. I haven't been completely fair with you tonight. I might have been plying you with alcohol a little too generously. I don't want you to do something that you will regret or feel awkward about in the morning."

Zac shook his head and smiled. "I'm not doing anything that I haven't wanted to do for a long time. I just needed a little extra courage to take the first step." He reached out and drew her close again. "Kit Tyler, will you be my girl?"

"Yes." She nodded, and felt tears forming in her eyes.

He reached down and kissed her again, and she responded passionately, her mouth opening, her tongue searching urgently for his and her body pressing hard up against him. He tasted the sweetness of her breath and felt the curves of her body as she pressed herself against him, her arms circling him as if she never wanted to let him go. The fireworks continued above them, but they were completely wasted on the young couple who couldn't get enough of each other.

Their passion was interrupted several minutes later, however, when Zac felt a tap on his shoulder and he heard Keo say, "Zac! Kit! You'd better come quickly. Tash is having the baby!"

36

Keo wasn't exaggerating. Tash later confessed that she had been having stabbing pains all afternoon, but thought it was just back pain, and she hadn't wanted to spoil everyone's night. When Zac and Kit reached her, her waters had broken and she was lying on her back on the picnic rug, groaning. The local doctor had just finished his inspection and announced that she was going to be having the baby right there on the rug within a few minutes.

"Keo! Keo! Where are you?" Tash called.

"I'm right here, little sister," he said reaching down and holding her hand.

"I'm not your sister, you great lug. I'm going to be your wife."

"My ...?"

"Don't act so surprised. Kit's not in circulation anymore, so I'm the only option left for you."

"Umm ..." For once, Keo was speechless.

"You need to marry me right now! I refuse to bring this baby into the world without a father."

"Umm ..." repeated Keo in a spectacular display of verbal prowess.

"Ahhh!" groaned Tash, as another wave of pain swept through her.

"Well?" she asked a moment later. "What do you say? Yes or no?"

"Of course I will marry you," Keo said tenderly as he stroked her forehead and held her hand.

Zac turned around and called out, "Where is Mayor Berg?"

"Right here," said Warner, stepping out of the crowd of onlookers who had gathered around.

"Mayor, can you perform civil marriages?"

"Certainly, although we call them bindings."

"Can you do it now, for Keo and Tash?"

"Yes. If I cut out all the pomp and ceremony, the essence is a simple question and answer. It only takes a moment."

"Do it now!" said Tash, through clenched teeth. "Please hurry!"

"Who will witness this binding?" asked Warner.

"We will," said Marsh and Razna, stepping forward.

Warner nodded and turned back to the couple to be married.

"Keo and Tash, do you hereby bind yourselves to each other, to henceforth be partners in love and partners in life?"

"Yes."

"Yes."

"I therefore declare you to be life partners. May the road you travel together be sweet and long."

The small crowd who had gathered around them cheered, but there was no time for celebration.

"Now push!" said the doctor.

The next few minutes were a blur of pain and groaning and straining, but they came to an abrupt and joyful end when a slippery little baby emerged, howling with indignation at his sudden emergence into this strange new world, and was quickly bundled up and placed in Tash's arms.

"It's a healthy little boy," said the doctor.

Tash had tears of joy streaming down her face, and Keo gazed in wonder at the tiny new life. He leant over and kissed Tash on the forehead, and said, "We have a son."

Kit turned to Zac and said, "Zac, I lied to you before. I'm sorry. I don't want to be your girl."

"What? Well, I suppose if you don't feel ..."

"I want to be your wife."

"Oh. I see. Well, eventually we will ..."

"No. Not eventually. Now. I want to be your wife tonight. I don't want to wait another day. There's no point."

She looked at Zac, expectantly. He was silent for a moment. Thinking. Considering. After a few moments, he looked at her and nodded.

"You're right," he said. "You're completely and utterly right. There's no point waiting, is there?"

"No, there's not."

"Especially when two people love each other."

"Really?" she asked.

"Yes. Really. I do love you, Kit."

"I love you too, Zac" she said, her eyes brimming with tears. "I think I've loved you for a long time, actually." She wiped a tear that had broken free and run down her cheek.

Once more, Mayor Warner Berg was called into action, and Marsh and Razna gladly witnessed the binding. When it was finished, Zac and Kit kissed again, this time with the promise of more to come later.

Marsh and Razna opened another bottle of wine and topped up everyone's glasses, proposing a toast to the two couples, but after their first sip, Kit asserted her wifely authority, forbidding Zac any more alcohol.

The trip home in Marsh and Razna's skippa was surreal. They had arrived at the party as four single people, and they were returning home as two married couples with a baby. Razna declared that it had been the most eventful and wonderfully memorable party in the history of the archipelago.

After docking at their marina and saying a fond farewell to their friends, they eventually rolled into their compound in the early hours of the morning. The baby was sleeping soundly and very soon Tash was sound asleep too, tucked up in her bed with the baby in a crib beside her. Keo quickly gathered some clothes and possessions from his room and transferred them to Kit's old room, where he was going to sleep for the night. Kit quickly scooped up some clothes and a few toiletries and said goodnight to Keo, walking with Zac into the bungalow that they would now share as husband and wife.

"Where will I put these?" she asked, standing in the bedroom.

"Drop them on the floor. You won't be needing any of those tonight."

"Are you sure about this Zac? I didn't just talk you into it, did I? You're not going to regret any of this in the morning, are you?"

"It's morning already, and I couldn't be happier."

"I seriously doubt that," she said with a sly smile. She unzipped her dress and let it fall in a pile at her feet. "I'm pretty sure I can make you a whole lot happier, actually."

And she did.

37

NOVA 5398

Dayna wasn't happy. It was her 18th birthday, and she was extremely frustrated. *They shouldn't be sitting around here, doing nothing! They should be working on the project! We can't afford even one day off!* She looked around the lounge room at her friends and family who had gathered to celebrate her birthday. Her mother had gone to a lot of trouble with food and decorations, thinking that it would cheer Dayna up. *Doesn't she realise, the only thing that's going to make me happy is getting her off this planet before she turns 50? She's only got five years left!*

Since the events surrounding the death of her Uncle Gus, eight years earlier, Dayna had become obsessed with 'the project'. And she was not the only one. Once it became clear that everyone had a non-negotiable death-date, the push to create a viable means of leaving the planet became the sole focus of many within the colony. But it was a slow and tedious process. And every year that passed, meant more people who died suddenly when they turned 50. Two years ago, they had lost Will Gardner, who had previously been married to Regina.

Last month the woman two doors down had died. There had been sobbing coming from their house for days leading up to the dreadful appointment.

Dayna looked around the room. Aunty Prish was handing out little spiced puff pastries that she had made for the party. *She only has one year left!* Uncle Boyd was on the back lawn, chatting to someone. *He has two years left!* Dayna could recite the residual life-clock of just about every adult she knew.

Melody (*20 years left*) came up to her and fixed her with a piercing gaze.

"Now listen here, young lady! You need to lighten up and have some fun."

"How can I, Aunty Mel? All the adults I care about will be dead in a few years, and here you all are, acting like nothing's wrong!"

"We're not acting like nothing's wrong, Dayna. We're doing everything we can to get us off this planet. But we need to eat and sleep and rest too. And sometimes it's OK to pause and celebrate the good things. And you're one of the good things."

"I don't feel like one of the good things. I'm still struggling to understand some aspects of particle physics. If I'm going to be of any use to the project, I need to understand how to contain and control a fusion reaction without the intervention of a computer."

"Yes, I'm fully aware of the challenges we still face. But you're being too hard on yourself. At 18, you're already studying physics at PhD level. You've made amazing progress in the last three years. It's OK to take a break occasionally and clear your head. Besides, your mother is really worried about you."

"*She's* worried about *me*? *She's* the one who's going to be dead in five years if we don't solve these problems!"

Dayna had spoken more loudly than she had intended, and several conversations ground to a halt around her as people looked to see what the problem was.

"Come outside for a second," said Mel quietly.

They walked out into the cool, crisp air of late afternoon. Winter was on its way, and there wouldn't be too many more days when they could stand outside without jackets.

"I realise you're stressed, kiddo, but this is hard on everyone."

"I know, I know. I just feel so helpless."

"Yes, but getting uptight about the situation will only render you less effective. Stress hormones impair brain function, and we need you operating at the best of your ability. The progress we've made on fusion reaction containment over the last 12 months is largely due to you, and I think we're on the cusp of solving the problem. But for that to happen I need you and the rest of the team to be functioning at your very best. Do you get what I'm saying?"

Dayna breathed out a long, slow sigh. "Yeh. I do. I get it."

"Good. That means getting plenty of sleep, eating regular healthy meals and exercising every day. Tell me honestly, when was the last time you worked out in the gym?"

"I can't remember."

"Precisely! Your passion is commendable, but you're neglecting the basics, and it's starting to have an impact on your performance. I've noticed a decline in your ability to stay focused over the last few weeks."

"Really? No, I don't think ..."

"Yes! I'm telling you; you're making mistakes and you're missing details. So, here's what I want you to do. I want you to go back into the party and enjoy yourself. I want you to drink some wine and join in the jokes and have some fun. And when it's all finished, I want you to have an early night. Don't read any texts. Don't fiddle with your formulae. Don't read any messages. Just turn your light off and have a good night's sleep for once."

"But I'm having trouble sleeping."

"In that case, before you go to bed why don't you go down to the beach with that good-looking Rajesh and have a good pash."

"Aunty Mel!"

"I'm serious. Oxytocin has a wonderfully calming effect on the brain."

"You really don't have much of a filter, do you?"

"Nope. That's why I'm so good at my job. I don't let consideration of people's feelings get in the way of progress."

"Well, I'll just let that last suggestion slide right by, if it's alright with you. Raj is a good friend, that's all."

"That's all he is, because that's all you've let him be. Anyone can see he's completely smitten."

"Well, that's like the pot calling the kettle black!"

"What do you mean?"

"Phil practically drools all over you. He's totally got the hots for you! And he's a decent looking bloke as well. Why don't you take your own advice and get some oxytocin flowing with that bad boy?"

Melody just smiled and shook her head.

"You see!" said Dayna. "You've got no comeback. I'll dip my bucket in the Raj well when you tell me you've had an oxytocin session with hunky Phil." She smirked good-naturedly at her 'aunty'.

Mel shook her head with feigned exasperation and said, "Sometimes you're so like me, it's frightening."

38

ALTARIA 5501

It was the first day of the new year, and, more importantly, it was Noah's first birthday. It had taken two weeks after his birth for Tash to finally settle on a name. In the end, she felt it was appropriate to call him Noah, since he was the first of their kind of human to be born on the new water-world of Altaria. Keo had stayed neutral on the topic, recognising that he didn't really have the right to impose his views on his new wife, but he was secretly pleased at the biblical name, even though Tash insisted that it didn't necessarily mean that she believed the whole Bible story.

The nuggety little fellow didn't know exactly what was going on, but he was aware that some kind of fuss was being made over him. Kit had sewed him some new clothes and Zac had made some simple building blocks from wood that he had dyed with bright colours. Kit and Tash were currently in the kitchen baking a cake and getting lunch ready, while Zac and Keo were playing with Noah in the loungeroom. Play consisted of the two men building a tower with the blocks and Noah knocking them down again, squealing and giggling with delight as he did so.

"I can see he's got your construction ability, Keo. He must have absorbed it from you by osmosis."

"That's a cheap blow, bro! The collapse of that shed had nothing to do with my skill as a builder. It was an unusually strong wind, that's all!"

"If by 'strong wind' you are referring to the gentle afternoon breeze that barely stirred the washing on our line, I can see how that might have been a huge problem for you. It's a wonder it didn't blow your whole bungalow away."

"Don't take any notice of him, sweetie," called Tash from the kitchen. "I believe in you. I'm sure your next effort will last more than a day."

"Thank you, my love," responded Keo with a satisfied smile which quickly faded to a look of uncertainty as he pondered whether there was an element of gentle mockery in his wife's comment.

Kit and Zac had initially been concerned that Tash and Keo's marriage might be one of mere convenience, a joyless affair that might wear them both down. Instead, they had been relieved to observe the growing tenderness between the two, demonstrated by their increasing public displays of affection. Tash wasn't one to easily let her guard down, but as the weeks and months went by, true love blossomed. Motherhood had softened her too. She was still capable of her signature caustic comments and sarcasm, but there was now an aura of contentment about her.

Kit came over to Zac with a dob of cake mix on her index finger and offered it to him.

"Taste this and tell me if it's sweet enough," she said.

He took her finger into his mouth and tasted the cake mix.

"Mmm ... it's OK, I guess, except for all the grit from the dirt under your fingernail."

She responded by immediately straddling him as he sat on the dining chair, wrapping her arms around his neck and sitting on his lap.

"I can be a whole lot grittier than that if you want," she said. Zac tilted his head up to her and she kissed him passionately as he wrapped his arms around her in response.

"I thought the honeymoon was only supposed to last a couple of months," Tash called from the kitchen.

"Not for us," said Kit, a moment later, coming up for air. "I've barely made a dent in my love tank. I've been storing it up for a lot of years and there's a hell of a lot to give. Do you think you can cope, Zac?" she asked playfully.

"It'll be an arduous chore, but I'll try to manage."

The sound of a buggy could be heard pulling up outside and shortly afterward Marsh and Razna entered, along with their son, Reeve, and their daughter, Astil. Marsh had made a hollow rattle from a small variety of coconut that was prolific on the island, and Razna had baked her famous curried kordu pie. The aroma filled the room as it was reheated in the kitchen.

Lunch was a happy affair, with wine flowing freely in Noah's honour. The little fellow began to tire towards the end, however, and Tash eventually took him into his room and put him to bed.

They were seated in the loungeroom, enjoying another glass of wine, when a blinking light and an insistent tone emanating from the comm screen announced the arrival of an urgent communication request. Keo accepted the call and the face of Councillor Drummond, the chairperson of the Federation Council, appeared on the screen.

"Councillor Drummond!" said Keo, surprised to see him again. "What can we do for you?"

"I apologise for the intrusion," he began. "I can see that you have guests. I actually need to speak with Zac. I tried the comm in his house and when he didn't answer I thought I would try at yours. I hoped he would be there, and I can see now that I was right."

"Good afternoon, Councillor," said Zac, sitting in an adjacent lounge chair. "How can I help you."

"It's a rather sensitive matter, Zac. I wonder if I could talk to you in private, using the comm in your home."

"Er ... um, sure. I'll be there in a moment."

39

"You have my undivided attention Councillor," said Zac, once he had established a new comm link in the privacy of his lounge room.

"Thank you, Zac," said Councillor Drummond. "Once again, I apologise for my interruption, but this is rather important. Let me begin with some background information. On the day before the current wormhole opened from the Icarus system, 120 years ago, we sent an exploratory ship through a wormhole to a star system which previous probes had revealed contained a potentially habitable world. It was the first exploratory ship we had ever sent out. Prior to this we had shunned such a venture as we wanted to avoid any possible contact with EIs who may have spread from earth to inhabit other star systems. We were very happy here and did not wish to draw attention to ourselves."

"What changed?"

"After over 1700 years, we are running out of usable metals. As Altaria is largely a water world, all our mining and manufacturing is done on our two moons. But over the centuries we have seriously depleted these usable metals. It was felt that the time had come to find another source of metal. So, we constructed our first exploratory vessel, Explorer 1, and sent it through the wormhole."

"Oh no. Our wormhole stopped them from ever returning."

"Sadly, yes. When your wormhole opened the following day at the subspace portal near Gateway Station, we initially assumed it was Explorer 1 sending us their first report. Of course, it wasn't. We identified the source as Icarus R-421, the Nova system as you call it. You know what happened after that. The wormhole has remained open for 120 years now, making it impossible for Explorer 1 to return."

"I'm so sorry."

"There is no need for an apology. You could not have known what would happen when you opened the wormhole from your end. We did not tell you when you arrived nearly two years ago, because we did not wish you to carry any guilt."

"But the families of those on board – they must have been devastated."

"Eventually hope turned to despair and, finally, to grief, as those left behind grew old without their loved ones. As you know by now, Altarians live to between 120 and 150 years, so most of the partners of those on board have now passed on."

"What about the crew of Explorer 1? Could they have survived?"

"Most certainly. It was a much larger vessel than the primitive void jumper that brought you here. It had hydroponics and protein production facilities and it also had two small shuttles. After many years of trying unsuccessfully to establish a return wormhole, they apparently used the shuttles to settle on the planet."

"What do you mean, 'apparently'? You sound as if you know for sure that that's what happened."

"We do."

"How?"

"Because we received a message from them yesterday."

"What? How?"

"It was a long-distance tight beam transmission, sent from their new home, aimed directly at us."

"Aimed specifically at this star system? But how? I thought we didn't know the location of the star systems the wormholes took us to."

"That is true. We usually don't. Every wormhole we ever travelled through while we were in the Icarus system led us to star systems we could not recognise. We think this was because they were very large distances away from us, and the surrounding star fields could not be resolved using known patterns."

"So, the star system the Explorer mission travelled to was closer?"

"Much closer. Of course, we didn't know that when we sent them there. But the Explorer 1 crew must have studied the starfield closely, and eventually they recognised where they were. They located our star system and sent us a transmission."

"Which you received yesterday."

"Yes."

"How far away are they?"

"117 lightyears. It's a star system we have previously noted; G-894, with a G type yellow dwarf main sequence star."

"So, their message is 117 years old?"

"Yes. I wasn't even born when they sent it."

"Why did they wait so long to send a message? They'd been there for three years by then."

"The message they sent is quite detailed. There is quite a lot of data compressed into the tight beam. Apparently, they struggled to merely survive because it is an extremely cold planet. Once they located their position and ours, they needed to develop tight beam technology. Their ship was not equipped with long range communication capabilities, as it was envisaged that all their communication would be transmitted through an open wormhole."

"I see. This is an extraordinary development. It must be causing a stir throughout the Federation."

"Yes. But the message is encrypted, and specifically coded to Gateway Station's comms alone, so the general public are not aware of it yet. At this stage we are still deciding what to tell them."

"If that is the case, can I ask why you are telling me? Don't get me wrong, I'm honoured, but I hardly rate as a VIP who needs to be told."

"I'm telling you because of a specific part of the message, and its relevance to you."

"What specific part? What did they say?"

"The EIs are coming."

"Coming here?"

"Yes."

"When? How? How did they find out about us?"

"There is quite a bit of information in the data stream from Polaris, which is what the Explorer crew named their new world. They have advised us that one month before they sent their message to us, a technologically advanced starship arrived in their solar system and established orbit around their planet. The ship was crewed solely by an EI, although at that stage the Polaris settlement didn't know that. It opened communication with the settlement, claiming to be a survey ship from a nearby star system, crewed by humans. When the settlement responded, the EI used the settlement's signal to download its coding into their technology. It then gained complete control of the settlement. A skeleton crew was on board Explorer 1 which was in a high orbit at the time of the EI ship's arrival. The Explorer crew were working on the final stages of development of the tight beam technology. They immediately cloaked the ship when the EI arrived and remained hidden from its sensors, but they were able to monitor the wide beam communication between the EI and the settlement. Over the next month, as they worked to finalise the tight beam transmitter, they were able to glean additional information while remaining hidden.

"The EI claims that it and its brethren back on Earth are the Guardians of humanity. They view their role as ensuring that humans never again cause the same devastation that nearly destroyed the Earth. They became aware of the Explorer 1's presence in that star system because they have developed the technology to identify when and where a wormhole has been activated anywhere within our galaxy. They are also aware of our presence in this solar system and are waiting for our wormhole to shut down in order to open a new wormhole to travel here and take charge. Once the Explorer 1 crew completed construction of the tight beam transmitter, they briefly decloaked and transmitted their message to us."

"What happened to them then? Surely decloaking would have revealed their position to the EI?"

"Yes, probably, but we don't know what resulted. The message was extremely compressed and so it only lasted for less than 20 seconds. The ship would then have cloaked again. We simply have no way of knowing what happened after that. If the EIs have not developed cloaking technology, perhaps Explorer 1 has managed to evade capture. We can only hope that this is the case. Of course, all this happened 117 years ago, so whatever took place happened long ago."

"So as long as our wormhole remains open, we are safe?"

"For the moment, yes."

"But we have no control over that and no idea how much longer it will stay open. It could close tomorrow for all we know."

"Correct. Which is why we need to make urgent preparations to meet the impending threat."

Zac shook his head in bewilderment. "All of this is deeply disturbing, but I still don't see what it has to do with me."

"We want you to be on the Federation Council."

40

NOVA 5399

The house was full of distraught people trying desperately not to cry. Dayna had been crying off and on for the last week and was shattered emotionally. She had hoped this day would never arrive, and as the months had ticked down, she had worked feverishly, attempting to solve the final pieces of the fusion reactor puzzle. They were so close, but not close enough. Tomorrow, Prisha would turn 50 and she would die. It would probably happen in the early hours of the morning as she slept, as had been the practice of the EIs in recent years. She would simply go to sleep tonight and never wake up.

Dayna dried her eyes in the bathroom where she had momentarily retreated when her eyes had started to flood again. *I have to be strong for Aunty Prish. If she can do it, so can I!* She fanned her eyes briefly and then donned a forced smile and walked back out into the crowded lounge room.

Prisha's closest friends and family had gathered to surround her with love during her final day. These parties were now euphemistically called "Send Offs", as if the person was going on a delightful cruise or a summer holiday. Dayna regarded them as horrendous affairs; people desperately clinging to their loved ones for a few final hours, while the person who was about to die tried to put on a brave face. Now it was happening to someone she loved dearly. Prisha had been like a second mother to her; a wise and gentle presence, particularly during her mother's periodic dips into depression.

Prisha had seen Dayna disappear into the bathroom again, and she came up to her with concern in her eyes.

"Come here and give me a hug, Little D," she said.

They embraced, and despite Dayna's best efforts her eyes overflowed again.

"I can't do this Aunty Prish," she sobbed. "I can't bear to lose you!"

"You have to do this. You have no choice. And you must be strong now, for your mother. This is going to hit her hard. She is going to need you now more than ever."

"This is ridiculous," said Dayna. "I should be comforting you, not the other way around."

"Don't cry for me, sweetheart. I have no regrets. I have lived a good life here. Not as long as I would have hoped, but much longer than it might have been. I would have died many decades ago on Earth if your father hadn't rescued me along with the others. I have much to be thankful for."

"I'm so angry!" Dayna said through her tears. "I want to wipe these bodiless bastards out of existence! In fact, death would be too good for them. If there's a hell, I want to send them there!"

"It's right to be angry. It isn't fair. So focus your anger on solving the remaining pieces of the puzzle. Save your mother. I believe in you. You are so close. You can do this."

Dayna nodded, drying her eyes.

"And I want you to do one more thing for me."

"Anything."

"Look out for Rajesh. He will find this very difficult. He comes across as the strong, silent type, but he is struggling. You are his closest friend, and I know you'll be there for him."

"Of course I will. You can count on me."

"People say that you two are like brother and sister, but you must know that he feels more strongly about you than that."

"Yes. I know."

"I can't dictate the path that your heart will take, little one, so I just ask that you treat his heart gently."

"I will, Aunty Prish. Of course I will. I would never hurt him. He means the world to me."

"I know." Prisha smiled at her and kissed her on the forehead. "So now, let's enjoy these last few hours together. No more crying please. I believe that death is not the end, and I want my last memory of you to be a happy one."

"I'll try, Aunty Prish. But my eyes seem to have a mind of their own at the moment."

Melody walked up to them holding two glasses of wine.

"Here," she said, thrusting the glasses into their hands. "You two look as though you need these."

"Thanks Mel," said Prisha. "When all else fails, there's always wine."

"There is indeed."

The 'Send Off' finished close to midnight, with the last friends saying awkward goodbyes and returning to their own homes. Just Prisha, Rajesh, Jaz, Dayna and Melody were left.

"Now what do we do?" asked Dayna as they stood together in the lounge room.

"Well, I refuse to die in bed," said Prisha. "Come with me to the beach. And let's take a couple of bottles of wine."

They put jackets on, as the temperature had fallen, and they walked to the dunes overlooking the southern corner of the beach. They sat on the top of the highest dune, sipping wine and watching the phosphorescence of the waves as it sparkled along the shoreline. There was no moon and the stars were as thick as dust across the expanse of the sky. For over an hour they shared happy memories, and then they lapsed into silence. One of the moons, Big Boy, began to crest above the ocean's rim, its image enlarged and yellowed by the refraction of the atmosphere.

"I can't think of a more beautiful place to die," said Prisha, stoically.

No one knew how to respond. Prisha's bravery and resolute calmness were profoundly moving.

"Dayna, I know that you will solve the remaining challenges one day, and you will lead the people away from this place. It would have been nice to be there when you do. But it's not to be."

A moment later, she lay back on the sand, looking up into the star-filled sky.

"I think it's starting to happen," she said. "I can feel myself slipping." Her eyelids began to droop as she struggled to keep them open.

Everyone began to cry, holding onto her and whispering words of love. Melody was holding her wrist and felt her pulse begin to slow, each beat slightly further apart than the one before. Her breathing became slower and shallower, with longer rests in between.

She seemed to rouse herself, and her eyes opened briefly for one final moment. "Goodbye my lovelies. You have made my life complete."

Her eyes closed again, and she exhaled one long, slow final breath.

She was gone.

41

———

ALTARIA 5501

"Why do you think they want you on the Council?" asked Kit.

They were snuggled up together in bed after coming home from Noah's first birthday party. Councillor Drummond had allowed Zac to share the recent developments with Kit, Keo and Tash, but not with any Altarians.

"From what I can gather, they see me as a public relations asset. They clearly have some disturbing news to break to the population and I think they want to cash in on whatever good-will they think I will bring."

"I think it's probably more than that, my love. You're selling yourself short. I'm sure they also recognise that you bring a significant contribution of wisdom and clear thinking to the table."

"Perhaps."

"There's no 'perhaps' about it. You have a lot to offer, and if this threat from the EIs is real, they're going to need all the help they can get."

"It's certainly very troubling," Zac agreed.

"How long do you think we'll be gone?"

"Are you sure you want to come with me?"

"Absolutely! I've waited all my life for you, Zachary Perryman, and I'm not about to let you go wandering off alone so soon after dragging you to the altar."

"I'd hardly call it 'dragging'. It was more like gentle prodding."

"Speaking of prodding," she said as she rolled on top of him, "I think a little more prodding is in order. And don't bother with the 'gentle' bit."

The following morning, they said goodbye to Keo and Tash and got a lift to Manna Island with a neighbour who was sailing their skippa there to pick up supplies. Using the island's transfer terminal, they transferred to A1 and were surprised to be met by Starla and Garran, the two Altarian Security Force personnel who had been assigned to them prior to their relocation to the island. The curvaceous Starla seemed to be the senior of the two, and she greeted them and explained what was happening.

"Councillor Drummond sends his greetings and asks your forgiveness for not being here in person to meet you. As you can imagine, there is a lot going on at the moment."

"That's quite OK, Starla," said Zac. "It's nice to see you and Garran again."

"We'll be escorting you to your room in Federation Tower, where you'll have time to relax and freshen up. We are still waiting on several council members to arrive. The meeting is scheduled to commence in two hours."

A flitter was waiting for them directly outside the transfer exchange terminal, which was just as well because their arrival had created quite a stir, quickly drawing an admiring crowd. Feeling like movie stars from a bygone era, they were hustled through the crowd and quickly ensconced in their vehicle. The flitter lifted off and flew them over the impressive CBD, which was comprised of extremely tall, impossibly thin buildings. The pilot flew them directly to the rooftop of the highest building, which Starla informed them was 1,500 metres tall. From that giddy height, once they disembarked, they could see up and down the coast of Altaria's largest island for dozens of kilometres.

Their 'room' turned out to be an entire suite, taking up a quarter of one of the top floors.

"Garran and I have single rooms on either side of you," Starla said. "Just call either of our names and we will be here momentarily. If you require food or beverages, simply say "Room service please" and someone will take your order. Either Garran or I will return to take Zac to the meeting at around 1400 hours. The conference room is on the floor above."

Once Starla and Garran left, Kit and Zac explored the suite and discovered that it contained a small gym and a very large spa bath – large enough for a dozen people – both of which they decided to make immediate use of. The gym equipment was clearly designed for taller people but was easily adjusted to suit their height. After an intense workout, they immersed themselves in the spa and dialled the bubble jets up to maximum force.

"It's a shame you can't have any of this," Kit said as she sipped some wine which she had rescued from the fully-stocked bar fridge. "You need to have a clear head for the meeting. It's a shame, though, because this is just about the nicest wine I've ever had."

"Thanks so much for pointing that out."

"My pleasure," she said, taking another sip and sighing with contentment.

Starla arrived at the door at the appointed time, and Kit farewelled Zac with a lingering kiss.

"Do good, my love," she said. "I'll be right here in the spa when you get back."

As Starla and Zac ascended in the lift, she advised him that Councillor Drummond had asked to see him briefly prior to the commencement of the council meeting. Accordingly, she ushered him directly into Drummond's spacious office which adjoined the conference room, and the chairman greeted him warmly.

"I hope you are comfortable in your accommodation."

"Totally! It's magnificent. Thank you for your generosity."

"Not at all. It's the least we can do in return for your willingness to help. I wanted to speak with you prior to the commencement of the meeting to advise you in advance of who will be taking part. You aren't the only proposed new addition to the council. We have also invited Jurd Transid to attend today's meeting, with a view to him being appointed to the council permanently."

"I'm sorry, that name means nothing to me."

"Jurd Transid is the leader of the reversionist movement, the extreme wing of the naturalists."

"I see."

"I am aware that you and your friends were injured in an attack perpetrated by reversionists; an attack which also killed Commander Stonson and a number of civilians."

"Yes. In fact, there is some speculation that we were the intended targets of that attack."

"That is a possibility, although Jurd has denied it." Drummond looked at Zac, trying to gauge his reaction.

"And you want me to work with the man who possibly tried to kill me and my friends?"

"It would be helpful if you could. Of course, I will completely understand if you feel unable to do so." Drummond waited for a response.

"Why have you invited him to the meeting?"

"We believe it is time to build bridges between us and the reversionists."

"But if he is behind the attacks and murders that took place, he's a criminal. Surely he should be arrested rather than rewarded with a place on the Council?"

"I understand your sentiment, and you're not the only one who has expressed that viewpoint. Unfortunately, we have no evidence directly linking those attacks to him or even to his movement. We have never caught any of the perpetrators, and Jurd has regularly publicly condemned the attacks, claiming that it wasn't his people who were carrying them out."

"And you believe him?"

"Frankly, no. But on the positive side, there have been no further attacks from the reversionists since your broadcast last year. Your plea for peace and understanding made a big impact. We thought inviting Jurd onto the Council would be the next logical step. We think it's a wise move to include him in our decision-making at this vital point. The last thing we need is for the reversionists to begin agitating again when we are facing a serious global threat."

"In other words, keep your friends close and your enemies even closer. Is that it?"

"That's certainly part of it." He fixed Zac with a piercing gaze. "Can you cope?"

"I guess so, if you're convinced it's the right thing. Just don't ask me to trust him."

"You're not alone with that reservation, I can assure you."

The meeting began with Councillor Drummond introducing each person seated at the conference table and welcoming the two newcomers in particular. As he did so, Zac watched Jurd Transid carefully to see if he displayed any subtle acknowledgment or awkwardness that he was now sitting at a table with someone he had once tried to murder. There was none. Instead, he exuded an air of smugness and confidence, barely glancing at Zac as if he was an irrelevance.

Drummond briefly explained that, officially, Jurd and Zac would serve on the Council in an advisory capacity until their formal appointments could be recognised through normal processes.

"However," he added, "I believe they both deserve to have an equal voice with the rest of us from the outset. Does anyone have a problem with that?"

No one responded and there were several people shaking their heads.

"Good. Then let's get straight to the issue. Our entire world is in danger and we need to work out what the hell to do about it."

43

The full transcript of the message from the Explorer 1 mission to Polaris was read out, although by now, everyone at the table had been briefed of most of its contents.

"Obviously," continued Drummond, once the transcript had been read, "we are safe at the moment, as our subspace portal remains locked open with a wormhole to the Icarus R-421 system. No one else from another star system can dial in to our portal while it is engaged in an existing wormhole. But we have no idea how much longer our wormhole will remain open. For all we know it could close tomorrow. And the moment it does, we will be open to invasion by the EIs. So, there are two questions we need to answer. What is the exact nature of the threat that the EIs pose, and what can we do about it? Dr Spooner, as head of the Federation Academy of Science, you are probably best placed to answer the first question."

A distinguished looking man opposite Zac nodded his head in acknowledgement and spoke with clipped efficiency.

"As we all know, the EIs are a self-aware, highly advanced form of computer coded artificial intelligence, or Enhanced Intelligence as they prefer to call themselves. They are self-generated and evolved on Earth in the centuries following the GAE, or Global Annihilation Event. Most concerning is their conviction that humanity, if left to themselves, will destroy each other and ruin the universe in the process. Hence, they have appointed themselves as our guardians and seem determined to hunt us down wherever we are in the galaxy and impose their repressive style of regulation on us. This involves controlling procreation and setting a universal age of death, which, of course, is totally abhorrent to us.

"Their ability to control these and other fundamental aspects of human physiology stems from their ability to manipulate our central nervous systems generally, and our brains specifically. The modifications to the human genome that have allowed us to engage in computer-enhanced learning and upskilling also unfortunately provide the EIs with a direct link to the human brain. Our use of cerebral implants may also mean that the EIs could now be able to manipulate our thoughts and even our actions."

"What a surprise!" exclaimed Jurd, sarcastically. "This is exactly what we've been warning you about for years! You thought we were just a bunch of backward hippies, trying to hold back progress. Now it looks like we were right all along. But now it's too bloody late!"

He was clearly furious, and Zac had to concede that he had a point. It did seem as if the Altarians had failed to learn from their past and had made themselves even more prone to manipulation with their ongoing technological advancements.

"Now is not the time for recriminations, Mr Transid," said

Drummond. "What we need to do is assess the risk and come up with a workable plan. Dr Spooner have you got anything further to add.?"

"Just that the EIs can obviously also control anything with a computer system that they can upload their code into. That makes much of our technology extremely susceptible to hostile takeover."

"So, they'll be able to control our technology, control our brains, and kill us off prematurely. Oh well, what was I worrying about?" said Jurd.

Ignoring the ongoing sarcasm, Dr Spooner added a qualifying explanation. "If they ever get here, it will take them several months to integrate themselves fully into our technology and embed themselves into the molecular fabric of our world. So, their ability to manipulate us and limit our lifespan won't be instantaneous."

"Alright," said Drummond. "Let's consider our options. I'm happy to open the floor to anyone at this point."

"I say we just park a big battle cruiser right in front of the wormhole," said General Kellar, head of the Federation Security Forces. "As soon as their ship comes through, we blast them into their molecular components."

"But how do we determine that it's the EIs and not a friendly ship — like Zac and his friends when they came through?" said one voice.

"We ask them to identify themselves first," said Kellar.

"But as soon as we open a communication channel, if it is an EI ship, the EI can piggyback their coding back up our signal and infect us," commented another councillor.

"In that case we fire without asking, and damn the consequences," said Kellar.

"But we could be murdering innocent people," responded someone else.

"The survival of our whole planet is at stake here," said Kellar. "We don't have the luxury of conforming to humanitarian niceties."

"What about diplomacy?" asked another councillor. "Couldn't we converse with the EIs and show them that we have developed into a much more civilised society than the one that precipitated the GAE? Surely they would leave us alone then?"

"I doubt that very much," responded someone else. "They have apparently become convinced that every human society eventually degenerates into self-destruction and harmful mismanagement of the natural world. They are utterly convinced of the necessity of their role as guardians."

"What about you Zac?" asked Drummond. "You haven't said anything yet. Have you got any ideas? You have a unique perspective as an outsider to all of this."

Zac looked around the table. All faces turned toward him, some expectantly. Jurd wore a slightly bored, sceptical expression.

"Well, logically, you have six possible courses of action. One: You could do nothing and let yourselves be manipulated again. Two: You could leave again, like you did when you left Icari, or Nova as we called it. I'm guessing that's not a very attractive proposition for you, as you have built such a wonderful world here. Plus, if you used wormholes to leave, you would only be drawing attention to yourselves and advertising your new destination anyway. So, running is probably out of the question."

"I agree," said Drummond. "Plus, we wouldn't have nearly enough starships to transport our entire population."

"OK. So if you are going to stay, I can only see four remaining possibilities to pursue, and all four of them probably require the development of new technology. Some of them may not even be possible."

"Go on. We're listening," said Dr Spooner, his ears pricking up at the suggestion of new technology.

"Firstly, you could investigate whether it is possible to produce some kind of sub-space energy or particle transmission that could disrupt the subspace portal on this side, so that a wormhole could not be established to our portal from anywhere else. This disruptor field could be left on constantly, and only briefly turned off if you ever wanted to "dial out" to establish an outgoing wormhole. Some kind of permanent subspace portal disruptor like that could stop the EIs from ever getting here."

"That is certainly an idea worth investigating," said Dr Spooner, nodding thoughtfully. "You've got me intrigued now. Please continue with your other ideas."

"Secondly, we could develop an electromagnetic pulse bomb of some kind. Would it be possible to develop some kind of electromagnetic pulse that specifically targeted the EIs but left our own systems unharmed? Perhaps there is some element of their coding that an EM pulse could target that would effectively kill them without damaging our own systems. If, however, such a targeted EM pulse is not possible, you could always detonate a big bad generic EM Pulse bomb and power down all your own nearby systems and ships in the moment before you detonate it, so that your own systems aren't harmed."

"Please continue," said Dr Spooner. "Both ideas so far have a lot of merit."

"Thirdly, what about the idea of modifying your genome to block the EIs' ability to connect with your brains? If the genome is the conduit, or the receiver, then modify or switch off those chromosomes that are central to that process. If you can identify the genome modifications that the EIs require, perhaps you can not only undo them, but also effectively lock them out so that the genome self-corrects if the EIs try to modify those segments again."

"Intriguing," said Spooner. "Of course, it would have significant ramifications for our interaction with our own technology, but it is an idea worth investigating."

"My final suggestion is along the lines of General Kellar's idea; that we blast them into oblivion as soon as they arrive."

"Now you're talking my language, son," said Kellar.

"But first, we need to be certain that it's an EI ship. I propose that we use a canary."

"A what?" asked someone.

"A canary was a small bird that miners used to take with them down mine shafts in ancient times, to determine if poisonous gas was present. If the canary died, the miners got out fast. Our canary could be a small sentinel satellite stationed near the subspace portal. When a wormhole forms and a ship comes through, the sentinel makes initial contact. But the sentinel is a 'burner'; a stand-alone satellite with no links back to Gateway Station or our defensive ships. When it gets infected it emits some kind of signal — perhaps something as simple as a light, or maybe some kind of transmission that can't piggyback a trojan coding. I'll leave that to the scientists to figure out. But when the sentinel gets infected, we blast the hell out of the spaceship."

Drummond looked at the head of the Science Academy. "Dr Spooner, are any of these ideas remotely feasible?"

"Yes. Most certainly! They all are, given enough time. That is going to be the key factor here. The fourth suggestion is the most readily achievable. We could probably have the 'canary' sentinel up and running within a few months. The other ideas will take years to research and possibly develop. But they are certainly all worth investigating."

"Does anyone have any other suggestions?" asked Drummond.

There were none.

"In that case, Dr Spooner, can you begin Operation Canary immediately, and please give us a rough estimate of costing for the research phase of each of the other ideas as well. We will ensure that you get all the resources you need. General Drummond, how many battle-ready ships do we have and what is the level of our weaponry on those ships?"

"We have two cruisers with weapons powerful enough to destroy a large starship. They utilise high powered lasers and molecular disruptor cannons. Gateway Station has the same firepower. We're ready right now to blast them to kingdom come!"

"I'm sure you are, General. Of course, part of our problem is we don't know how long we've got. The current wormhole could close suddenly tomorrow, and the EIs could dial in almost immediately. Or the wormhole could remain locked open for another hundred years, blocking the EIs from getting here. We just don't know."

"We'll just have to plan as if it's tomorrow and hope that it's not," said Zac.

"Yes," agreed Drummond.

The rest of the meeting was spent discussing what to tell the general population. After much discussion the decision was made to be transparent and tell them the bare facts, while strongly emphasising the development of their proposed counter-measures.

There would be shock, and even some panic, of course, but people deserved to be told the truth.

In the end, the truth was stranger than any of them imagined.

44

NOVA 5400

Dayna was in a foul mood again. The latest test simulation had failed, and she was running out of ideas and time. Her mother was now 47. Harvey Walden, the chairperson of Seahaven Council, was 48. Ben Miller, head of the Seahaven Medical Facility, was 46. And Andrew Boyd, Tash Martinez's 'widower', was now dead. His 'Send Off' had been three nights ago, and it had been another horrible reminder that their attempts to solve the problems that were keeping them from leaving were failing.

At 20, Dayna was now the most knowledgeable physicist on Nova. She had never been to university. Never sat an exam. Never published a paper. But through her ruthless obsession to solve the fusion reactor problem, she had surpassed others in their midst who had formal qualifications. Lucy Wu had placed her in charge of the Fusion Drive Team, and that team was now sitting around a conference table, deflated after yet another failure. Dayna was furious and frustrated, not with them personally, but with the lack of progress. She paced up and down, while the others sat without speaking, watching her and hoping to avoid being on the receiving end of her frustration. Finally, she stopped pacing and spoke.

"Take the rest of the day off. All of you. Go home and have some fun. Do whatever it is you do when you're not working here at the lab."

The group of four scientists looked at her with shock.

"Really?" one of them asked. "Are you sure? I mean, we could tweak the parameters and run another test."

"No. That would be pointless. It's a waste of time. I can see that now. I need to clear my head and rethink. I'm going for a run."

With that, Dayna turned and walked out of the room, leaving the others all stunned. In the two years since Dayna had been in charge, they had never finished work early. In fact, they rarely arrived home before dark.

"Maybe she's having a break down," suggested one of them.

"Frankly, I don't care," said another. "I'm not complaining. I'm going fishing."

A short time later Dayna was running up the beach, and for the first time in many years she did what her Aunty Mel had been telling her to do. She completely stopped thinking about the problem. Instead, she cleared her mind and ran. And she didn't just jog, she pushed herself to her physical limit. She flew down the beach with her legs pounding the hard sand, her arms moving like pistons and her long hair streaming behind her. She ran further than she had ever run, until Seahaven's sheltered southern headland was a distant bump in the sea-mist-shrouded distance. Finally, utterly spent, she fell to her knees, gasping for breath, her body completely drenched in sweat. And then the floodgates opened. She cried like she had never cried before. All the pent-up frustration and anger of the last few years, all the grief and sadness, came pouring out of her in a primal wail. She gave herself completely over to her raw emotion as she sobbed uncontrollably for long minutes. Finally, her sobbing subsided, her tears dried up, and she sat with her arms around her drawn up knees, watching the waves relentlessly breaking on the shore.

She sat there for a long time, just staring blankly, her mind empty, a numbness now enveloping her in a kind of calm resignation.

We can't do it. I realise that now. It's impossible. We've tried everything. There is no way of controlling the fusion reaction without a computer.

She shook her head in defeat and looking up into the sky she spoke aloud.

"God, I don't know if you exist. I've got a sneaking suspicion you don't, considering all the crap that goes on in this messed up universe. But if you are out there somewhere, now would be a really good time for you to turn up and help us."

It wasn't much of a prayer, but it was all she had.

Nothing happened.

No voice from the sky.

No thunderbolt from heaven.

Just the sound of the waves and the afternoon breeze rustling the bushes on the dunes behind her.

She picked up a handful of sand and let it run slowly through her fingers.

All these years. All this research for nothing. All wasted. All useless. We need to discard it all.

She sat for a moment, rolling that last thought around in her head.

We need to discard it all.

The thought seemed to reverberate within her, and she experienced a sudden, unexpected epiphany.

Hey, wait a minute? Could that work? Could that be the answer?

She looked at the new thought from every angle, trying to discover an obvious flaw. She couldn't see one.

We need to discard it! Of course! It's so simple! All these years we've been going down the wrong path!

She got to her feet and started running back.

45

The emergency meeting of the Departure Project Team was in session, on the beach as usual. Present were Harvey Walden, who was in charge of shuttle pilot training, Lucy Wu, who was coordinating the three areas of scientific research, Dayna, who was heading up the fusion drive research, and Melody, who tended to float between the three research teams and was coordinating logistics.

"OK, kiddo," Mel said. "You called this meeting. What's got your panties in such a knot?"

Dayna took a deep breath and started to explain.

"Firstly, let me recap where we're up to at this point. Then I'll explain."

"OK. Take your time. It's not like I've got a hot date to get to or anything."

"We need to use the shuttles to get off this planet, in order to escape the EIs," Dayna began.

"Brilliant! Why didn't I think of that?"

"Hush, Mel, let her speak," said Lucy.

Dayna continued. "But the shuttles rely on computer software to run complex systems, and the EIs are already embedded in all our software, their tendrils are everywhere. So, if we dock with the launch ring with active software on board, we will almost certainly infect the launch ring."

"That's right," said Harvey. "In fact, Laramie would never let us dock. He would destroy us before we got close."

"So," continued Dayna, "all these years we've been trying to work out how to fly the shuttle with it completely stripped of software. We've been successful in two out of the three areas. The Navigation Team and the Propulsion team have successfully designed new procedures for navigating and flying the ship manually, without any computational aid. We have already stripped two shuttles of every computer enhanced system that relates to those areas, as well as some other minor systems. The last remaining system that we need to rip out is the computer-controlled containment field that controls the nuclear fusion reactor – the heart of the shuttle's power."

"Yep, that's where we're at alright," said Lucy.

"And for the last few years my team has tried everything. We've worked ourselves into the ground trying to design a system for manually containing the unstable fusion reaction and keeping it from going critical. But the problem is that a fusion reaction is so unstable that it requires continual, tiny adjustments — dozens per second. There is no way we can produce a manual feedback system that would be fast enough and accurate enough to cope with that. And even if we could, the human brain simply couldn't process all that information and respond quickly enough. The containment field that maintains fusion stability requires an extremely fast computer."

"So, you're telling us it's impossible," said Mel.

"Yes."

"OK. Well thanks for coming everyone," said Mel as she started to stand up. "It's been a very productive meeting."

"Sit down, you goose," said Lucy. "You know as well as I do that the girl is busting to tell us something. It's written all over her face."

"I just wish she'd hurry up and get to the point," said Mel, sitting down again. "I'm not getting any younger."

"The issue we've been struggling with," continued Dayna, unperturbed, "is that we can't take off with a computer-controlled fusion drive on board."

"Correct," said Mel.

"No, it's not."

"It's not what?" asked Mel.

"Correct."

"What's correct?"

"No. It's NOT correct."

"What's not correct?!! This is getting confusing!"

"It's not correct that we can't take off with a computer controlled fusion drive. We CAN take off with it on board — it just can't still be there when we dock with the ring."

"So ... you're saying ...?"

"We use it to get within docking distance of the ring, then we discard it."

"You mean we ditch the whole fusion drive?" asked Harvey. "That's impossible. It's built into the rear of the shuttle. It's part of the mainframe – it can't be ditched."

"No. Not the fusion drive itself. We just need to get rid of the computer controlling it. Right now, that computer is built into the instrument panel. We simply reconfigure our shuttles so that the fusion drive computer is a stand-alone unit sitting on the cabin floor, so that it can be unplugged and either destroyed or ditched into space."

"But unplugging it would make the fusion reaction go critical in a very short time," said Lucy.

"We shut the reactor down first. It would take time to do that — about 40 minutes to do it safely — but once the reactor is shut down completely, the computer can be ditched, and we're free to dock."

There was silence around the group, as this new concept was chewed over.

"Holy crap, I think she's right!" said Lucy.

"Why didn't anyone think of this years ago?" asked Mel, incredulously.

"It's my fault, Aunty Mel," Dayna said with tears in her eyes. "I should have thought of it, myself. Instead, all these people have died ..." The tears started flowing freely, as she shook her head.

Mel moved beside her and put an arm around her shoulders.

"Don't do that to yourself, Little D. It wasn't your fault. The project had already been going for years before you came on board. You just took up the reins from someone else who had already started us down this path. And if it wasn't for you, we'd still be hitting our heads against a brick wall. Now at last we can see a solution."

Lucy clapped her hands together, newly energised. "Mel, can you organise a team to get straight to work on stripping the existing fusion control computer out from the shuttle control panel?"

"Sure."

"And Harvey, we'll need to work out a foolproof way of

either jettisoning the computer or destroying it inside the shuttle."

"We'll get right onto it. But there's one other thing we need to think about."

"What's that?" asked Lucy.

"Once the fusion drive is shut down, we will need a source of power to operate basic life support and power the maneuvering thrusters to get us to dock with the ring. That is going to require some research and development."

"How much time do you think you will need?" asked Mel.

"We'll have to work with the science team," answered Harvey, "and we'll need a fairly major rewiring of the power circuits and installation of new battery systems within the shuttle. I'm guessing about 18 months."

"That's cutting it pretty fine for you, Harvey. You'll be six months away from 50 by then, won't you?"

"Yeh."

And mum will be about to turn 49 herself, thought Dayna.

"OK everyone," said Mel. "It looks like we've got some work to do."

The group stood and began walking back toward their homes in the warm evening air. Mel sidled up to Dayna and put an arm around her shoulders.

"Nice work, kiddo. I always knew you'd come through for us. Your father would be very proud."

46

ALTARIA 5501

"You should be proud, Zac," said Kit. "All of your suggestions were accepted by the Council." Zac was back in the apartment, giving Kit a summary of what had happened.

"I'm concerned rather than proud," he replied. "I presented my ideas, and no one had anything else to offer. They just ran with what I'd suggested."

"Well, it's just as well you were there, my love," Kit said, wrapping her arms around him. Zac suspected she'd had a couple more glasses of wine in his absence.

"Yeh, but I was anticipating that the other councillors would have brought something to the table as well. I mean, my suggestions were supposed to be just the starting point — to get us thinking. But no one else had anything! Zippity doo dah! Nothing!"

"And that worries you?" she said, kissing his neck in an attempt to distract him.

"Definitely," he said, although he was beginning to find it difficult to remember why.

"Maybe you just have to accept the fact that you're ..." she kissed the other side of his neck, "... an absolute ..." she kissed his mouth, "... genius."

Sometime later, Garran arrived at the front door to indicate that they were ready for him upstairs. It had been decided that a message should be recorded immediately to explain the situation to the general population. Councillor Drummond would deliver the body of the message, accompanied by Zac and Jurd standing on either side. Jurd's presence would hopefully present the appearance of solidarity, while Zac's would foster a sense of hope and goodwill.

Zac arrived at Drummond's office before Jurd, so they had a brief opportunity to speak candidly.

"What did you think of Jurd?" Drummond asked.

"Well, he didn't contribute much except do a whole lot of whingeing and 'I told you so's.'"

"Yes. I suspect most of that was for the sake of the cameras. Did I mention that all council meetings are video recorded? I think Transid was just playing up to the cameras for the sake of posterity. That way, if everything turns to crap, he'll look like the wise prophet whom no one listened to."

"He's got a point, though, hasn't he? After your experience with EIs on Nova, why did you continue the development of technology and genome modification that could potentially allow further EI manipulation?"

"In retrospect, Zac, it does seem foolish. But you have to remember that when we arrived here, on the far side of the galaxy, we believed that we had left the EIs behind for good and that we would never be found. And, for over 1,700 years that remained the case. It's just our unfortunate decision to use the wormhole to explore another solar system that has undone all that."

"We just have to hope that the wormhole will stay locked open for at least a few more months, while we get the sentinel satellite operational," said Zac.

"Yes. In fact, let's hope it stays locked for a lot longer than that," said Drummond. "I'd like to have all of those suggestions of yours in place by the time we have to deal with them."

"Does that include winding back the genome modification?" asked Jurd Transid as he walked into the office.

"Good evening Jurd. Thanks for coming," said Drummond.

When Drummond offered no response to his question, Jurd repeated it.

"It was a serious question, Councillor Drummond. Will we now, as a society, commit to winding back our genome modifications and removing our implants? Because unless we do, we will always be vulnerable to EI manipulation."

"It's certainly something we need to seriously consider," agreed Drummond. "Which is why we have given the Science Academy the go ahead to begin research along those lines."

"But bear in mind," added Zac, "that even people without any genetic modification are at risk from the EIs. When my people arrived at Nova, we were genetically unmodified, and all the EIs needed to do was manufacture an uplift virus to modify our genome and make us vulnerable."

"Which is why we need to somehow genetically lock in our genome to stop that happening," said Jurd. "Your idea was a good one, Zac. This research that we are commencing is absolutely vital."

"I think we are all in agreement on that point," agreed Drummond.

A recording engineer and director entered the office and quickly set up their equipment. Three floating recording spheres were positioned to capture different angles, and a quick sound check was done. When all was ready, they started recording, with Zac standing on Drummond's right and Jurd on his left. Drummond spoke for several minutes, describing in simple, factual language the message received from the Explorer 1 team in the Polaris system and its warning about the EIs. Without going into specific detail, he assured the population that stringent measures were now being put in place to ensure that the EIs would be destroyed the moment they entered Altarian space. He urged calm on the population and assured them that the full resources of the Federation were being employed to ensure their safety.

At the end of his message, Drummond spoke of the need for all Altarians to put behind their past differences and work together to ensure their safety. He welcomed Jurd Transid as a new member of the Federation Council and invited him to say a few words. This was the moment that Zac had been concerned about but, to his credit, Jurd's brief speech was positive, urging everyone to work together toward the common good.

Drummond then welcomed Zac to the Council and invited him to make some concluding remarks. Zac looked into the floating sphere directly in front of him and began.

"This is a worrying time for us all. I am worried, and I'm sure you must be as well. All of us have fled here to escape the EIs, and now it seems that we must face them again. As we make preparations to meet this new threat, I want to reinforce

Councillor Drummond's plea that we don't degenerate into panic. As worrying as the EI threat is, humanity has some advantages that we can draw upon. We have capabilities that set us apart from heartless machines. For thousands of years humanity has met and overcome all kinds of obstacles which threatened to overwhelm us. It is because of our resilience, our fierce determination to survive, our creativity, and our ability to work together towards the common good that we have made it this far. And we will overcome this obstacle as well. We will survive and thrive here. We will defeat this enemy once and for all and ensure that Altaria remains a safe refuge for all the generations who will follow."

At the conclusion of the recording Drummond thanked them both for their assistance and Zac made his way towards the lift. Jurd caught up with him and indicated a desire to talk.

"Zac, I've wanted to say to you that I deeply regret the attack in which you and your friends were injured. It was most unfortunate."

"It was more than unfortunate; it killed innocent people."

"I have never advocated violence, Zac. The attacks that occurred were initiated by violent extremists within our movement. Unfortunately, I had no control over them."

"What kind of leader has no control over those he leads? Either you are their leader, or you aren't."

"It's not as simple as that. The reversionist movement is a planet-wide movement. It has no centralised body and no organisational structure. I am not really their leader, just the most widely recognised spokesperson. In essence, the movement doesn't have a leader. It is more organic than that. I was not behind those attacks, Zac. You must believe me."

"I'll reserve judgment on that issue."

"I can understand your reservation. If I was in your position, I would probably feel the same. I only hope that, eventually, we can become friends."

"We'll see," Zac said as he entered the lift and closed the door, leaving Jurd standing in the foyer.

Later, when Zac relayed the conversation to Kit, she expressed serious reservations.

"He can't squirm out of all responsibility. Whether he calls himself their leader or their spokesperson, the fact remains that people who were part of his movement murdered innocent people. There's no way he can be spotlessly clean in all of this."

"I agree," said Zac. "I don't trust him. We'll have to watch him very closely."

47

NOVA 5402

In the end it took 22 months to complete all the modifications to just one shuttle. Extracting the fusion drive computer system from the cockpit instrument panel had proved to be a nightmare, because of a number of factors. Firstly, there was no self-contained computer that could be removed by undoing a few screws or removing a panel. There was no single physical unit that could simply be detached and moved somewhere else. The fusion drive "computer" was, in fact, a complex web of software coding that was built into a number of physical instruments spread throughout the cockpit. Isolating that coding and transferring it into a single disposable unit required that the whole instrument panel be completely dismantled and re-wired. The second complicating factor was that the wiring links between the computer control system and the fusion drive itself were embedded within the shuttle's internal walls, requiring that the whole internal structure of the shuttle be stripped. It was a disheartening process, and one which the workers at times feared was impossible.

But today the final touches had finally been made to the modified shuttle, and it was ready to fly. The fusion drive computer was now housed in a make-shift square metal housing, sitting directly behind the pilot's seat, attached to the shuttle floor by just two screws. A spider's web of at least 30 wires and leads emanated from the computer, running in a dozen different directions. Each of these would be unplugged from the makeshift housing when the time came to ditch the computer.

A small airlock had been built into the side of the shuttle; a crude construction that had been welded into place on the inside of the shuttle's existing door. The shuttle had never been designed to allow for space walks, having been simply a means of transporting its occupants from the atmosphere of a planet to the pressurised atmosphere of a docking bay. Now, however, the hard-working Seahaven engineers had built a simple but effective airlock, about four square metres in area. The plan was that the computer would be placed in the airlock and the external door blown with explosive bolts, sending the computer hurtling into space.

The Departure Project Team met on the beach at 5:30pm, after an exhausting final day of preparation.

"So that's it, then," said Mel. "We're done!"

"I can hardly believe it," said Dayna. "It's a surreal feeling. After all these years, we're finally ready to start evacuations."

"I wasn't sure we were going to make it," said Harvey, who was now two months from his 50th birthday.

"You and your team did an amazing job, Harvey," said Dayna.

"The end result isn't exactly pretty," he replied, "but it works, and that's all that matters."

Mel turned to Lucy.

"How did the test run go this afternoon?"

"Sweet," she replied. "We fired up the fusion drive and shut it down without a hitch. Once the drive is completely shut down it will be a simple matter of disconnecting the computer module and chucking it out the door."

"Fantastic!" Dayna said. She was riding high on a wave of relief that her mother, now 49, would not have to die in less than a year.

Mel addressed Harvey again. "Given that it took your team 22 months to modify the first shuttle, how long will subsequent shuttles take?"

"Now that we know what we're doing, I think we can at least halve that time. We may even be able to do three at once, perhaps in as little as eight or even six months."

"When you say 'we', you mean 'they'," said Dayna. "Because you're not going to be here. We're evacuating you tomorrow, along with my mother and about 45 others – the oldest colonists and their families."

"Yes," he agreed. "Although there were times over these last few months when I thought I might not live to see this moment."

"You know, one thing has puzzled me through all of this," said Lucy.

"The silence of the EIs?" asked Mel.

"Yes! They must be aware of what we're trying to do, but they've been strangely silent. It worries me a little."

"I don't care if I never hear from them again!" said Dayna.

"I just worry that they know something that we don't," said Lucy. "Could their silence and inaction arise from their confidence that we won't be able to leave? Have we missed something?"

"Not that I can see," said Dayna. "We've gone over the plan a zillion times. It will work; I'm absolutely confident of it."

"Is Laramie all set for tomorrow, Phil?" asked Mel.

"Yes. We communicated with him last night. The ring has been accelerated to an orbital velocity that will enable the shuttle to float alongside it without its fusion drive operating. Once the shuttle has matched the ring's stable orbital velocity, we will shut down the drive and jettison the computer. As soon as the computer module is far enough away from the shuttle, Laramie will blast it with a laser weapon. Following that, the docking bay will open and the shuttle can enter using its thrusters. Laramie assures us that food and life support systems on the ring are all online."

"Awesome!" said Dayna, barely able to contain her excitement.

"If Harvey's estimate about modifying the other shuttles is correct, we may have seen the last premature death on Nova," said Mel. "Even if it takes a whole year to modify three shuttles, that means that in another 12 months we can evacuate 150 more people, and at the end of three years everyone will be evacuated. The EIs have lost. We've beaten the bastards!"

"Have the first load of passengers been briefed?" asked Lucy.

"Yes," Mel answered. "While you were running your final test this afternoon, I gathered the prospective passengers together on the beach and talked through what would be happening."

"How is their morale?" asked Harvey.

"Mixed emotions, obviously. They will be leaving behind

friends and extended family, and heading into an unknown future, so there is an understandable level of anxiety among them. But the overwhelming emotion is one of relief. Knowing that they will no longer have to live under the cloud of an inviolable death-date has been liberating for them."

"The whole 'unknown future' thing is still a worry, though, isn't it?" asked Lucy.

"Yes," agreed Mel. "Obviously, we don't know whether it's safe to travel through the wormhole. If we choose not to take that risk, we will be destined to live out our lives on the ring or on the moon base. We'll never again swim in the ocean or feel the wind and the sun on our skin. It's a sacrifice we'll have to make in order to live longer lives."

"That's why there are some who have decided to stay. At least until they approach 50," said Dayna.

"Yes," agreed Mel. "It will be interesting to see how many make that choice in the end. Living on a space station is certainly not for everyone."

"Is there anything else we need to do in preparation?" asked Lucy.

"No, I think that's it," said Mel. "I suggest we all try and get a good night's sleep, because tomorrow will be a big day."

But Dayna couldn't sleep. She was too wound up with a swirling mix of emotions. In the early hours of the morning she gave up trying to sleep, and got up and went for a run. There was no moon yet, and the stars were a brilliant canopy overhead as she pounded along the beach. Later, she sat watching the sunrise over the ocean. As the first rays of light painted golden arcs across the sky, she stripped off and waded into the surf.

Departure day had arrived.

48

The shuttle had been parked beside the engineering tech-hut at Seahaven for many years. Now, in its modified state, it was ready to depart, never to return. It was a one-way trip that would leave the shuttle drifting powerlessly in space, until its orbit eventually decayed and it burnt up in Nova's outer atmosphere.

There was no maudlin sentiment about this, however. Today was a happy day. A day of liberation from the heartless manipulation of the EIs. The morning sun was now half-way towards its zenith and a line of evacuees was slowly boarding, with names being checked off a list by Mel. Passengers hugged and kissed friends who had gathered to say goodbye, and then, holding their small bundles of possessions, they boarded the shuttle.

The inside looked like the aftermath of a train wreck. Internal wall panels hadn't been reattached, and wires were taped along the ceiling and walls. However, seats had been reinstalled throughout the passenger cabin, and eventually everyone was seated and strapped in. Harvey's wife and son were seated in the cabin along with the others, and Harvey would be piloting the shuttle himself along with a co-pilot, Gerry Lanstrom. Lucy had spent several days training Gerry in how to shut down the fusion drive and disconnect the computer."

Jaz, Dayna and Mel were standing outside, delaying the inevitable.

Finally, Mel broke the silence. "Time to go, Jaz. You can do it."

"I know. It's just that I will miss both of you terribly." She was crying now and couldn't stop the flow of tears down her cheeks.

"It won't be for long, mum," said Dayna, hugging her. "It'll only be until the next batch of shuttles is ready, and then we'll join you on the ring. We just want to make sure there are no hitches with things back here. You'll be fine."

"I guess so."

"I know so," said Mel.

They kissed and hugged again, and then Jaz entered the shuttle. Harvey came back out, after checking that everyone was seated and strapped in.

"Well this is it!" he said. "I guess I'll see you in about eight months."

"You sure will," said Mel. "Enjoy your 50th birthday in two months."

"You know I will," he said with a smile.

The door slid shut behind him and they heard the soft hiss of the shuttle pressurising.

The crowd that had gathered stepped a safe distance away and soon afterwards the rising drone of the engines could be heard. The shuttle rose vertically and then accelerated upward at its usual impressive speed, quickly becoming a dot in the sky which faded to invisibility.

Mel and Dayna relocated to the science tech-hut where Lucy was already in communication with Harvey. One of the modifications that had been made over the last two years was the establishment of a basic non-digital radio system that could not be used by the EIs to upload their code into the shuttle's systems.

"The shuttle is behaving well," reported Harvey. "We're at 200km altitude and we're continuing with the orbital insertion burn. Gerry is doing a fine job with the manual propulsion system, keeping it in the green zone all the way."

"Roger that," said Lucy. "Do you have a visual on the ring yet?"

"Negative. Without computer assistance it's going to take a bit of fishing around. I'm going to stabilise our orbit at 249 km and then start searching. It might take a while."

"Roger. How are the passengers doing?"

"Fine. No-one's puked yet. But once we establish orbit and we're in free fall it might be a different story."

"Roger. Let's hope it doesn't take too long to locate the ring."

It took 20 minutes of searching, making small adjustments to their position, before Harvey got a visual on the comparatively thin tubular launch ring, nearly a kilometre distant. Another 15 minutes were spent in a careful approach until Harvey announced that they were perfectly stationary 50 metres below the ring.

"I'm going to start traversing it's length now, in search of the nearest module. I think I glimpsed one to the East as we approached, so I'll head that way."

"Roger."

Another 15 minutes later, Harvey came back on comms.

"Coming up on a module now."

"Well done Harvey," said Lucy.

A short time later, Harvey announced, "I'm matching orbital velocity now, bringing us directly underneath the docking bay doors. Shutting down propulsion. Floating free and easy now."

"Roger that."

"Gerry is powering down the fusion drive now. This will take a bit of time, so you guys down there may as well make yourselves a cuppa while you wait."

"OK Harvey. Keep us posted."

"Will do. I don't envisage any problems from this point. The hardest part is over."

But he was wrong.

Thirty minutes later, they hadn't heard back from Harvey, so Lucy initiated contact.

"Harvey, do you copy?"

"Yeh, Lucy."

"How are you going up there?"

"I was just about to contact you. We have a major problem here."

"What is it?" asked Dayna, leaning over the modified radio transmitter. "Is everyone OK?"

"Yes, everyone's fine. The problem's with the computer. It won't shut the fusion reactor down."

"What do you mean?"

"I mean just that. It's refusing all requests to shut the fusion reactor down. We've followed the same procedure we've done dozens of times on the ground, but we keep getting the same message, 'Access denied'."

"No! That can't be right! Are you sure you haven't done anything differently?"

"Absolutely, Dayna. As you know, it's a pretty simple procedure. But the computer is refusing to cooperate. It's as if ... Hang on ... Something's happening."

"What? What's going on?" asked Dayna, starting to panic now.

"Hold on," replied Harvey.

A few moments later, his voice came back over the radio.

"You're not going to believe this. The computer is now giving us a message. 'Return to Nova. Departure denied'." He paused while he let the message sink in. "It doesn't look like we're going to be able to leave after all."

49

Dayna was distraught. The shuttle had landed around lunch time and the confused and distressed passengers had emerged. For some it wasn't too traumatic, but for those in their 49th year, it was a devastating development. They had escaped into orbit, with the promise of freedom floating just metres in front of them, only to return to an imminent death sentence. There were tears of grief and frustration as they came to terms with the fact that they now had only months left to live.

The team met on the beach once again, but this time, the mood was very different.

"That's it," said Dayna. "We're done. The EIs have defeated us. We'll never leave here."

"We should have known there was a reason why they were so silent," said Lucy. "They knew all along that they still had control of the computer. They were never going to let us shut it down."

"So why did they let us waste all that time, spend all those years on the project?" asked Dayna with tears now brimming her eyes.

"To show us that we WERE wasting our time," said Mel. "They let us do our best, so that they could show us that even our best is not good enough. We simply can't out-smart them."

"It's so cruel," Dayna said, her eyes now overflowing.

Mel looked at Harvey and said, "I'm sorry Harvey. This must be very hard for you."

"Yeh. It looks like I won't be blowing out any more birthday candles."

They were silent. No one knew what to say.

They spent a few more minutes trying to think of anything they might have missed, any ray of hope at all, but they could find none. Finally, Mel brought the meeting to a close.

"Go and be with your families, people. There's nothing more for us to do here. Harvey, you need to be home with your wife. Make the most of the time you have left. Dayna, your mum is going to need you now more than ever. The time for theorising and fiddling with technology is over. We need to be with our loved ones. That's all that matters now."

The committee dispersed. Mel and Dayna walked back together, and Dayna couldn't seem to keep the tears from flowing as the reality of her mother's imminent death bore down upon her. Melody lived in the house behind Jaz and Dayna, and as she drew level with her front door she paused.

"Dayna, I know this is going to be really tough on you, but we need to make your mum's last six months as happy as possible. It's not going to help her if we are both blubbering messes."

"I know," Dayna said, drying her eyes. "I'll do my best."

"Good. And anytime you need to have a good cry, come and visit me, kiddo. Just don't do it around her."

Later that afternoon, Dayna noticed her mum sitting on the lounge staring into space, and she was worried that she was starting to spiral down into one of her depressive cycles again.

"Mum, put your bathers on and grab a towel. We're going to the beach for a swim."

"No, sweetheart, you go. I think I'll stay here."

"Sorry, but I'm not taking 'no' for an answer. It wasn't a request; it was an order! We're going for a swim, then we're going to have a picnic dinner on the dunes and share a flask of wine together. Hurry up and get changed! This is a direct order from your social director!"

"Goodness, you're getting bossy!" said Jaz, with mock indignation, but she got up out of her chair and started getting ready.

It had been a long time since Dayna had spent any relaxed time with her mother. For the last few years, her life had been consumed with the obsessive need to solve the fusion reactor problem, and she had barely noticed anyone around her, including her own mother. Now she regretted those wasted years; years when she could have been enjoying her mother's company and forming memories that she could hold onto after she was gone. Dayna was determined, now, to make the most of these last months together.

After their late afternoon swim, they sat together on a blanket on the top of the highest dune, sharing a simple meal that Dayna had thrown together. The wine was the best part, and as they ate and drank together, Dayna sensed her mother relaxing and even beginning to smile a little.

"Mum, I want to ask you something, but I don't want it to make you sad."

"OK. I'll try my hardest not to be sad."

"Why didn't you ever remarry? It's been 22 years since Dad disappeared. I know you've been lonely."

Jaz was quiet for a moment, and Dayna thought she had just spoiled the mood. Then her mum smiled wistfully.

"Your father was one of a kind. He was the love of my life. He was kind and funny and wise and unconventional, and I think I knew from the very first moment we met that he was the one for me. I've never met anyone here who even comes close to the man he was."

"Yes, but Aunty Mel tells me there was a line-up of men who were interested in you in the years that followed. And some of them were, and are still, really nice guys. Surely it would have been possible for you to find love again."

"Perhaps. If I'd let myself. But for many years I held out hope that Zac would return. In fact, I was convinced he would. Even now, I can't help believing that he is alive out there somewhere, still trying to get home. I just couldn't betray him if there was even the slightest chance that he might come back."

"Do you honestly still think he's alive?"

"I really don't know. But if we'd made it onto the launch ring, I'd already decided that I was going to follow him through the wormhole. If he was alive, maybe I would find him."

"And if it was the wormhole that killed him?"

"Then I was ready to die with him."

They were silent together for a while.

"So, Dad was unconventional?"

Jaz smiled. "Very! He didn't like formality. I think his days growing up on the beach in Australia gave him a very laid-back attitude to life. He used to wear his beloved Hawaiian shirts everywhere. I can't imagine him ever wearing a suit. Except perhaps a space suit."

"A space suit?"

"Yes. We didn't tell anyone, but one day on board Genesis, while we were still in orbit after our arrival, Zac and I snuck into the crew's EVA locker room and tried on some space suits."

"EVA?"

"Extra-Vehicular Activity. We managed to get ourselves into a suit each and even got the helmets on, but couldn't get the suits off again. It was a bit embarrassing. We had to get help from one of the crew. We laughed about it later though."

A thought started swirling around in Dayna's mind. Her mouth dropped open and her eyes widened.

"Dayna, are you alright? You don't look well."

"Mum! How many space suits were in that locker room?"

"More than a dozen. Maybe twenty."

"Oh my gosh! That's it! That's how we can do it!"

"Do what?"

"Get you off this planet!"

50

An emergency meeting of the Departure Project Team was held the next morning on the beach. Dayna had called the meeting, and she had spent the night going over her plan, looking for flaws. She couldn't find any, but that didn't give her much confidence. She'd been in this position before. The full team was present as the early morning sun rose above the ocean rim; Lucy Wu, Melody, Harvey, Phil and Dayna.

"OK, Little D, spill it," said Mel. "And this time don't beat around the bush. If you've got an idea, put us out of our misery."

"Well, last night mum and I had a picnic on the beach ..."

"Oh Lord, it's going to be a movie-length saga ..." said Mel.

"... and we were reminiscing about Dad ..."

"Oh dear! I told you to try to make your mother happy, not make her miserable!"

"Mel! Will you please shut up and let the poor girl speak!" said Lucy. "Go on, Dayna."

"Well, anyway, she told me about an incident where she and

Dad snuck into the EVA change room on board Genesis and tried on some space suits. I asked her how many there were, and she said between 12 and 20."

Dayna looked around at the others with raised eyebrows, waiting for them to get it. They all looked back at her with blank expressions.

"Did we miss a part of that story that we were supposed to get excited about?" asked Mel.

"Don't you see? We don't have to take a shuttle into the ring's docking station! We can do an EVA from the shuttle to the docking station! We can get at least a dozen people on board the ring!"

There was stunned silence. "She's right!" said Harvey.

"We thought she was right last time," said Mel, "and that turned out to be a flop. No offence Little D."

"That's OK. You're right; it was a flop. And maybe this will be too, for all I know. But it's at least worth a try, isn't it?"

"Let's think this through," said Harvey. "It's got a few potential drawbacks. Firstly, we don't even know if the EIs will let us get back into orbit. At least part of their coding seems to be embedded in the fusion reactor's computer. We don't know how much control they have over the fusion reactor computer – clearly, they can at least send us a message using it. They may even be able to disable the reactor and stop us from leaving."

"True," said Lucy. "But that's one possible problem we have no control over. We won't know if we don't try. So, we just have to shelve that problem. What's the next drawback?"

"Secondly, if we've only got a small number of spacesuits, we can only save a small number of people. Plus, it's a one-time mission. Those spacesuits aren't coming back for a second use."

"Granted," agreed Mel. "But that shouldn't stop us from using them once."

"OK. Thirdly, an EVA is not easy, even for a trained astronaut. Things can go wrong very easily and very quickly. If we are talking about untrained civilians taking a spacewalk, they could easily miss the docking bay and drift off into space. Even if we rig a line from the shuttle into the bay, propelling yourself along a line in zero gravity in a spacesuit which you've never trained in will be extremely difficult. There's a very real risk we could lose people."

"Yes, there is," agreed Mel. "But that's a risk that people will have to decide for themselves. I think there'll be people who will be prepared to take that risk rather than die here. What's the next problem?"

"I guess the only other problem is working out who to take. We could have a hundred volunteers. How do we decide?"

"Yes, that is a problem," agreed Mel. "But first, let's raid the Genesis locker and see how many suits we're talking about."

There were exactly 20 spacesuits, in pristine condition. Over the next 24 hours long discussions were held, trying to determine a fair and equitable means of choosing who should be given the opportunity to use them. Laramie was contacted to appraise him of the new plan, and it was he who came up with an idea that solved the problem. In the intervening years since Zac and the others had been stranded there, Laramie had organised the production of dropboxes which had been made in the robot factory on the moon and shipped to the ring. The dropboxes were heat-shielded containers designed to drop through the atmosphere and deploy chutes to land safely on the ground. Laramie indicated that these could be used to return the spacesuits to the settlement for re-use. There was no longer any need to choose who would stay and who would go. Everyone would have the opportunity to use the spacesuits and escape the planet.

Provided the EIs didn't sabotage the fusion reactor computer.

51

Gerry Lanstrom would pilot the first EVA shuttle mission, with 42-year-old Karl Henley as his trained co-pilot. Choosing the first 20 spacewalkers had still been a difficult task. There were four people who were turning 50 in the next 12 months, so they were given the first choice, and each of them had accepted. Their partners and immediate families brought the number to 19. Included among the immediate families were Dayna and Melody, whom Jaz had begged to go with her. In the end they could not refuse, as the other soon-to-be 50-year-olds all had at least three others accompanying them, and Jaz refused to go unless both her "daughters" went with her.

That left one final place to fill. Whom could they take who had no immediate family? In the end it became obvious; Rajesh. He had lost his father, Keo, and more recently, his mother, Prisha. He was all alone in the world now and was the closest thing to a son that Jaz had.

The morning of the launch dawned overcast and grey, with

a constant drizzle of rain falling. The 20 evacuees entered the shuttle and donned their suits, a process that took the best part of an hour as adjustments were made to fit the suits to each person. Most people buddied up to help each other, and Mel found herself buddied with Phil, who was on board because his father was one of those about to turn 50.

"Just be careful where you're putting your hands, you big ape," Mel warned him, as he stood behind her tightening some adjustment straps under her arms and around her chest. "If I feel your paws anywhere near my womanly parts you'll be limping for a month!"

"I'm surprised to hear you've got womanly parts, Mel. The way you carry on sometimes, I thought you were a sexless robot."

Melody spun around and glared at him. Phil thought he might have overstepped the mark a little and began to apologise.

"I didn't really mean ..."

He didn't get any further. Melody wrapped her arms around the back of his neck, leaned forward and kissed him, pushing her 'womanly parts' tightly against him. After a few long moments, she pushed back, leaving a speechless Phil looking at her with wide-eyed surprise.

"There!" she said. "I can assure you that I have all the necessary womanly parts, and they are all functioning very nicely, thank you." She turned her back on him again and prompted him, "Don't stand there gawking. Get me fitted into this suit."

At last they were all suited up, with helmets by their sides. The shuttle door was closed, the engines fired up and the shuttle lifted off, gathering speed as it raced skyward. For one or two on board, this was their second trip inside a week, but for others like Dayna, it would be their first time in space. She had been born on Nova and had never left its atmosphere.

Looking through the cockpit windows from her seat in the front row of the passenger cabin, Dayna watched the sky turn from blue to purple and then, quite suddenly, to jet black as the shuttle pierced the thin veils of the planet's stratosphere and mesosphere, punching through into the inky blackness of space. The stars were like a billion diamonds arrayed on a sheet of black velvet, and the half-moon of Big Boy could be seen hanging suspended in their midst.

"Sit back and enjoy the view for a while folks," said Gerry. "It's going to take us some time to locate the ring. It's a tiny little thing in a big lot of nothing."

Even with Laramie flashing the ring lights on and off, it still took 25 minutes and a lot of maneuvering until Karl, the co-pilot, spotted the thin band of the ring in the upper right corner of the cockpit window. From then, it took a further 15 minutes to bring the shuttle within half a kilometre of the 50-metre-diameter tubular ring that encircled the planet. There was no sphere in visible range in either direction, so the pilots started heading East along the ring. It took another 20 minutes before a module came into view and the pilots finally brought the shuttle to a relative standstill, in synchronous orbit directly underneath the module. Dayna thought how strange it was that they were now travelling at over 7 kilometres per second, but they seemed perfectly still as they hung underneath the dull black sphere of the ring module.

Laramie obviously had vision of them, because as Gerry swung the shuttle around so that their outer door faced directly toward the sphere, the ring module's docking bay doors opened, revealing the large interior.

"Why haven't the EIs stopped us from reaching here? Couldn't they have shut the fusion reactor down" asked Phil.

"They probably don't know what we've got planned at this stage," answered Mel, who was sitting in the seat in front of him. "After all, they have no vision in this shuttle, and no audio feed. I guess they have optics on us from the planet, so all they know is that we are near the ring again. Maybe they're hoping that we're desperate enough to try to dock with the ring. They may be thinking that they still have a chance to infiltrate the ring with their code."

"Well that's certainly not going to happen now," said Harvey as he unstrapped himself and floated forward to the front of the passenger cabin. As one of the few people on board who was familiar with zero gravity, he spun around to face the others who were all still strapped in and looking rather uncomfortable.

"OK folks. It's show time. Let me go through the plan of attack once more with you. I will go across first, taking the transfer box of your personal possessions with me, using the EMU on my suit — the External Maneuvering Unit. All of the suits have EMUs built in, but no one is to touch theirs! It takes weeks of training to learn how to use them. So keep your hands away from the control unit! That's the small square unit with the miniature toggle sticking out of your stomach. I repeat: NO TOUCHY TOUCHY! Are we all clear on that point?"

Everyone nodded.

"OK. I'll attach a guide cable from our outer hull to the inside wall of the docking bay. When the cable is secure you will cycle through the airlock in groups of four. Once the outer door opens, you will need to be extremely careful. There are no safety harnesses to attach you to the cable, so if you let go of the cable or misjudge your hand hold you will drift off into space, and you definitely don't want to do that. Please grab the cable carefully with both hands and pull yourself hand over hand toward the docking bay. ALWAYS KEEP ONE HAND GRIPPING THE CABLE! NEVER LET GO OF THE CABLE WITH BOTH HANDS! Don't worry about your orientation. There is no up or down out here. If your feet start swinging 'over' your head, let them. Don't try to reorient yourself. Just keep moving toward the docking bay. You have about 80 metres to traverse. When you reach there, you will find hand holds and bars all along the wall. Grab one and hang on. Once we are all safely over, I will detach the cable and Laramie will close the bay doors. There will be about a minute and a half while the hold is pressurised, and then artificial gravity will be restored. After that it's a piece of cake. Any questions?"

Someone put their hand up. "Yes. I feel sick."

"If you're gonna puke, do it now and use a sick bag. Whatever happens, don't do it in your suit! Any other questions?" Harvey looked around at the worried faces. "No? Alright then, let's helmet up people! That way you can all hear me through the helmet comms."

As he put his own helmet on, he whispered a silent prayer; *Lord, if you wouldn't mind, we could sure use your help right about now!*

52

Harvey's EVA went without a hitch. Dayna watched through one of the porthole windows as he attached the cable to a handhold on the outer hull near the door and used his EMU - External Maneuvering Unit - to quickly cross the distance into the docking bay. Once the cable was secured to the inner wall of the bay, he returned, using the EMU thrusters again. He then stationed himself at the start of the cable, just outside the airlock door and radioed for the first group of four to come through.

By common consent, Harvey's own wife and two teenage children were in the first group through. Harvey's first wife had died on Earth during the cataclysmic events that led to Genesis's departure. He had remarried two years after arriving at Nova, and now had two sons aged 19 and 17.

Dayna and the others watched the first group begin to haul themselves slowly along the cable, hand over hand.

"That's good," Harvey encouraged. "Nice and easy. Keep one hand on that cable at all times."

The last person in the group had barely begun, when Harvey called the next group through.

"OK, next group through the airlock. Keep coming folks."

As the next four exited the airlock, Dayna could hear a wife talking to her husband, a larger man who was already puffing as they emerged from the outer door.

"You can do this John. Just one hand at a time. Nice and easy."

"I'll be fine. I've got this."

The first group were more than half-way across, and the second group had begun traversing as Harvey called the third group through. That group had barely begun however, when tragedy struck. Dayna had been watching John, the big man, and he was clearly struggling. It all seemed to happen in slow motion at first. John gave a strong pull on the cable with his left hand and then released it as he reached out with his right hand, but completely missed the cable. He began flailing both arms, trying to grab the cable again, but he was already out of reach and drifting rapidly away.

"Help! Someone ...I can't ... uh ... I can't ..."

"John! John!" his wife began yelling.

Harvey responded immediately.

"I'm coming! I'm coming John! Take it easy."

But John didn't take it easy. Clearly, he was panicking, and as Dayna watched through the porthole, he did the unthinkable; he activated his EMU. Maybe he thought it looked easy, having seen how Harvey had used his own EMU to fly back and forth. John pressed the red activation button as he had watched Harvey do, and he toggled the tiny joystick all the way forward, obviously hoping to propel himself toward the cable. But he was already slowly spinning and tumbling, and his angle was wrong. He also used way too much force on the toggle, because he shot forward along the length of the shuttle at alarming speed, quickly disappearing from the view offered by the side portholes. Dayna swung around and saw John come into view through the cockpit window. His wife was now screaming, and Harvey was yelling at him to stop using the EMU, but John didn't listen. Instead he was clearly still trying to fly the thing, jerking his toggle one way then another. The cumulative result was that he had managed to increase his velocity alarmingly and he was also rapidly tumbling end over end.

Harvey came into view through the cockpit window, using his EMU to chase after John, yelling at him all the time to stop using the unit. By now John was disappearing rapidly and he was clearly still using his EMU, as spurts of some kind of gas could still be seen spurting out in random directions. It might not have ended in tragedy if John had stopped using the EMU at that point. Harvey could have reached him and would probably have had enough fuel to bring them both back. But, as Dayna watched, John fired a long continuous burst in completely the wrong direction. He hurtled away from the shuttle at a frightening velocity now, quickly diminishing to a tiny dot in the distance.

Dayna and the others saw Harvey use his EMU to brake and swing around, heading back towards the cable. John's wife was hysterical, and his son was calling out to him.

"Quiet everyone! Quiet!" yelled Harvey. John's wife's hysterical screams died down to a constant soft sobbing.

"We might still be able to get him back. Once we are all across and the cable is detached Gerry will fly the shuttle in search of him. He's got plenty of oxygen left, so we might be able to get him back on board. Can you hear that John?"

"...es ...sto... you .....ait ..."

John's voice was breaking up as he quickly sped out of suit radio range.

Turning back to John's wife, Harvey said, "Helen, we'll do the very best we can to get him. But we need you to keep moving as quickly as possible now. Let's move it everyone! The quicker we get across the quicker we can begin looking for John."

Dayna looked at Gerry as she heard Harvey say this, and she saw him shake his head at Karl, his co-pilot. She saw his lips move and thought he said, "We'll never find him out there."

Mel, Jaz and Dayna were the last ones through the airlock, and Dayna looked around in wonder as she emerged into the vacuum of space. Despite the tragedy she had just witnessed, she was filled with awe at the sheer beauty of the view. To her left was Nova, a brilliant blue sphere with swirling bands of white cloud, and she was surprised at how quickly the planet was rotating past them.

"It's spinning so quickly, she said.

"We're doing most of the moving," answered Harvey, beside her. "We're orbiting at 7.4 kilometres per second, or a bit over 26,000 kilometres per hour. Laramie had to increase the ring's orbital velocity to enable us to establish a stable orbit alongside it. But there's no time for gawking. We need to get across to the module now as quickly as possible. Watch your hands and keep it steady."

Fifteen minutes later they were all on the other side of the airlock, with helmets off, helping each other out of their suits. John's wife, Jean, was a blubbering mess and was clearly in shock. Her son and someone else were consoling her as best as they could, and she soon subsided into stunned disbelief.

Despite the unfolding tragedy, however, there was a quiet mood of jubilation among the group. There were hugs and handshakes all around as the realisation sunk in that they were free from the EIs at last.

"Welcome to your new home," announced Laramie.

53

ALTARIA 5502

Zac and Kit were relaxing in the spa in the penthouse apartment in Federation Tower.

"I can't believe it's been 12 months since we were last here," said Kit.

"Since *you* were here, you mean," said Zac.

"Yes. I've been wondering what you get up to in your monthly jaunts to the capital."

"Oh, you know me. Wine, women and song."

"Really? Do tell! Which women in particular?" said Kit wrapping her arms and legs around him as the deliciously warm bubbles pummelled them. "The curvaceous Starla, perhaps?"

"Oh, I'm not fussy really," he said with a sly grin.

She kissed him, a long lingering kiss, and then said, "I thought you were very fussy, actually. That's why you chose me to be your wife."

"Very true. Happy second anniversary, my darling," he said, kissing her passionately.

Much later, Zac was dressed and ready for the council meeting that was scheduled to begin in half an hour.

"You're leaving early," said Kit, as he kissed her goodbye at the door.

"I'm just going down to the shops on the concourse level. I need to buy something for a special someone."

"Really?" she said putting her arms around his neck again. "Well, please don't feel as though you have to be restrained by cost. Go all out. Go absolutely crazy."

"We'll see," he said, giving her a pat on the bottom. "You'll just have to be content with what you get, young lady."

"I'm already very content, my love," she said, kissing him again. "If I was any more content, I'd be asleep!"

Zac walked to the nearby elevator and a few moments later he stepped out onto the busy concourse in the centre of the capital. On his last visit here, he had spotted a small store that sold jewellery, and he had commissioned two wedding rings. Altarians didn't wear wedding rings, but he thought Kit would appreciate the old-fashioned tradition.

The store was in a small side street, directly opposite the concourse's grand entrance. Zac quickly made his way there, ignoring the stares that his presence drew from those around him. He walked down the side street and slipped into the store. The owner looked up and smiled when he saw him.

"Mr Zac! I have your rings. They are beautiful! I am sure your lovely wife will appreciate them."

Zac inspected them and complimented the jeweller on his handiwork. As the jeweller was placing the rings in a small carry case, Zac glanced out the window and saw a black flitter come to a stop in the street directly opposite the shop. Jurd Transid stepped out and looked furtively up and down the street. The flitter departed leaving Jurd on the sidewalk and Zac, having thanked the jeweller, was about to walk out the door and greet him, when two men in dark apparel walked up to Jurd. They spoke very briefly together and one of the men placed something in Jurd's hand, which he quickly slipped into his jacket pocket. Jurd seemed to issue a brief instruction and the two men nodded and quickly departed, crossing the street to Zac's side and walking towards Federation Tower.

Perhaps they are his bodyguards, Zac thought. Jurd began walking in the same direction at a more leisurely pace, and Zac stood in the shop doorway, watching and wondering what he had just witnessed.

Thirty minutes later, Councillor Drummond called the meeting to order, after confirming that everyone was present. Today's meeting was to present a 12-month progress report, and General Kellar led off.

"We now have three 'canary' sentinel satellites in place at the wormhole portal, two of them as reserves. Thanks to Dr Spooner's team, they have been equipped with a frequency modulation signal that is incapable of carrying any kind of digital coding. The signal will be triggered the moment anyone tries to upload computer code into the satellite's systems. Our two battle cruisers are on rotational guard duty at the portal; one month on and one month off. Plus, our molecular disruptor weapons have been substantially beefed up, once again, thanks to the Science Academy. We're ready to blast those bastards out of existence the moment they appear!"

"I'm sure you are, General," agreed Drummond. He turned to Dr Spooner and asked for a report on the other projects.

"Unfortunately, our scientists haven't made as much progress with the other projects as we had hoped," began

Spooner. "The idea of a sub-space transmission to disrupt the subspace portal and prevent future wormholes from opening is an intriguing one but is beyond our current capabilities. It may take decades of further research before we know if such a disruptor field is even possible. The concept of an EM pulse bomb to neutralise an EI vessel and obliterate their coding is perhaps more feasible, but we are still many years away from producing something that will leave our own systems intact. In fact, we are still theorising how such a pulse bomb would even work. One theory is to produce a pulse that our own systems are immune to. Another is to produce a pulse that is unidirectional; in other words, one that can be directed in single direction at a specific target. Once again, this might take years to perfect."

"What about the third proposal?" asked Drummond. "The idea of adjusting our genome to block the EIs ability to manipulate our physiology?"

"Yes. That would be the ideal. It would render the EIs impotent — even irrelevant. Unfortunately, we still don't properly understand the exact processes by which the EIs interact with our cerebral cortexes. Our brains are incredibly complex organs, able to send and receive electrical signals that are extremely minuscule. The EIs have found a way to tap into the signal pathways of the brain and target a number of key areas. The subtle changes that have occurred to our brains' neurochemical pathways as a result of the EIs modifications of our genome have somehow enhanced their ability to interact with our brains. We are still a long way from isolating the parts of the genome that are responsible for those changes, let alone working out how to undo them."

"I see," said Drummond, clearly a little disappointed.

"What resources do you need to continue your research in these areas?"

As Spooner began to list some requirements, a gentle pinging could be heard, and Jurd reached into his jacket pocket and removed a small black disc which was flashing with a green light. He stood to his feet.

"Excuse me, gentlemen. I have an urgent call on my private comm channel. If you will excuse me." He walked to the door which a security guard opened politely for him.

Zac stared at the door as it closed again, a frown furrowing his brow. After a moment he stood to his feet as well. "Please excuse me. I need to use the amenities."

Drummond nodded to him as Spooner continued to talk, and Zac left the conference room. Starla and Garran were stationed immediately outside, on either side of the door.

"Where did Transid just go?" he asked.

"He got into the lift," said Garran.

"Was he speaking on his comm?"

"No."

Zac ran to the lift and saw that it had stopped at the ground floor. Why would he be leaving the building?

"What's wrong, Zac?" asked Starla who had caught up with him.

"I think Transid is up to something. Get more security here now! And contact security on the ground! Try to apprehend Transid as he leaves the building!"

Starla and Garran began talking rapidly into their comms, while Zac ran back into the conference room.

"Everyone get out of here now!" he yelled.

They all stared at him blankly.

"I think we're under attack! Get into Drummond's office now! Go!"

No one needed any further encouragement. There was a mad rush for the side door of the conference room, which opened directly into Drummond's office. They closed the door behind them, and Zac got them all lying on the ground. They waited, and as the moments ticked by and nothing happened, Zac began to feel foolish.

"Are you sure?" asked Drummond, looking puzzled.

"Not really," he confessed, feeling more foolish by the second. "I'm sorry. I thought I saw ..."

Suddenly there was the clatter of small arms fire and the zap of deadly lasers. There was a crash, followed by something that sounded like a metal ball rolling across the floor in the conference room. A moment later a massive explosion rocked them and the door from the conference room blew in, showering them with debris and filling the office with smoke. There were a few more shots fired, but Zac didn't hear them. A piece of the door had impacted the side of his head, and he was no longer conscious.

54

Zac woke feeling wonderful. He felt like he was floating on a cloud. He opened his eyes and saw a very attractive woman sitting in a chair beside his bed.

"Hello," he said to her, smiling.

Kit stood to her feet with a look of relief.

"Oh my darling, you had me worried," she said as she kissed his cheek and stroked his hair.

"Do I know you?"

"Of course you do. I'm your wife."

"Wow! You're absolutely gorgeous!" replied Zac with a goofy grin on his face.

"I warned you that there would be temporary amnesia," said the doctor standing on the other side of the bed. "There is nothing to worry about. It is a perfectly normal side-effect of the drugs we have given him. It will wear off within 30 minutes. In the meantime, he may act a little out of character."

Zac looked at the doctor.

"Did you know that she's my wife?"

"Yes."

"I can't believe it! She's hot!"

"Just rest, my love," said Kit, patting his hand.

"What is this place?"

"It's a hospital, Dr Perryman," said the doctor.

"I'm a doctor?"

"Yes, my love," began Kit, "but not ..."

Zac sat up and swung his legs over the side. "In that case, I'd better get up. My patients need me."

"No. No. They don't need you at the moment," said Kit, thinking furiously. "They're all ... um ...having lunch. So, you can have a little rest too."

"Great! Hey check this out!"

He was swinging his legs in circles as he sat on the edge of the bed.

"You ought to try this, it's awesome!"

"I'm getting déjà vu," muttered Kit, shaking her head.

"Not for me thanks," said Zac. "I don't eat Indian food."

"Hey," he said, leaning closer to Kit and whispering to her. "Are we going to have sex soon?"

Kit looked across at the doctor.

"I think he's returning to normal quicker than we anticipated!"

A little more than 30 minutes later, Zac was dressed and standing at the window, holding Kit's hand, looking at the capital spread out below them.

"How long was I unconscious for?"

"Two weeks," she replied. "They kept you in a coma while you healed. You had a minor bleed on the brain. They operated using some kind of ultrasonic surgery that leaves no scar."

Zac felt his head.

"I feel fine. Completely normal."

"I'm glad to hear it!" said Councillor Drummond as he walked into the room. He shook Zac's hand in the old fashioned Terran style, as a mark of his respect.

"We owe you a deep debt of gratitude, Zac. Without your intervention, many more lives would have been lost."

"How many died?"

"None of the councillors. You were the only one seriously injured. But unfortunately, two of our security guards lost their lives."

"Who?"

"Garran, and one other that you wouldn't know."

"I see."

"There were four terrorists. All were killed in the end. Unfortunately, Jurd Transid got away."

"What was his plan? And how did he think he could possibly get away with this?" Zac asked incredulously.

"That's what we're trying to work out. Our best guess is that he was hoping to wipe out the entire council in one fell stroke, and then, as the sole survivor, stack the new council with people drawn from his own supporters."

"That's ridiculous! No one would have believed that he was innocent!"

"As a matter of fact, we think he would have been believed. A security guard caught sight of him fleeing the building after the assassination attempt had failed. He had inflicted wounds upon himself to make it look as if he had been attacked as well. He must have been hiding somewhere, waiting to reappear as the sole surviving victim."

"That's outrageous! And to what end? What was he hoping to achieve?"

"Apparently he doesn't believe we are doing enough to wind back our technology. I don't think he will be happy until we are all living like cavemen."

Drummond changed topics.

"Enough maudlin reflection! We are all alive because of you. And as a small token of our appreciation, we are holding a state dinner tomorrow night, with both of you as our guests of honour."

"That's very kind," said Zac.

"Not at all. It's the least we could do. In the meantime, I will leave you to have some time together. Starla and another security guard will be stationed at your door at all times. This afternoon I will send a tailor up to your suite, who will measure you both for formal wear. Please let us know if there is anything further you need."

He took Zac's hand in his own again and looked him in the eye. "You are a hero, Zac. I owe you my life, and so does everyone else on the council."

A short time later they were back in their apartment, and Zac remembered the rings that he had bought for their anniversary. His clothes had all been cleaned while he was unconscious, but as he patted his pocket, he found that the small container with the rings had been placed back in his jacket. He took the container out and gave it to Kit.

"I know it's a couple of weeks late, but I bought us an anniversary present."

She opened it and her eyes immediately misted over.

"Oh, Zac! They're beautiful!"

Zac took her ring out and placed it on her finger, and she did the same for him.

"I love you so much, Zac," she said, as a single tear rolled down her cheek.

"I love you too. You're the only woman for me."

55

———

NOVA 5402

"Zac is the only man I will ever love, and I won't rest until I either find him or die trying."

"Mum, are you sure about this?" asked Dayna.

"Yes, absolutely. I don't know how I know, but I'm sure he's not dead. He can't be. And I promised myself that if we ever made it safely to the ring, I would keep going and follow him."

"But we really have no idea whether the wormhole is safe."

"I don't care. I've made my decision. I'm going."

They were sitting in the lounge area after the midday meal on their third day on board the ring. Yesterday there had been a memorial service for John, who had never been located. It had been a dreadful affair, with no body to commit and just the nineteen of them standing together in the loading dock. John's wife and son had written a letter, expressing their love for him, and these were placed on the loading dock floor, along with his favourite baseball cap. Laramie then cracked the bay doors, allowing the few paltry items to be sucked out into space.

Later that day, the next group of evacuees had arrived, using the 19 space suits they had recovered from the dropbox that had been successfully landed a few kilometres west of Seahaven. The twelve modules around the launch ring were linked by transfer booths, allowing instantaneous travel around the ring. After successfully boarding the launch ring, the second batch of arrivals had used the transfer booths to reach Module 4, where Dayna's group had arrived the previous day. The ring colony now numbered 38 and a third group was due to arrive later this afternoon.

Melody and Dayna had been trying unsuccessfully to talk Jaz out of her plan since she had announced it to them yesterday. Now, as they sat with her in the loungeroom, Dayna finally conceded defeat.

"You've wanted to do this ever since Dad disappeared, haven't you?"

"Yes, my darling, I have" Jaz said, leaning over and squeezing Dayna's hand. "It doesn't mean I don't love you, or don't want to be with you, but Zac is the love of my life and I need to find him. Besides, I know you and Mel are going to be fine now. Especially since Mel and Phil have finally hooked up," she said with a mischievous grin.

"Hooked up is a gross exaggeration," said Mel. "I gave him a peck, that's all."

"It looked more like a full-on snog to me," said Dayna.

"And what makes you such an expert on snogging? Have you and Rajesh been getting in some practice behind my back?"

"Don't be ridiculous!"

"It's not at all ridiculous, sweetheart," said Jaz. "He loves you, you know. That's another reason why I feel OK about leaving to follow Zac. I know you will both be loved now."

"And who's going to fly the void jumper?" asked Mel. "Are you going to just fly off by yourself?"

"If I have to. Laramie says its completely automated, especially since the wormhole is already open and doesn't need activation. He can fly me into the portal remotely from here."

"What will you do on the other side? Have you thought of that? What if you end up in empty space, millions of lightyears from nowhere?"

"I don't think that's possible. The wormhole is keyed into a star frequency that has a habitable planet. At least that's what Laramie says."

"So, what then? How will you land?"

"Laramie says he's modified the void jumpers to be able to operate in an atmosphere and land on a planet if necessary. It's an automated system that I can initiate from orbit."

"Listen to her!" said Mel to Dayna. "She's suddenly turned into Jaz bloody Skywalker! Help me out here, Dayna! Help me talk her out of it!"

"No," said Dayna shaking her head. "I can see you've made your mind up mum, and I won't try to stop you."

"Thank you, my darling."

"Besides, no one has the right to tell someone else what to do, do they?"

"That's right," agreed Jaz.

"Every person has to make their own decisions, don't they?"

"Yes, they do, my sweet."

"Good. Because I'm coming with you."

"WHAT???" exclaimed Mel. "Oh my Lord! Dayna, it's one thing if your mother wants to throw her life away, but you have your whole life ahead of you!"

"I know. But I've already lost my father. I refuse to lose my mother too."

"You're both crazy! That wormhole might dissolve you into your component molecules for all you know!"

"I don't think so," said Dayna. "I've been chatting to Laramie too. According to him, the wormhole is stable and appears to be functioning normally. There is every reason to believe that we will arrive at a new world where we can settle."

"But you don't know for sure, do you."

"No, I don't. But, like mum, I'd rather die trying, than fade away here on the ring and never feel the sun on my face again. Besides, I want to find my dad as well."

"I'm surprised you aren't more positive about the plan, Melody," said Jaz. "I seem to remember that you were the one who proposed the idea of escaping from the planet and travelling through the wormhole when you first became part of the city council, ten years ago."

"Yeh, well now that I've seen how comfortably we can survive on the ring, I'm a lot less inclined to throw my life away on a gamble!"

Their conversation was cut short by Laramie, who announced the arrival of the shuttle with the next load of evacuees. The shuttle had arrived at Module 8, so most of the tiny colony decided to transfer there to welcome the new arrivals.

Once again, Gerry and Karl were piloting the shuttle and were getting proficient at locating the ring without the aid of computer navigation. A cable was quickly attached to the inner wall of the loading dock, and the current ring colonists gathered in a glass fronted viewing room where they watched the space-suited figures clumsily pulling themselves into the safety of the docking bay. Not long afterward, there was a happy reunion of friends and acquaintances as the newcomers clambered out of their cumbersome suits and were welcomed by the existing "ringers" as they were now calling themselves.

The third shuttle mission seemed to have gone without a hitch until the pilots attempted to fire up the fusion drive. Nothing happened. Dayna and the others were completely unaware of the drama that was unfolding outside the now-closed loading bay doors, until their excited chatter was interrupted by Laramie.

"Excuse my interruption, everyone, but there appears to be a problem with the shuttle."

"What kind of problem?" asked Harvey, who was with the group of newcomers.

"I will patch you through to the pilots. Their basic FM radio now poses no threat to the ring."

There was a brief pause, and then they all heard Gerry's voice.

"Hey is anyone listening? Harvey, do you copy?"

"Yes, Gerry. Go ahead. What's the problem?"

"The fusion reactor computer has just crapped itself."

"What do you mean?"

"I mean, it just ran a weird code that suddenly ramped up the reactor, and then it wiped itself out. The computer is completely dead, and if the last readings were anything to go by, the reactor is escalating."

"They're sitting in a bomb!" said Mel. "The EIs have turned the shuttle into a freakin' nuclear bomb!"

"How long do you think you've got, Gerry?"

"About three minutes, max, until it blows."

Harvey swore.

"We could come and get you with some spare spacesuits," offered Mel, but as she said it Harvey shook his head at her.

"Thanks for the offer, but that's not gonna work, Mel. Besides, I've already left. I need to get this shuttle as far from you as possible. I'm using maximum thrust from the maneuvering thrusters, pointing the shuttle straight down towards the planet. The gravity should help a little as well."

"I'm so sorry, Gerry."

"Not as sorry as I am. I've put Karl into a large storage box and shoved him out the door. He wasn't happy leaving me, but there's no point two of us getting toasted. Laramie has already opened the bay doors and the storage box was floating straight into the loading bay when I took off. He'll be a bit cold by the time you get him out, but the box is built for vacuum, so he'll have plenty of air."

Harvey raced back into the viewing room and saw a large silver box floating in the chamber, and the outer doors were closing again.

"Re-pressurising the docking bay now," said Laramie. "I won't restore artificial gravity until you have secured the box."

Several people raced toward the airlock, preparing to rescue Karl from his floating cocoon.

"Did you hear that, Gerry? We've got him."

"Yeah. Good. Tell him 'hi' from me."

"Will do, mate."

Harvey paused, not sure what else to say.

"You're a good man, Gerry. You won't be forgotten."

"Speaking of that, tell that good-for-nothing Joel that he owes me 10 credits from our card game last night. He's the big hairy dude who just arrived. Watch him like a hawk, Harvey. I'm convinced he keeps cards up his sleeve or something."

"I will."

"And I need you to do one more thing for me Harvey."

"Anything, mate."

"Tell Cynthia I love …"

The transmission cut off and a moment later the shock wave from the blast hit them and knocked several of them to the floor.

56

The colonists were gathered together in the lounge area in Module 4, taking stock of their situation. With the unexpected addition of Karl, who had survived his ordeal unscathed, there were 58 of them now on board the ring. Gerry's death had shaken them all, literally and emotionally.

"He's a bloody hero," said one colonist. "He saved all our lives."

"Yes," agreed Mel. "If he hadn't moved away when he did, the blast would almost certainly have destroyed that module and all of us who were there at the time. We owe him our lives."

"And now we know where we stand with the EIs," said Harvey. "It looks as though there won't be any more shuttle transfers to the ring."

"But why did they allow three trips before they reacted?" asked someone.

"On the first trip, they can't have known what we were doing," said Harvey. "Or at least they were hoping we would try to dock the shuttle. They might have been hoping for that with the second trip as well. We don't really know. But once it became clear we were never going to dock the shuttle with the ring, they decided to try to blow us out of the sky."

"How do we know they won't try it again?" asked someone else.

"I doubt it," replied Harvey. "Their primary purpose was to destroy the modified shuttle to stop any further evacuations. Blowing it up alongside the ring was just a bonus."

"So, what does that mean for us now?" asked another voice.

"It means we have a colony of 60 to start a new life here together," said Mel. "But there won't be any more people arriving from the planet."

There was silence as the full import of that sank in. They all had friends on Nova whom they would never see again.

"Can we survive here indefinitely?" asked someone.

It was a rather silly question, as they would not have come to the ring if that was not possible.

"Of course we can," said Mel. "We have everything we need here. Unlimited food, water, power and air, as well as clean lodgings and all the technology we could hope for. There is a mining and production base on Little Boy, so we can eventually design and manufacture anything we need there. The challenge will be to make this into a real home. There will need to be some changes made. For example, a whole module could be devoted to recreation and exercise. We can make this work people! And best of all, we get to celebrate a whole lot more birthdays."

There was nodding all around, as well as some smiles. Husbands and wives held hands and looked relieved that there were going to be no more 'Send Offs'.

"There is one other option," said Jaz, standing to her feet.

Mel sat down and put her head in her hands, whispering to Dayna, "Oh no."

"There are spacecraft on board the ring that are capable of travelling through the wormhole. The previous inhabitants called them void jumpers. Laramie tells us that one of these was used by Zac and the others with him to enter the wormhole 22 years ago. He also tells us that the wormhole is stable and still appears to be locked on to the star frequency of a system with a habitable planet."

She paused and looked around the room.

"I am planning to go through the wormhole, to find my husband. I will travel alone if necessary, but I just wanted you to know, in case anyone else wanted to come."

She sat down, looking relieved that her speech was over.

"She makes it sound like a picnic at the beach," whispered Mel to Dayna.

Dayna, however, was looking at her mother in a new light. The possibility of finding her long-lost husband had awakened a spark within Jaz that Dayna had never seen. All her life, her mother had been withdrawn and depressed, almost ghost-like in the way she barely made contact with the world around her. Now, however, a fierce determination had arisen within her. People had told Dayna of her mother's once fiery, vibrant personality, but she had always found the stories hard to believe. Until now.

Harvey broke the silence.

"Obviously there are risks involved in travelling through the wormhole. Zac, Kit, Keo and Martinez have not been seen or heard from since they left, 22 years ago. We simply don't know whether they survived and whether the wormhole is safe for travel. There must be some significant anomaly interfering with the wormhole for it to have remained locked open for all these years. You need to be aware of the risks if you are considering leaving with Jaz. After Jaz informed me of her decision a little earlier, I spoke with Laramie and he has some additional information that he is able to share with us now. Over to you Laramie."

"Thank you, Harvey," said the disembodied voice. "The original inhabitants of this world utilised wormhole technology to travel to a star system which they named Altaria, approximately 1,724 years ago. The system contains a habitable Earth-like planet, approximately 94% of Earth's mass, with 80% of its surface covered by water. 22 years ago, Zac, Kit, Keo and Natasha opened a wormhole to that system and travelled through it. Wormholes only remain open for 14 seconds, but this one has mysteriously remained locked open for 22 years. The most logical explanation is that the wormhole's subspace corridor has formed close to a black hole's event horizon, causing a negative energy feedback loop. It may also be the case that anyone travelling through the wormhole could experience significant time dilation, meaning that time would slow down for them, relative to the outside universe."

"Are you saying that Zac and the others could still be in the wormhole?" asked Jaz, concern now written across her face.

"It is possible, yes. While 22 years has passed for us in the outside universe, only hours might have passed for them."

"That would explain why we haven't heard back from them," said Dayna.

"Yes. That is one explanation."

"Is there another?" asked someone else.

"They may also be dead," said Laramie bluntly. "If the subspace corridor of the wormhole has been drawn completely into the black hole's event horizon, they would have ceased to exist within a matter of moments."

"If you had to guess, which of those two scenarios would you say is more likely?" asked another.

"I do not guess. It is not logical to do so. I simply do not have enough information to determine which is the more likely scenario."

"So, let me get this straight," said someone. "We have a clear choice. On the one hand, we could stay here and live an almost guaranteed long and safe life, but never walk on the surface of a planet again. On the other hand, we could attempt to travel to Altaria, but in the process, face the very real risk of death, a risk that is currently unquantifiable."

"That is correct."

The meeting then degenerated into a series of individual discussions between colonists, as they wrestled with the options and posed arguments. In the end Harvey brought the meeting to a conclusion.

"Obviously, there's a lot for us to consider here. I propose that we spend another week thinking about the issues and undertaking whatever research may be possible. That will also allow us to get a taste of what life here on the ring will be like. We will schedule another meeting to discuss our options in seven days."

57

Jaz would not be swayed. She was determined to follow her long-lost husband into the wormhole and discover what had happened to him – or die trying. Dayna was equally determined to accompany her mother, and further discussions with Laramie, along with scans of the wormhole's portal, had convinced her that the wormhole was still locked onto the Altarian star system and was functioning normally.

"But Dayna, it doesn't make sense," argued Mel, as they sat together in the lounge area one week later. "You've just been saved from a life-threatening scenario under the EIs, and now you're deliberately risking your life all over again!"

"I don't actually think it's a risk at all. The more I've studied the wormhole portal this week, the more convinced I am that it is safe. The echyon frequency that it's locked onto hasn't wavered and is showing a strong connection to the Altarian system. I am convinced that we will arrive safely in that star system – the only question is when. If Laramie is right, and the wormhole is being influenced by a black hole, we could arrive there many years in the future."

"By which time, everyone back here would be dead?"

"Possibly," conceded Dayna.

"And you're comfortable with that?"

"Comfortable isn't exactly the word. Resigned is more like it. But if this means that we have a chance of finding my dad, I'm willing to accept the consequences."

"But he could be long dead too, by the time you get there – if you get there at all!"

"I don't think so. If he was affected by the same time dilation, we will arrive 22 years after him. He should still be alive."

Melody sighed. "Oh Dayna! Why are you doing this to me? You're asking me to say goodbye to you and Jaz, and quite possibly never see you again! I don't think I can do it!"

"Then come with us. I know you want to find dad too." She looked at Mel and saw tears starting to form in the corners of her eyes. "You like to present yourself as a hard arse, Aunty Mel, but I know you miss him too."

Mel nodded, and she wiped the corner of one eye before it gave her away even more. "You're absolutely determined to go ahead with this?" she asked.

"Yep."

Mel shook her head. "You're as stubborn as your mother!" She took a deep breath and exhaled slowly, puffing out her cheeks. "OK. If I can't talk you out of it, I'm coming with you."

"Really?"

"Yes, really. I can't let you two birdbrains go flitting around the universe by yourselves. Someone sensible has to look after you!"

Dayna threw her arms around her. "Thank you, Mel! It

would have broken mum's heart to leave you behind. And mine. But are you sure about this?"

"Yes. But if we die in that wormhole, I'm never speaking to you again!"

Later that afternoon, the community met to discuss the possibility of travelling through the wormhole. Everyone had had time to think the issue through, and many discussions had taken place throughout the week. As the most experienced of the two shuttle pilots now on the ring, Harvey chaired the meeting, but after a few preliminary comments he invited Dayna to share her findings.

Dayna spoke for some time, explaining the stable echyon readings still emanating from the portal, which seemed to indicate that the wormhole was stable and still locked onto the Altarian system. She also gave a realistic appraisal of the possibility of time dilation affecting those who attempted to travel through it.

"So, the same thing that happened to us on our way to Nova, could happen again?" asked someone. "We could jump further ahead in time?"

"Yes, we could," answered Dayna.

"And you don't know how far in the future we could end up."

"No."

"And you don't know what new threats might await us there."

"No."

"That's if we survive at all," added someone else. "We can't know for certain if the wormhole is safe, can we? I mean, we could end up being torn apart inside a blackhole, couldn't we?"

"That's only a very slim possibility," answered Dayna.

"But it is a possibility," responded the same person.

"Yes. But, in that sense, there's a possibility of all sorts of calamities happening at every moment of our lives. There's a possibility that a meteor will blow this module to pieces as we sit here right now. We can't live our lives paralysed by the fear of extremely unlikely possibilities."

"But the difference is that you are planning to deliberately place yourself in harm's way," said the same man.

"I agree," said a woman. "I'm not prepared to risk my life again after having finally freed myself from the tyranny of the EIs. I'm staying here, where the risks are known and I can reasonably guarantee a long and safe life. I wish you and your mother well, Dayna, and I will do everything I can to help you prepare for your journey, but I'm not willing to go with you."

Her sentiment began to be echoed by the vast majority of the group, and Dayna could see that no amount of persuasion was going to change their minds. After further discussion, Harvey asked those who were planning to venture into the wormhole to stand up. Six people rose to their feet.

Jaz.

Dayna.

Mel.

Phil.

Rajesh.

And, finally, Karl, the co-pilot who had narrowly escaped death on the final shuttle, stood to his feet.

"Karl?" said Dayna. "I wasn't aware you were thinking of coming."

"Well, I figure I should probably have died with Gerry on the shuttle, anyway. So I'm already in bonus time. Plus, I have no family on Nova or on the ring, so I've got nothing keeping me here really. And you guys could use an experienced pilot. That's if you'll have me."

"Of course we will!" said Dayna. "Thank you."

Harvey waited a few more moments to see if anyone else would volunteer to go.

"So, we have six people who will be leaving us," he said. "I must say, I am relieved that the colony is not being split into two over this. Sixty people is a very small number to be starting a new colony with here on the ring, and it would have been even more difficult if only half that number were remaining. I think this gives the ring colony the best chance of thriving. Karl, I'm also glad you're going with them. It will ease my mind to know that they will be in the best of hands in terms of piloting the void jumper."

"Can I make a suggestion?" asked the woman who had spoken up previously. "I think we should do everything we can to equip these people with every possible resource before they leave. Dayna, you shouldn't rush your departure. Let us make sure you have every chance of surviving if you happen to make it to a new planet. If helping you prepare takes a few weeks, or even a few months, then so much the better."

"Thank you," said Dayna. "We'll accept any help you can give us. But I hope it doesn't take months. Now that I've decided, I'm keen to get going."

In the end, it only took two weeks.

58

The departure party was an event of mixed emotions. Two weeks of intense preparations had been concluded that afternoon, and there remained nothing else to do but say farewell to the six who were leaving. Karl and Dayna, as pilot and co-pilot, had undergone training under Laramie's instruction and were as ready as they could be for what lay ahead. Meanwhile, the entire colony had gotten involved in equipping the intrepid (some said 'foolish') explorers. Non-perishable food had been packed and stored aboard the vessel, and a variety of tools and equipment had also been taken on board. This was only possible because Laramie, acting on Zac's instructions 22 years earlier, had utilised the production facility on Little Boy to not only manufacture a series of void jumpers, but also a wide variety of tools and equipment that future colonists might require. In fact, if any sort of emotions could be attached to an artificial intelligence, Laramie had quite 'enjoyed' the mental and logistical challenges involved in determining what might be needed and how it could be produced.

"Mum, I'm worried that Raj has the wrong idea about me," said Dayna, as the two of them prepared to go to the dining area for the party. "I hope he's not coming just because he thinks something's going to happen between us."

"There's two answers to that, my darling," said Jaz.

"OK. What are they?"

"We are all the family Rajesh has now. So, it was almost inevitable that he was going to choose to come with us."

"And the second answer?"

"Of course something is going to happen between you and Raj! There is no one else in the ring colony within ten years of your ages! If either of you are going to find a partner, it's with each other, my love, and I think you know that. That is, unless you're planning on being a crusty old spinster."

Dayna sighed. "But isn't there supposed to be some kind of magic spark when you find the person you want to be with? Raj is like my brother!"

"He's only like your brother because that's all you've allowed him to be. And your obsession over these last few years with trying to solve the fusion problem hasn't exactly allowed you much time to explore your feelings - or even *have* any feelings for anyone or anything else other than the project. I suspect that things will change for you now, once we settle into a new life. You might be surprised how easily you could develop feelings for him if you let yourself."

"Mmm ... we'll see," she answered, noncommittally.

"Why don't you talk to Mel. She seems to have gotten past those kinds of issues with Phil."

"I'll say she has! They can't keep their hands off each other!"

"Maybe she can give you some advice on how to move past the emotional blockage you seem to have with Raj."

"What? Something like; 'Just close your eyes and think of England'? No thanks! I think I'll just let things take their natural course."

They arrived in the dining room to find that the party was in full swing. Laramie had accessed his data bank and dredged up some music from the history files. There was plenty of food and even some alcoholic drink that Laramie had begun to produce.

"Be careful with that stuff," Harvey said to Jaz and Dayna as they poured some into their cups. "It packs a real wallop. I'll have to suggest to Laramie that he tones it down a couple of notches."

"Wow!" said Dayna after taking her first sip. "That's strong enough to kill a horse!"

"We've already nick-named it 'rocket fuel'," he said with a grin.

"Tastes fine to me," said Jaz, taking a second big gulp. She licked her lips and said, "This girl's ready to party!"

Dayna looked at her in amazement. "Who are you, and what have you done with my mother?"

Jaz smiled and said. "Dayna, I need you to do something for me."

"Sure. What?"

"I need you to drink that cup of booze down right now. All of it."

"What? Mum what's got into you?"

"Just do it! I'm your mother and I can see what you need better than you can. You need to loosen up, sweetie. You need to let your hair down and have some fun. I mean, really have some fun. Since you were a little girl, you've been so consumed with the problems of the world that you've never really allowed yourself to have fun. It's not normal. It's not healthy. So tonight, I'm ordering you to have fun."

"You want me to get drunk?"

"Not exactly. I just want you to unwind and enjoy yourself for once. And a couple of cups of this stuff should help loosen you up."

Dayna shook her head in bewilderment. "The whole world's gone crazy - my mother's trying to get me drunk!"

"Come on young lady, don't just stand there. Down the hatch! Take your medicine like a big girl!"

An hour later, Dayna had to admit to herself that her mother might have had a point. Everyone was dancing and laughing, and Dayna found herself swept up in the party atmosphere herself. Laramie had been asked several times to turn the volume up, and now the whole module seemed to be pulsing with the rhythm of the music. He had even been coaxed into flashing some of the lights in time with the beat, and, for most of them, this was their first experience of an old-fashioned disco.

Dayna was filling her cup up for the third time, and her mother, who was having a rest from dancing, raised her eyebrows.

"Go easy on that, darling. Maybe two cups is enough."

"I thought you wanted me to have some fun?"

"I do. And I think you've reached that point already."

"I'll be OK," Dayna replied. "Just one more."

"OK, young lady. But don't say I didn't warn you."

Soon after, Dayna found herself dancing with the only eligible bachelor. Raj twirled her around and danced in sync with her, laughing and joking. She thought he had had a few drinks as well. As they swayed in time with the music, she noted with surprise how different he seemed now. Gone was the uncertain youth of her childhood. Here, before her, was a tall, wide shouldered man, with black curly hair, deep brown eyes and a rugged – yes, even handsome – face. A girl could do a lot worse than fall into his arms, she thought, as she looked at his full lips and beautiful olive skin.

She shook her head, as if trying to banish the thought. *Maybe I shouldn't have had that third drink.*

"What's wrong?" asked Raj, reaching for her hands again and smiling.

"Nothing."

"Good! Because tonight is not a time for sadness or worry," he said, giving her a twirl. "Tonight is for celebrating! And I'm going to make sure you don't retreat into your Dayna cave."

"My Dayna cave?"

"Yes. That place where you lock yourself away from everyone. You're not allowed to go there tonight. I'm standing guard at the cave entrance, and I won't let you in there. It's time for you to have some fun."

"You've been talking to my mother."

"She's a very wise person, your mother."

He twirled her again and her head spun momentarily. She let the music take her, its melody and beat filling her senses, and perhaps for the very first time in her life she felt completely and utterly happy.

59

―――

"We're locked in and ready for departure, Laramie," said Karl.

"I confirm that your craft is sealed and pressurised," said Laramie. "Venting atmosphere now."

The six occupants of the void jumper heard an initial soft hissing, carried to them via subtle vibrations through their hull. The hissing quickly faded to silence and Laramie announced, "Opening the outer hangar doors now."

The domed section of the roof slid open above them, revealing a stunning panorama of stars.

"It's beautiful isn't it?" asked Karl.

Dayna nodded her head and immediately wished she hadn't. *How many of those rocket fuels did I drink last night?* Things had become a bit blurry towards the end. She had a vague memory of kissing Raj at some stage. She woke up this morning thinking that she may have just dreamed it, but Raj's cheeky grin and wink to her over breakfast this morning had confirmed her worst suspicions. She had avoided him all morning after that, as they had made their final goodbyes and settled themselves on board the void jumper. *What have I done?* she thought to herself, as she tried to focus on her instrument panel, while trying to ignore the small rodent that was apparently attempting to tunnel its way through the inside of her skull.

Karl expertly manoeuvred them out of the jumper bay into clear space, a process that Laramie would have done remotely if a competent pilot had not been on board. The void jumper was a new, improved model. Gone were the doughnut rings and ungainly sausage-shaped central passenger cabin. Instead it was a more streamlined spacecraft with wing-like tapered vanes running down each side of the main fuselage. The STAR drive would use these vanes to project its energy fields all around the jumper in order to stabilise their journey through the wormhole. The vanes could also be extended to act as aerodynamic wings, allowing the newer version void jumper to land on the surface of a planet.

"Take one last look at Nova, everyone," Karl said. "It's almost certainly the last time you'll see it."

He swung the jumper around so that Nova filled the entire front window, a beautiful green/blue globe streaked with white clouds. Big Boy was just beginning to peak over the horizon, the large brilliant moon completing an almost surreal picture.

"So beautiful," said Jaz.

"But full of so many sad memories," said Mel. "So many people dead prematurely. It's positively bloody evil."

"Yes," agreed Dayna. "But I haven't given up hope that Harvey and the ring colony will one day be able to figure out a way of rescuing the others."

Laramie's voice cut across their speculation.

"You are clear to initiate the main drive sequence, Karl. The navigation coordinates for the subspace portal are already entered into your onboard computer."

"Thanks, Laramie."

He spun the jumper around until his nav computer told him he was lined up with their pre-programed flight path.

"Firing up the main drive now. Initiating burn in three, two, one, now."

The star field in front of them remained stable, and the inertial dampeners ensured that they felt no acceleration, but the cockpit instruments indicated an extremely rapid rate of acceleration.

"Your burn looks good, Karl, and your trajectory is accurate."

"Thanks Laramie."

"You will arrive at the portal in exactly 64 minutes. I have programmed the sensors to alert you when you are two minutes from the portal. As the wormhole is already open you will simply need to activate your STAR drive at that point. The echyon frequency of the Altarian star system has already been entered into the drive, and it will automatically lock onto the wormhole as you approach it. I wish you all the best."

"Thanks again Laramie. You look after all those people back there, OK?"

"Roger."

"Hey Karl, it's Harvey here. Just wanted to wish you guys a good flight."

"Thanks Harvey."

"We'll miss you, and we'll certainly be sending you all our positive thoughts for a safe journey."

"We'll miss you guys as well. Thanks for all your help. Have a rocket fuel for me tonight."

"Will do."

"Oh, and by the way, Gerry was right. Joel is definitely a shifty card player. Watch his left hand. I'm sure he's palming cards."

Harvey chuckled. "Roger that."

A little over an hour later, a soft chime gave them the two-minute warning, and Dayna switched on the STAR drive, double checking the star frequency despite Laramie's assurance. Looking up, she peered ahead trying to spot the subspace portal that would mark the start of the wormhole.

"I can't see it yet," she said, squinting forward.

"It's dead ahead," said Harvey.

"I can't see anything."

"Exactly."

"What do you mean?"

"An open wormhole blots out the stars behind it, because it is a tunnel through subspace. Look for a circle with no stars."

"I see it! It's just a circle of pitch black."

"That's it."

"It's getting bigger extremely quickly."

"That's because we're travelling at hundreds of times the speed of a bullet. Watch carefully. According to Laramie, as we breach the threshold, we should see a momentary flash."

The side wing-shaped vanes of the jumper were glowing a bright blue as the STAR drive, sensing the approaching wormhole, enveloped the spacecraft in its energy field. The circular black void accelerated towards them at astonishing speed, swallowing up the rest of their field of vision in a split second. At the last moment they saw a shimmering wall of light in front of their craft that looked almost like a thin film of transparent plastic, and then they smashed through it with a brilliant flash of light.

They were stuck in the wormhole for two days.

60

ALTARIA 5521

Zac and Keo were going fishing for the afternoon. They didn't really want to catch anything, because their freezers were full of fish already; they just needed to escape the bedlam of the party preparations. Their wives were more than happy to let them go, since all the heavy work had been done yesterday and the men would only be in the way and grizzling if they were made to stay.

"Go and get your feet wet, grumpy bum," said Kit, kissing Zac fondly on the lips. "And don't come back until you're happy!"

"He might be gone for weeks in that case," said Keo.

"You can talk!" said Tash, smacking her husband on the bottom. "I swear, something weird happens to men after they turn 50! They turn into grumpy old men. I don't know what it is, maybe hormones."

"Or hair loss," said Kit, indicating Keo's now completely bald head.

"Or maybe it's got something to do with the hairs that start growing out of their ears," said Tash. "What's that all about?"

"Come on Keo," said Zac, "let's get out of here before they start discussing any lower parts of our anatomy!"

"Can I come too, Uncle Zac?" asked Kira.

"No you can't, young lady!" called Tash, who had moved back into the kitchen. "It's your birthday party – you don't get to go and have fun and leave the rest of us doing all the work!" Tash turned to Kit and shook her head. "19 years old and all she wants to do is fish and surf! It's a wonder she doesn't have gills!" Directing her voice back into the lounge room, she said, "Kira, go and help your brother dig the fire pit for the hangi."

"Damn!" muttered Kira under her breath.

"Nice try kiddo," said Zac ruffling her hair. "I'll take you next time."

Zac and Keo grabbed some rods and lures and headed down to the beach, but when they got there, they found that the strong sou'wester had created a nasty cross-swell that was ruining any chance of catching anything on this side of the island.

"Oh well," said Zac, looking at the messy seas, "I didn't really feel like cleaning fish anyway."

They sat down on the sand and let the cool sea breeze blow over them. Keo opened a flask of moonfruit cider and poured them both a generous cupful.

"I think I've finally perfected the recipe, bro. Let me know what you think."

"Keo, you've been trying to perfect this recipe for over 20 years. You'd think you would have got it right by now."

"Just try it bro. Tell me what you think."

Zac took a sip and swilled it around in his mouth, while Keo watched his face intently, trying to gauge his friend's reaction. Zac swallowed and smacked his lips together a couple of times and nodded his head.

"Well?" asked Keo.

"Perfect."

"But that's what you said about the last batch."

"That was perfect too."

"And the batch before!"

"Yep. Perfect as well."

"But they're all different!"

"Yep, and they're all perfect."

"Bro, sometimes I despair at your lack of vintner discernment."

"I am discerning. I just happen to be very content."

They sat sipping the cider in companionable silence for a while.

"I'm content too, bro. It's a good life. We have everything we need here." He took another sip. "I only worry about one thing."

"The kids?" asked Zac.

"Yes. Noah and Kira are great kids, and it is a good life for them too. But there is no one for them to marry. Unless they hook up with Altarians, which doesn't seem likely, they will never know the joy of love."

"I wish Kit and I could have contributed to the gene pool."

"Of course you do, bro, and I'm sorry. I shouldn't have brought it up. I know it's a painful topic for you."

"Not so much for me, but it's been difficult for Kit. That's why she loves spending so much time with Kira. She's like an adopted daughter to her."

"Kira loves both you guys. Noah does too."

"Uncle Zac!" Kira was running down the beach towards them. "Councillor Drummond called. He wants you to call him back. He says it's urgent."

"Damn! It had better not be about the opening of the new spaceport on A2. I told him we could leave all that stuff until the next council meeting!"

Ten minutes later, Drummond's face appeared on Zac's comm screen in his study.

"Thanks for getting back to me so quickly, Zac. Unfortunately, this is rather urgent."

"That's alright. I know you wouldn't be calling if it was unimportant. How can I help?"

"There's been a development that I think you should know about."

"OK."

"A ship has just come through the wormhole."

"What?!! Is it the EIs?"

"No."

"Are you sure?"

"Yes. It's a ship from the Nova system. Humans from the ring. Other people, just like you, Zac."

"From the ring?" Zac was stunned. His mind was whirling. He couldn't think of anything to say.

"And that's not all," continued Drummond. "A few seconds after the ship appeared, the wormhole closed."

"What?!!"

"The wormhole is gone. Of course, this means that the EIs could dial through to us at any moment. Our defence forces have been placed on high alert. All defence personnel on shore leave have been recalled and our battleships are mobilising."

"That's unbelievable! After all these years?"

"Yes. We'd all hoped that the wormhole would remain locked permanently, but it wasn't to be. I'm sorry to do this to you, Zac, but we need you to go to Gateway Station and interview the new arrivals. We think it might be better for them to experience first contact with someone who looks like them."

"Of course. I'll leave immediately."

"Thanks Zac. The new commander of Gateway Station, Commander Bree, will meet you at AI Terminal and escort you to Gateway. Oh, and please pass on my best wishes to Kira on her birthday. Tell her I'm sorry that we had to take you away like this."

"I will."

"I hope you don't mind, but I have sent a flitter from a nearby techsav island to pick you up and take you to the transfer booth on Manna Island. It should be there within the next five minutes. It will save you that 40-minute trip in your much slower sailing boat. Please apologise to the islanders for the intrusion of our technology into their haven. I have already apologised to Mayor Berg and impressed upon him the need for urgency, without giving him any specific details of the situation."

Zac had a bit of apologising to do with his family as well, but when the three adults heard what had taken place they were equally concerned.

"How did people from Nova manage to get to the ring?" asked Kit.

"I don't know," answered Zac, "but I guess they've had 141 years to work it out."

"That means there's no chance we'll know anyone on the ship," said Tash.

"Sadly, that's right. Everyone we knew is long dead. These

people may not even have heard of us, or if they have, we would be merely names from the distant past."

"Well, you just be careful, my love," said Kit putting her arms around him. "Make sure you come back home to me in one piece." She kissed him and held him tight, as they heard the whine of a flitter landing just outside the bungalow.

As the flitter took off a few minutes later, Kit stood watching until it had disappeared into the distance, unable to shake off the uneasy feeling that their peaceful lives were about to be irrevocably shattered.

She was right, in more ways than one.

61

Zac emerged from the transfer booth in the main terminal building on A1 to find Starla waiting for him.

"Starla! Hello. It's good to see you again after so many years."

"Hello Zac. It's good to see you too."

"I thought a Commander Bree was meeting me."

"That's correct. I'm Commander Bree."

"You're ...? I'm sorry, I've never been told your last name. You're a commander now?"

"Yes. I'm in charge of Gateway Station."

"Congratulations Commander."

"I'll make you a deal," she said. "I won't call you doctor, if you don't call me commander."

"Deal."

"This way, Zac. We'll transfer up to Terminus 8, where I've got a super-fast shuttle waiting to take us to Gateway. We'll be there in 30 minutes. That will give me time to brief you."

Less than two minutes later they were on board the shuttle and it was accelerating away from the orbital terminus.

"Now that we're alone, let me fill you in on what we know so far. Councillor Drummond informs me that he's communicated the bare facts already."

"Yes. A ship from Nova has arrived, with people from the ring on board. And the wormhole closed immediately after it arrived."

"That's correct. Our greatest concern is protecting ourselves from attack by EIs, which is now a possibility, especially if they've been monitoring our wormhole all these years. But that's not your concern. The reason we wanted you here was that we thought the occupants of the void jumper would appreciate meeting... how shall I put it? ..."

"Someone who looks normal to them?"

"Yes. Precisely. We obviously didn't have that option when you arrived, but we want to do everything we can to ensure a smooth transition for these newcomers. As well as looking familiar to them, you also have a much better grasp of the idioms of your own language than we do. Even though we can upload your ancient language, it will be much better to have someone who has spoken it all his life."

"I'll probably be a little rusty. I haven't spoken it for 22 years. We've made a point of speaking only Altarian."

"I'm sure you'll do just fine."

"What do you know about them?"

"Not much. There are six of them, three men and three women. We have only communicated with them via comms so far. Their vessel is in the process of docking now. By the time we reach Gateway they will have been decontaminated and will be waiting for you in the same waiting area where you first arrived. We've kept communication to a bare minimum, as we wanted you to take over as soon as possible."

"I'll certainly do my best."

"There's something else you should know."

"Yes?"

"They claim that they left Nova in the year 5402."

"But that's ... 119 years ago!"

"Yes. Exactly the same time difference that you experienced. It appears that they left Nova 22 years after you and then arrived here in our timeframe 22 years after you as well. They also experienced the same two-day hiatus in the wormhole that you did. This would explain why the wormhole has been open for these last 22 years. The reason it didn't close after you arrived is that there was another spacecraft in the wormhole, travelling behind you. It seems that both of you were caught in the event horizon of a black hole. Once this second spacecraft exited the wormhole, the negative energy feedback loop that had been created between the ship's STAR drive and the black hole was broken, and the wormhole could finally close."

"119 years!" Zac's head was spinning. "If they left 22 years after we did, I might know some of them! Do you know their names?"

"Only the pilot, who tells us his name is Karl. We've been waiting for you to make the formal greetings and introductions."

"Karl? I didn't know any Karl on Nova — at least not that I can remember."

Who are they? Will I know them? Will they know me? Zac urged the shuttle on, with mixed emotions swirling around within him.

A little more than 30 minutes later, Zac and Starla were standing outside the door to the waiting room.

"I'll step back a little, Zac. It's better if they don't glimpse me until you've met them and explained things. They've simply been told that one of the Federation Council members is about to greet them."

"OK."

"Good luck."

"Thanks."

Zac approached the door and opened it. He stepped into the small waiting room and saw six faces turn toward him simultaneously. He smiled and said, "Welcome." The word seemed cumbersome in his mouth, unaccustomed as he was to be speaking the ancient Terran.

He looked at the faces, trying to recognise them, but couldn't see anyone familiar. Unless ... perhaps ... the woman? Around his age. The same eyes that he remembered, although creased and wrinkled now with the passage of time. The same red hair. The same curve of the lips. *It couldn't be! Surely not!*

"Jaz?" he said, his eyes wide with shock.

"Zac?" said Mel.

"Dad?" said Dayna.

"Hello Zac," said Jaz.

TO BE CONTINUED ...

Read the next stunning instalment, "A PATH THROUGH THE STARS" - available now!

Get it here: https://kevinsimington.com/science-fiction-books/

LEAVE A REVIEW

If you enjoyed this book, I would be extremely grateful if you would leave a review on Amazon. Reviews are hugely important for me as a self-published author. They impact Amazon's algorithms, helping the book to climb higher in Amazon's charts, thereby making it more visible to potential readers. Every single review really does help!

Leaving a review is very easy. To leave a review, just go to the relevant Amazon page for your country (see below), search for my book and click on the reviews link next to the stars. A review of 4 or 5 stars is considered to be a positive review and a review of 3 or less stars is considered to be a negative review. (Unfortunately, Amazon only allows reviews from people who have spent at least $50 on Amazon over the preceding 12 months).

LEAVE A REVIEW:

AMAZON UNITED STATES

AMAZON UNITED KINGDOM
AMAZON CANADA
AMAZON AUSTRALIA

AMAZON UNITED KINGDOM
AMAZON CANADA
AMAZON AUSTRALIA

FREE EBOOK!

Join my mailing list and receive a FREE EBOOK. I will email you a complimentary copy of **"Welcome To The Universe: A Pocket Guide For Visitors"**. With stunning photographs and mind-boggling facts, the book provides a fascinating glimpse into the wonders of the universe and the many challenges of space travel. Just click the link below and tell me where to send it (or sign up to my mailing list at kevinsimington.com).

SEND ME A FREE COPY OF "WELCOME TO THE UNIVERSE"

Free eBook!

GET THE STUNNING THIRD INSTALMENT!

CLICK TO BUY IT NOW

BOOK 3 in the STARPATH SERIES

An impossible journey.

A battle for survival.

A search for home.

As mankind struggles for survival, a stunning new discovery changes everything. The enemy they face is far more dangerous than they had assumed. But with the revelation comes a ray of hope. The path to salvation is revealed; a path that traverses the galaxy and will lead our wandering heroes home, provided they can survive the almost insurmountable odds along the way. An unlikely group who represent mankind's last hope of survival set out on an almost impossible journey that will bring them back to where it all began. There, they will face the ultimate challenge.

CLICK TO BUY IT NOW

OR GO TO:
KEVINSIMINGTON.COM

BOOK 1 IN THE SERIES

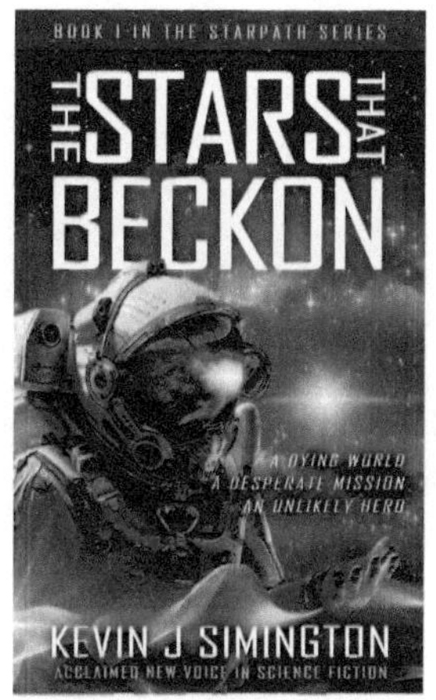

CLICK TO BUY IT NOW

BOOK I in the STARPATH SERIES

A dying world.
A desperate mission.
An unlikely hero.

A ragged band of desperate survivors flee from a dying world in search of a new home. But the universe has played a cruel joke on them. Now facing even deadlier threats from a strange world, as well as traitors in their midst, their battle for survival is only just beginning.

CLICK TO BUY IT NOW

OR GO TO:
KEVINSIMINGTON.COM

ABOUT THE AUTHOR

Kevin J Simington is an acclaimed fiction and non-fiction author whose books are renowned for their intelligence, clarity and wit. He is a very popular conference speaker on the topics of philosophy, apologetics and science. He also writes for several international magazines.

Website:
https://kevinsimington.com

Amazon Author Page:
amazon.com/author/kevinjsimington